FRANKLIN

First Edition.

ISBN: 978-9-0831367-4-5

Cover Design: © The Pretty Little Design Co.

Editor: Kim BookJunkie

Formatting and Proofread: Katie Salt at KLS Publishing

FRANKLIN

BILLIE LUSTIG

AUTHOR'S NOTE

I don't want to ruin the experience, but I also don't want a claim up my ass because you went in unprepared.

Even though I don't consider this very dark, I feel obliged to tell you: they fuck, they say 'fuck', they shoot, and there is blood.

If your reaction to those things isn't: yes, fuck yes, yes please, and hell yes?

Then this ain't for you.

Abort mission, or read at your own risk.

I'm dedicating this one to me. That's right, you heard me. This one's for me. Because I'm fucking proud of myself for publishing my third book in the last six months.

I hope you are ready for more, because like Franklin Wolfe—there is no stopping me.

1

FRANKLIN

I lean against the doorpost of his office, my hands in the pocket of my coats, examining him while he's hovering above some papers with a pen in his hand. His greasy, gray hair flops in front of his face when he draws the occasional line through the words in front of him.

There was a time I respected this man. He helped me get us Wolfes where we are now, but I guess somewhere along the road he decided we weren't good enough anymore.

Shame.

"Good evening, David."

He looks up with a slight frown before leaning back in his desk chair, his lips shaped into a friendly grin.

"Franky! Social call?" He beams, referring to the nights I used to crash his office and we would talk about the best ways to do business. I think back to those nights, when moments of weakness crept in, making me believe that he was my friend. When I thought trust wasn't solely a thing I could expect from my brothers. When I thought I could form connections with people I don't share blood with.

Silly me.

I match his smile, amused by his oblivion, clearly unaware that I'm not alone. I saunter into the room, my leather shoes tapping sinisterly against the hardwood floor with every step I make. He holds my gaze in anticipation until he notices my brothers walking through the door behind me. His face falls when he sees they are followed by two more of our men, placing themselves in the corners of his office while Reign and Killian take the chairs in front of his desk. Connor closes the door behind him, placing himself against the door as a barrier while I walk towards the window. I close the curtain before turning around, leaning my back against the window frame, then folding my arms in front of my body.

"W-what's up, guys?" David's eyes move back and forth between the four of us, nervousness marring his chubby face, while his stutter makes me smile on the inside. They say I'm ruthless and severe. That I have no mercy for those who piss me off.

It's true.

But what everyone fails to see is what happens before I reach that point of no return. I take care of the people around me, the people who deliver good work for my companies and therefore are good for my brothers and me. It's when they decide to no longer return the unspoken courtesy, the loyalty I demand, that reason is no longer in my vocabulary and they are no longer a priority.

They become a liability.

"Oh, you know," Reign starts with his famous, boyish grin, running a hand through his honey brown hair, "just doing the rounds. Seeing who's paying, who's doing their job, who's running their mouth." He casually shrugs his shoulders, holding David's gaze, which is getting more tense by the second.

"Got any info from the street, David?" Killian pitches in, cocking his head a little in a mocking way. Killian and Reign are the most easygoing of us Wolfe brothers, but a lethal team when put together.

"N-no, all good. You know, no one dares to talk shit about the Boston Wolfes." He starts to fumble with the pen in his hand, tapping it against the armrest of his chair. The gesture is noticed by Killian, and a pleased look appears on his face.

"Are you nervous, David?" He nods at the tapping of the pen, making David abruptly stop the movement, suddenly completely aware of his stance.

"I think he is," Reign states with a slight chuckle.

He has the biggest heart out of the four of us, always wanting to have proof before any retaliation is executed. Though Killian's extensive knowledge of body language makes him judgmental in general, both of them are pretty forgiving people. Connor and me? We are unforgiving. We don't give second chances. We don't listen to excuses when people fuck up. Simply because we won't allow *fuck ups* to mess with our family. If there is even a slight chance someone's a threat to my brothers and me, we will eliminate them without question. I look at Connor, who meets my eyes, waiting for a signal for how we will proceed.

To be honest, I haven't decided yet. In any other situation, I would've let Connor have his way and be done with it. But you see, David made this personal.

He messed with my favorite girl.

He crossed a line he can't come back from.

A line I can't pretend wasn't there.

He knows this. You don't mess with my girl.

I watch him, swallowing hard while a drip of sweat runs down his neck.

Literally sweating like a pig with his beer belly being hugged by his tight dress shirt.

"I don't know, David. I've been hearing some wicked confusing rumors running around." Killian gets up, heading to the liquor cart in the left corner while David's eyes follow his movement.

"You want one?" he asks, holding up a bottle of scotch. "I think you should have one." Without waiting for any response, Killian pours the contents of the bottle into two tumblers before handing one over to David.

He reaches out his now slightly shaking hand before bringing the rim of the glass to his mouth.

"You wanna know what I've been hearing lately?" Killian asks while he takes a seat on the corner of David's desk, his glass resting on his dark jeans.

David takes another sip of his drink before lifting his chin, looking like he's pushing out his last ounce of bravery.

"Sure." His voice squeals a little, with audible fear.

"I heard Emerson got a new accountant. You know Emerson, right? Emerson Jones? Short hair, ugly face, sounds like a redneck?"

"I've heard of him," David admits hesitantly, then wipes his forehead with one of his sleeves.

"I sure hope you do, because your name seems to occur in the same sentences as Emerson's a lot."

"I-I d-don't—" David stammers before being silenced by Killian slamming his glass against the side of his head, the sound of glass falling echoing through the room as the shards fall to the ground. David cries out in pain, clutching his head while the liquor drips down his disgusting face.

"This is not the part where you say you don't know what we are talking about, Dave." Reign lets out a sigh, obviously bored with the conversation. "I have proof. Otherwise, we wouldn't be here. You know this. Just like you knew we would find out."

"But you got greedy, didn't you? How much did he promise you?" Killian hisses, hovering above David's face, his hands resting on the armrests.

"I-I'm s-s-sorry," he pleads, bringing his arms together as if he's praying for a way out.

Connor growls from the other side of the room. He's always impatient, so he's probably eager to make David shut up, but I lift a finger, telling him to not make a move. My eyes meet Killian's. He assesses my gaze, then turns the chair, forcing David to look at me.

As soon as his eyes lock with mine, noticing the fury in my eyes, his face pales, the blood draining from his skin.

"Please, Franklin. Please, you have to listen."

"I would've listened if you'd come to me telling me you weren't happy with the way we're running our businesses," I reply, clearing my throat before continuing with the same calmness in my voice. "I would've listened if you'd told me you wanted a raise."

"Franklin. Please." He starts to sob, his body shaking as tears stream down his fat cheeks.

"But you chose to talk to Emerson Jones, giving me no chance to listen to you. Sorry, Dave. It's too late for me to listen now. You made your choice. Now I've made mine."

His eyes widen at my words. Then, without hesitation, I

reach into the holster on my side and take out my gun, ignoring the frantic pleas of the man I'd once thought was my friend. I pull the silencer out of my pocket before I screw it on unhurriedly, looking into David's bloodshot eyes as I slowly close the distance between us. A pleading look runs through them, desperation dripping from his face.

"What will you tell Marie?" he asks, his voice breaking more with every word. "And Tyler?"

He gives me a hopeful look, knowing it's useless for him to pray for another outcome yet desperate to know what will happen to his family.

"That, David," I drawl, "you'll never know."

Without giving him a chance to react, I bring up my gun with rapid speed and pull the trigger, running a bullet through his head. Instantly, it jerks back, a perfectly round circle in the middle of his forehead as his entire body goes limp.

"For fuck's sake, Franklin," Connor booms through the room, "I wanted to punch him."

"Well, you can still do that," I deadpan, making Killian chuckle.

"Not the same, asshole." Connor scowls.

I look at Reign, who's staring at a now dead as fuck David, his green eyes looking hollow and troubled.

"Hey? You good?" I snap my fingers in front of his face, trying to get his attention as he moves his face towards mine.

"He deserved this," I remind him. He rubs his face at my words.

"I know. I know." He nods, the disappointed expression still on his face as he straightens his shoulders. "I'm outta here."

I nod in agreement before moving my head back and forth between the other two men in the corner.

"Get rid of him," I command.

2

I hold up the bottle of brown rum in the air, looking at the extremely intoxicated man in front of me.

"You want another one, Larry?"

He raises his wobbling head when the sound of my voice reaches his ears, his eyes trying to keep up with my movements but failing miserably.

"Sweetheart, I want anything you pour me!" he replies with a slurred tongue while making an effort to shoot me a wink as he takes a toke of the cigarette dangling between his thin lips.

I smile, tipping the bottle to splash two fingers of brown rum in his tumbler as he blows smoke directly in my face.

Instinctively, I shut my eyes while my hand reaches up to wave away the smoke that makes my throat sore while I try to suppress a cough.

I thought I'd be used to it by now, working four days a week in a bar that decided to ignore the Massachusetts law about smoking in bars. In general, I'm not really bothered by it. I don't mind being surrounded by the smoke. It's just the dickheads who blow it right in my face that I want to slap. Not sure if they think it's sexy to watch as their drunk faces are being blurred by an air of smoke or they're just morons.

I'm guessing the latter.

I look back at the man in front of me.

Larry, looking like a drunk Santa Claus from hell, can barely hold up his head while he's rambling shit about the manager of his day job.

I just chuckle at the sight of him, knowing there is no point in a lesson on respect when he probably doesn't even know how to use his brain, anyway.

I pick up the dishcloth off the workstation, running it over the bar, cleaning the contents that slid down the glass from his shaking hand when I hear the door open with a loud screech. Cold air sweeps through the room, bringing goosebumps to my skin as my head turns towards the entrance where I'm met by a set of mesmerizing, green eyes.

The whole bar turns silent as the leader of the Boston Wolfes saunters over the hardwood floor, making his way to the bar while being followed by four of his men.

I've never met the man, but I know exactly who he is.

Franklin Wolfe.

You can't live in South Boston and not know who the Wolfes are. They run the city, even though the American Government likes to pretend that's not the case. But if you're from around here, you know exactly what the deal is.

Rumor is he even has dinner with the mayor once a month.

I try to keep my focus on cleaning up the bar since my shift is about to end, but I can't help but glance at the tall man getting closer by the second. His black coat brings out his broad athletic shoulders, showing off his fit physique, while his chocolate brown hair is perfectly styled in a fringe up.

He's fucking handsome.

If you see him walking down the street, you'd never suspect his involvement in the underworld of Boston. His appearance is not the same as the rest of his crew who wear black leather jackets, looking like the street gang they really are. He stands out, but he doesn't stand out the way they do.

Although he's sophisticated like a businessman with his perfectly trimmed five o'clock shadow and his expensive clothes, something about him still makes him just as street as his boys.

A perfect blend between both worlds.

Franklin slowly pans around the room, taking in the customers silently staring at him.

"Alright, carry on." He waves his hand in the air as his booming voice fills the room with the order, yet the bar remains deathly silent. Apparently, no one has the guts to actually make a sound.

My eyes move back and forth across the room, anxiously waiting for everyone to keep minding their business, making sure the Wolfes don't start trashing the place.

"Carry on!" His powerful voice holds a clear threat, making me drop the dishcloth, wincing as my heart starts to race in my chest. I bend over to pick it up before straightening my body, watching while the rest of the room starts to mumble again, obeying Mr. Wolfe's order.

He gives Larry a friendly slap on the back, making it clear they know each other. I realize I'm still holding my breath, wondering if this is a social call or one that comes with chaos and destruction. If there are Wolfes in the house, you never know.

"How are you doing, Larry? Drinking away this week's wages?" he teases as he takes the seat next to him, giving him a friendly smile. His men are staying close, keeping an eye on the rest of the bar.

"It's all her fault, Wolfe! She's like a siren. I can't say no when she offers," he explains this with the same slurred tongue while I offer him a tight smile.

Thanks for bringing the attention towards me, dickhead.

"You keep paying, I keep pouring." I shrug, insecurely crossing my arms in front of my body while my eyes glance at the gorgeous man in front of me.

"Is that so?" Franklin Wolfe reaches in his pocket, holding my gaze before pulling out a pack of cigarettes and dropping it on the bar.

I try to keep breathing while his eyes remain fixed on mine and he pulls a hundred-dollar bill out of his pocket.

"There. Tonight is on me," he declares, slamming the bill on the wooden surface.

He turns his body towards Larry, who's grinning from ear to ear.

"Now, go on," he continues, motioning to the door. "Get going before she pours you another one and your wife makes you sleep on the couch." He looks at two of his men, snapping his fingers.

"Boys, make sure Mr. Brown here gets home safe, will you?"

They nod in agreement before helping Larry off his bar stool, escorting him out of the bar. I watch as they help him stumble through the door before my attention moves back to the man in front of me. My heart almost stops when I realize he's been staring at me the entire time.

His piercing eyes are locked with mine, drawing me into his energy as he pulls a cigarette out of the pack and lights one, softly blowing the smoke towards the ceiling.

The smoke moves between us, leaving nothing other than his green eyes glaring at me like he's about to eat me alive.

Now that's fucking sexy.

Once the smoke has completely cleared, I take a deep breath and reach down to pull a glass out of the water filled sink, then start to dry it with my cloth, anything to keep my hands busy.

"I'm looking for Kenny." He cocks his head a little and gives me the tiniest smile. It's barely noticeable, yet my heart stops when the name Kenny rolls off his tongue, making me want to drop my panties.

Fuck.

From what I've heard about Franklin Wolfe, I was expecting a scary crime lord who'd give me the creeps and make my skin crawl if I ever had the unfortunate luck of meeting him. But in reality, he's scary in a whole different way.

Mesmerizing.

Compelling.

Sexy.

The kind of man who can reach your heart with his eyes and crush it with his hands. But I vowed to never be dominated by a man again, that I wouldn't crumble under a man's gaze ever again.

Prove it, Kendall. You've got this.

I hardly believe myself, but I dig deep, scraping out every

ounce of confidence I can find in my body, determined to hold my own against men like this.

I suck in a deep breath, then lean over, resting my elbows on the wooden surface of the bar.

Our faces are only a few inches away from each other, and I can smell his fresh cologne as I stare into his eyes. They are green like a saltwater lake with specks of amber around the edges.

"What do you want with Kenny?" I ask boldly, biting my lip in a daring way, not sure where my sudden bravery is coming from.

Franklin's eyebrows rise slightly with amusement while his men instantly snap their heads towards me, each of them inching closer to the bar, scowling at me like I'm their next kill.

"That's none of your business, *little girl*." One of them growls. I just glare at him, refusing to let him affect me.

Franklin's hand lands on the guy's upper arm, silently telling him to calm down and resulting in him moving back to his seat. I can feel Franklin's breath slightly fanning my face while my heart continues beating like a sledgehammer. Every bone in my body tells me to run and hide, walk away and make sure I stay off his radar for the rest of my life. But his eyes pin me down, making me feel like my feet are cemented to the floor, unable to walk away or look away.

When he moves his hand up to cup my throat, my mouth turns as dry as sandpaper, making me realize it's too late to back down now that I've dared him with my stance. The sudden yet soft touch makes me gasp while the feeling of his skin connecting with mine burns through my body like a flaming arrow mixed with a hint of fear.

Fear that he may snap my neck at any second.

Fear that any minute now, he will control me like I have no spine left, showing me that I'm nothing more than a little girl in a big man's world, like I've been told many times in my life.

I hold still, somehow hoping I don't piss him off, like prey waiting for the hunter to make the next move.

"Do I make you nervous, pretty girl?" he rumbles. He moves in a little more, his nose almost brushing mine, his hand still covering my neck.

"No," I answer firmly, bluffing, like I'm in a game of poker with my life at stake.

The corner of his mouth moves a little, as if a smile is trying to sneak through before his face returns to the stoic look he's allegedly famous for.

"Your throbbing pulse tells me otherwise."

Feeling busted as fuck, I quickly straighten my back, untangling myself from his grasp. He purses his lips in annoyance, his hand still up in the air where my neck was, so I'm expecting him to flip any second now. Instead, he drops his hand and takes another drag off his cigarette, moving on as if he didn't feel that electrifying spark between the two of us.

"You see, we would like to offer him a job," he explains.

"What kind of job?" I raise my brows, my hands on my hips.

"An accounting position. We heard he's the top of his class at Northwestern."

"Ugh, who told you that?" I huff out uncomfortably. "No, let me guess. It was Mr. Garrison, that nosy teacher, wasn't it?"

It's frightening to have the most powerful criminal of Boston in my bar, but there is something about this man that makes me think it's fair game to blurt out what I want. I'm not sure why. Or if my intuition is right. Fingers crossed it doesn't get me killed.

"You know Mr. Garrison?" Franklin asks.

He keeps looking at me, and I feel my skin getting more damp by the second, just from holding his gaze.

"Kenny, love, just help me change this barrel, then you're free to go!" Harry, the owner of the bar, yells as he rolls a barrel of beer out of the stockroom. "My back is killing me."

Fuck, fuck, fuck.

I glance at Harry before my eyes are drawn back to the man in front of me, the man who is now glaring at me like I'm a schoolgirl in need of some serious punishment.

Shit.

3

Franklin

I glance at the old man coming from the stockroom before realizing what he just called her. A frown pulls at my lips, annoyed by the play she just performed.

"*You* are Kenny?" I ask, calmly blowing out the smoke from my lungs while I keep my eyes on the stunning brunette in front of me. I went to Northwestern, looking for a replacement for David. Figuring students always need the extra cash and are a lot more flexible in closing their eyes to certain things than an experienced accountant will be. However, I did *not* expect 'Kenny' to look like *that.*

Her Bambi looking blue eyes are glowing as she gives me a stiff smile with guilt dripping off her face.

"It's Kendall, actually," she clarifies before she walks away to help the old man with the barrel of beer he's struggling with.

I keep a straight face even though the corners of my mouth itch to curl into a grin, a little stunned by the fact that she had the guts to try to trick me. My eyes roam over every curve of her body while she drags the barrel behind her, the muscles in her toned legs flexing as she places it under the bar. Her black jeans hug her curvy hips, which are perfectly displayed since she has knotted her red flannel shirt in front of her belly button, revealing a small strip of skin. Just enough for me to want to find out what the rest of her body looks like. What it will feel like under my palms. She reaches her hands up to pull her dark brown hair into a high ponytail, unintentionally showing me even more of her delicate skin.

For fuck's sake.

I rub my forehead while holding my cigarette, ignoring the way my jeans are getting uncomfortably tight.

My eyes are glued to the perky little thing as she installs the new barrel with an ease that shows she's been a bartender for a long time before walking back to me.

"Can I get you anything?" Her eyes give me a kind smile, all the provocation she gave me when her neck was under my palm now completely gone. She's clearly hoping I'll ignore her little stunt.

"Three bottles of Budweiser." I raise my three fingers in the air before taking another toke off my cigarette.

The nicotine fills my lungs as I try to ignore the weird feeling under my skin while I watch her move.

She turns around then bends over, giving me a complete display of her peachy ass. I can't help but lick my lips at the sight of it. When she turns back to face me with the three bottles in her hand, her eyes quickly lock with mine in a questioning look. Probably wondering if I was checking her out from behind.

Yes, pretty girl.

Shameless, I lock my eyes with hers while she unscrews the bottles, then places them in front of us.

"There you go. These are on the house. Have a nice evening, gentlemen." She glances between the three of us before quickly walking away.

"Hold on," I call out, my voice filled with demand.

I like her small acts of rebellion, but I'm certain I didn't tell her this conversation was over.

She stops hesitantly, giving me a demure smile as she slowly turns around while taking off her apron.

I make her uncomfortable. Part of me likes the fact that I seem to have at least some power over her.

"I still want to offer you a job." I suck in another toke of my cigarette before putting it out.

"I already have a job, but thank you for the offer, sir." There is a finality in her answer that makes my men next to me growl in response, while a frown appears on my face.

I am stunned by her answer, but I'm also amused by her confusion in thinking it's optional.

If she was a guy, I would just offer more money combined with a little force and he would be in my office by morning, doing whatever the fuck I tell him to do. But I don't lay hands on women, and she must know I pay more than her bartending job, yet she's standing in front of me rejecting me like I've asked her out on a date.

I don't do rejection.

Ever.

The fact that she now is on my radar only reinforces that.

You see, when you get on my radar, there are only two outcomes for me: you either will be eliminated by my circle or incorporated into my circle.

Considering my dick already made its preference perfectly clear, I'm going for the latter.

I force out a friendly smile, leaning over the bar and offering her my hand.

"I'm sorry, I haven't probably introduced myself. I am—"

"I know who you are," she interrupts, a provocative look creeping back into her ocean blue eyes that remind me of sapphires, luring me into their beauty. "But I'm not interested." I resist letting my jaw drop to the floor, amazed by the amount of attitude she's giving me, even though she is clearly uncomfortable with it. She rapidly walks towards the door, grabbing a black coat off the rack, then putting it on before waving at Harry.

When the door closes behind her, I shake my head, realizing what just happened. Unable to mask the angry look on my face, I quickly get up and storm through the door while my two guys follow right behind me.

The freezing February cold hits my flustered face while little snowflakes blur my vision.

Snapping my head frantically from left to right, I search for her on the street before I spot her cute physique strutting away from me, her hips swaying with every step.

There is a burning desire to run up to her and pull her back by her hair, telling her it's unwise to fuck with me unless she actually wants to get *fucked by me*. But the warm feeling that image elicits is quickly snuffed out by the cold breeze, reminding me that I will never get what I want from her if that's the route I choose to take.

And I'll definitely get what I want from her.

"You want us to give her a little scare, boss?" Nigel nudges his head towards her while I watch her move farther away from us.

"Yeah, what do you think, boss?" Thomas adds, they're

both looking at me with questioning expressions while a grin stretches my lips. I need to know more about this girl.

I push Nigel against the building, my head moving between the two of them before turning my head back to the brunette.

“I think, boys … I’m going to marry her.”

4

The morning light is shining through my small bedroom as I'm woken by some annoyingly loud knocking on my door. I do my best to ignore the loud sounds that quickly become loud bangs.

"For fuck's sake," I grumble.

"You talking to yourself again, darling? You know you need to stop doing that because people will think you're madder than a hatter." Josie's thick Southern accent yells through the door, a smile audible in her voice.

I look at the alarm clock on my nightstand.

"J, it's fucking eight in the morning. Let me sleep!" I sink deeper into my soft sheets. There is a reason I locked the damn door, because I knew she would be jumping on my bed like a five-year-old on Christmas morning if I hadn't.

"No, can do, sugar pie. I've got Dunks. And I stood in the damn line for half an hour, so you better get your ass out before I use my spare key to drag you out."

"What? You have a spare key to my bedroom?!" I shout incredulously.

"You bet your ass I do. What if you have a heart attack or something? Now get the fuck out, you lazy fuck."

"You're the one giving me a heart attack," I bellow.

Slightly irritated, I lift myself out of the bed before jerking the door open.

"You do realize I got in bed at two, right?" I glare at her, wishing my death stare would silence her.

I turn around to put on a hoodie, covering up my tank top before turning my attention back to her.

"Oh, good, you're up!" she quips, holding a box of Dunkin Donuts in front of her, looking like a damn Girl Scout ready for a bake sale.

But let me tell you something: Josie Montgomery is anything but a Girl Scout. She curses like a sailor, eats like a construction worker, and is a total maneater, yet she looks like a fucking dark angel with her dollface, dark blue eyes, and her long black hair.

I love her, but she's a lot at times.

"Shut up." I roll my eyes at her before I move past her into the hallway, strutting towards the kitchen in need of some serious coffee.

"Fine, but I need *you* to talk." She trails behind me before I take a seat at the breakfast bar that separates the living room from the kitchen. Josie walks around the bar, taking the seat opposite me after she holds up a cup of fresh Dunkin Donuts coffee in front of my face.

"Gimme, gimme." I show her grabby hands while she holds it up in the air as leverage.

"Are you going to stop growling at me?" Her brows are

lifted up in a reprimanding look. I purse my lips to suppress a chuckle.

"Yes."

"Are you going to answer my questions?"

"What questions?" I frown.

"Are you?!"

"Fine," I comply, rolling my eyes. "Now give it to me!"

She hands me the cup, and I eagerly take a sip as I feel my irritation fade away as the taste of the nutty sweetness hits my tastebuds. I close my eyes, savoring the moment before Josie shoves the box of donuts in front of my face.

"Why are you buttering me up? What's going on? Are we getting kicked out?" I grab a donut with pink glaze and sprinkles before sinking my teeth into it.

She grabs a chocolate one out of the box, giving me a knowing look, as if I'm supposed to know whatever she wants to know.

"What?" I ask again, my eyes widening in anticipation.

"So," she starts, a suspicious look on her face, "I heard a little rumor while waiting in line this morning."

"Oh, yeah? What's the latest chit chat?"

Josie has a habit of going into town every single morning to get fresh breakfast since she's always up at the crack of dawn. Apparently, that's the time the gossip around Boston is at its peak, so she always comes home with details on whatever's currently going around town like wildfire. Considering she woke me up for it, this must be a big one.

"They were talking about how Franklin Wolfe made an appearance in The Library last night."

My eyes snap up to hers quicker than I want her to notice before I try to casually put my focus back on my donut, plucking off a piece of the sweet dough. My heart starts to race as if the compelling man is in front of me once again, so I take a deep breath to calm myself down.

Goddamn, it's only been six hours, yet Franklin Wolfe's latest appearance is already the talk of the town. This just proves how important and influential the Boston Wolfes are once again.

"Yeah, he was," I admit, knowing there is no denying it.

"They say he offered the girl behind the bar a job."

"Hmm, he did. So did you watch the game yesterday?" I'm staring at my donut like it's the most fascinating thing I've ever seen, trying to change the subject even though I know there is no chance in hell she'll let this slide.

"Kendall!" she blurts out, making me wince a little.

"What?!"

"It's true? He offered you a job?"

"Yes, he offered me a job." I let out a sigh.

"As what?"

"His accountant. Apparently, Mr. Garrison recommended me."

"Well, I'll be damned." She sets her coffee cup on the white marble counter as her jaw practically dislocates. "You're going to work for the Boston Wolfes?"

"What? No!" I screech.

No fucking chance in hell am I going to work for the biggest crime lord in town. That would be asking for trouble.

Specifically because I almost got lost in his green eyes, ready to hand over my soul if he'd asked me to as he pinned me down with his hypnotizing gaze.

Think about your spine, Kendall.

If I had to see those eyes every day? I would have no life left. I'd become a slave to the specimen that is called Franklin Wolfe, just like the rest of Boston. I'll pass.

Besides, I'm still recovering from the last man who walked into my life. I don't need another one messing with my head.

"No?" she repeats, shock evident on her face.

"No."

"No?"

"I'm sorry. Do they have another word for 'no' in Boston that I missed? Because I'm from Alabama, and we just stick to the word 'no'. No. N period. O period."

She places her elbows on the bar, pointing her finger at me with a skeptical look.

"So let me get this straight. You told Franklin Wolfe no?"

"You're starting to sound like a fucking parrot. Yes, Josie. I declined his offer," I snap.

I know it may be rare to hear that word out of my mouth since I'm a pleaser in general, but I'm pretty sure I didn't start speaking French overnight.

She shakes her head while I drop the last bite of my donut in my mouth, still glaring at her.

"You don't say 'no' to Franklin Wolfe." The sound of her voice is resolute, as if she is stating a fact.

Okay, I know he's the biggest fish in town, but surely he can't *make* me work for him if I don't want to.

Right?

An uncertainty creeps into my body, and suddenly, I don't feel so sure of myself.

"I vowed I wouldn't let a man control me ever again, so how about trying to help me keep that promise. You know? Show that I have at least some backbone left in my body." I shrug, taking another donut from the box.

"And you chose Franklin Wolfe as the first man to show the *new you*?" Incredulity washes over her face. That or she's thinking I've lost my mind.

"I'm not going to work for the biggest crime lord in town," I state carefully, wondering if this is the smartest decision. I felt confident about it last night, proud of my resolute stance, but looking into Josie's worried face makes me think I'm more stupid than smart at this point.

"Oh, please," she huffs, bringing her cup to her pink lips, her eyes filled with disbelief.

"What?"

"Yes, you will."

"No, I won't." I cross my arms in front of my body in a defiant way, hoping to convince her of the new me, just like I'm trying to convince myself. She mirrors my posture, giving me a look like she knows it all. She may know it all, but I'm not the same girl I was a year ago.

This is the new me!

I think.

"Darling, he may have let you go with a 'no' last night, but he sure as hell won't do it again."

"I'm not going to let another man dictate my life," I avow firmly, still trying to hold on to my attitude.

"I don't know, I wouldn't mind letting Franklin Wolfe dictate my life." She gives me a swoony look like the maneater that she is, hoping to soften my mood.

"Well, you take the job then." I chuckle as I take another sip of my coffee.

"He didn't offer me one."

"Right. It doesn't matter, anyway. "

"No, because you *will* take that job."

Her smug grin is pissing me off, and I want to slap it from her face. I know she knows exactly what goes on in this town, but I know enough to believe he won't hurt me by simply telling him 'no.' He's got a hand in basically every business in this town, but he also has a reputation of being just and fair. For treating women with respect and doing his best to keep his staff happy. I'm sure he won't force me to work for me.

Right?

"I'm not taking the job, Josie. And I doubt he'll put a gun to my head to tell me otherwise."

"Oh, honey, bless your heart." She shakes her head as she gives me a sympathetic look. "Your first mistake was thinking you can say 'no' to Franklin Wolfe. The second one is thinking he'll let you walk away now that you're on his radar. You *will* work for him, and he won't even have to put a gun to your pretty little head. He'll make you believe it was all your own choice."

I stare back at her in annoyance, my lips thinning as I let her words sink in, wondering if maybe she's right. If maybe my behavior put me on his radar and is now entwined with the wills and wants that are Franklin Wolfe.

5

Franklin

I open the door to The Library, my eyes assessing the area with my chin held high. The bar is mainly filled with blue-collar workers having a drink after a day of hard work. I quickly scan their faces, making sure none of them is from a rival gang before I move my attention to the reason for my late-night visit.

My stern face relaxes a little when I notice the perky brunette from last night on her tiptoes trying to get a bottle of liquor on the highest shelf. Her jeans are hugging her curves, and she's wearing a t-shirt that shows some of her light beige skin every time she reaches up. I quietly walk towards the bar, then take a seat on one of the barstools in front of her. She slightly rocks along to a country song coming from the speakers, completely oblivious to my presence until she turns around to pluck a clean glass from the shelf in front of her.

Her eyes widen in shock as she winces, almost dropping the glass.

"H-hi, Mr. Wolfe. Good evening." She flashes me a timid

smile before she sucks in a breath of air, pulling herself together.

My hand reaches into the pocket of my coat, and I pull out my pack of smokes, setting it on the bar after I take a cigarette out of the pack. I light it, sucking in the nicotine filled air, my eyes never leaving hers. I notice her swallow while she starts wiping the bar in a frantic way, and I can't help but imagine how she would look swallowing me.

"Do I make you nervous, Ms. Ryan?" I ask, repeating my question from last night, despite knowing what her answer will be.

Her head darts towards me as she gives me a slight glare. I have to press my lips together to keep a straight face.

She's cute when she's pissed, a little endearing even. I wonder if she's pissed at me or at herself. Seconds pass while she holds my stare, finally letting out a deep breath as she continues wiping down the bar.

"Yes."

I cock my head, surprised by her honesty. When I had my hand covering her slim neck last night, I'd enjoyed the defiance that she tried to push through her insecurity. It had me thinking about all the ways I could push her further before stripping her naked. Surprisingly, her being honest turns me on even more.

A small smile twists my lips while I give her an approving look.

"A whiskey please, Ms. Ryan." I take another toke of my cigarette while she nods and grabs a bottle of whiskey off the shelf behind her.

She splashes two fingers in a fresh glass, glancing at me before she screws the cap back on.

"Why?" I ask.

Her eyes find mine in confusion before she shakes her head and pours a second glass of whiskey, as if this situation is too much for her.

"Why what?" she fires back before pouring the whiskey down her throat in one gulp, making me chuckle inside.

"Why do I make you nervous?" The smoke of my cigarette lingers between us, like a smoldering curtain that blurs the features of her pretty eyes and the emotion that seeps through them. I put out the cigarette, feeling the need to see every single detail of her face before taking a sip of my whiskey.

"I see it now," she starts, doing her best to hold my gaze even though I can see she's having a hard time with it. "Why they call you the leader of the pack? It's your eyes."

"My eyes?" A hint of amusement etches my voice.

"Hmm," she hums in agreement. "Your eyes are like those of a wolf in a dark forest, compelling. Drawing you in. You know that you have to run, but something has you freezing to the spot."

"Are you saying I'm an animal?"

"No," she replies with certainty, even though her eyes tell me yes.

Wrong answer.

I *am* an animal.

I'm not the kind of animal half of my boys are. I don't feel the need to throw out a few punches on a Friday night just to release the tension. I rarely give people that amount of my energy, simply because my energy is worth more than beating up some morons. But push me too far, make me decide that loss of energy is worth it, and I'm the worst animal out there. I'm the animal that will tear you apart, leaving nothing other than pieces of flesh scattered around the particles that were once your soul.

"Do you wanna run, Ms. Ryan?"

She bites her lip at that question, stirring my dick to attention as I contemplate what her answer will be. She should run because I will destroy her. But maybe she's smart enough to realize it's already too late for that.

"Should I?" she questions, swallowing hard, as if she can read my mind.

"It's up to you, Ms. Ryan."

She holds my gaze before letting out a deep breath, a bit of the tightness releasing from her shoulders.

"Please, just call me Kenny," she says, changing the subject as she looks towards the clock hanging above the door. "So, are you walking in at midnight to force me to work for you?"

Her look is stern, the small scowl on her flawless face forcing my respect while her fingers nervously tap the bar as she waits for my answer.

And to thank her for her effort, I give it to her.

"I thought about it," I admit.

"What part?" Her face softens a little, and a string of her brown hair falls over her face, making her run a hand through her hair.

"Forcing you. My men were eager to show you there is no saying 'no' to the Boston Wolfes."

She swallows hard, tension clearly entering her body again.

"Are you going to?"

I hold her gaze, not saying a word, just shamelessly staring at her while I think about all the things I want to do to her. She has a bright spark in her eyes that is filled with pride, making her put in her best effort to hold her own against me. It's a spark that I want to set on fire. I can tell there is also a fear in her that is fed by insecurity, making me curious to find out what the root of her lack of confidence is.

"To force me, I mean?" she continues when my silence becomes too much for her.

"No," I answer truthfully, bringing my eyes to my glass before lifting it to take another sip, glancing at her from above the rim of my glass.

She frowns in confusion as I tap the empty glass to request another.

"No?" She fetches the bottle and refills my glass.

"Even though I know there are many ways I can get you to work for me by tomorrow, I'm convinced none of those ways will give me *'you'* the way I want," I explain, licking my lower lip.

My gaze locks with hers, my eyes pinching to make it perfectly clear what I'm talking about. Her mouth opens slightly, shallow breaths leaving her lips while her cheeks start to blush.

Fuck, that's sexy.

"Instead, I'm going to sit here," I point my finger at the bar, "at this bar, every night, until the day you agree to work for me."

"You can't be serious?" she scoffs incredulously.

"I'm always serious, Ms. Ryan."

She tilts her head as she examines my face.

"What if I never agree to work for you?" She cocks an eyebrow, presumably feeling more secure now that she knows I won't hurt her.

Cute.

"You know I always get what I want, right?" I counter with a straight face.

"Must be boring?" She rolls her eyes while a small smile creases her face.

"You're bold, Ms. Ryan."

She huffs in response, "I'm definitely not *bold*, Mr. Wolfe."

"Please, call me Franklin. And I beg to differ, *Kenny.*" I shoot her a wink, complying with her request, hoping it'll be enough encouragement for her to do the same with mine. "You defy me, even though it makes you uncomfortable. That's pretty bold to me."

"Is that a good thing or a bad thing?"

I let out a soft chuckle.

"Definitely good."

6

Kendall

He made good on his word. He's been sitting at my bar for the last seven nights. Always coming in at eleven at night, not leaving until I close it down. I still get a nervous flutter in my stomach when he watches me work, but I've learned to ignore his staring eyes. Sometimes he comes in with other Wolfes, I think one of them is called Nigel. Sometimes he comes in alone, though it wouldn't surprise me if he has some undercover back-up nearby. But he always focuses his attention on me, speaking to me any moment I'm not pouring drinks or waiting on the other guests. At first it was uncomfortable, feeling like he was grilling me every single chance he got, but now we just talk. Mostly about me.

Tonight is no exception, I realize, while he stares into my eyes. He weakens me with his burning gaze until I have no resolve and will answer any question he has.

"Where are you from?" he asks, his face stoic as ever.

"Why? My Boston accent need more work?" I taunt,

taking his glass from the bar and pouring him his second and final glass. He never drinks more than two glasses before switching to sparkling water, making me wonder why that is.

"Your Boston accent is nonexistent, pretty girl." He softly chuckles while his nickname for me warms me inside. Chances are he uses that for every woman he talks to, but I've caught myself pretending it was reserved for only me more than once this past week.

I grab my heart, feigning offense.

"How dare you, Mr. Wolfe? You break my heart." My real accent is on full display, subtly telling him where I'm from.

"Ah, see!" He points his at me while still holding his cigarette between his fingers. "There it is. You're a Southern belle. What brings you to The Olde Towne?"

The interested look on his face makes my stomach flutter, and I show him a genuine smile in response.

"Followed an old flame, eight years ago."

"An old flame?" He cocks his head slightly, his lips pressed firmly together in displeasure for two seconds before his face goes back to its usual impassive expression. I wonder if that was jealousy I saw creeping in or if my mind's playing tricks on me.

"How old?" he asks, taking a puff of his cigarette.

"Ancient." I smile, hoping to relax him again.

He waves his hand, requesting more confirmation.

"Another lifetime. Forever ago, in the past." I add, watching his green eyes sparkle as the words leave my lips.

"Good." He looks content as he holds his eyes locked with mine. I wonder if he's flirting with me. The thought alone has me swallowing that same curiosity away, feeling kinda scared that he really may be.

"You've been sitting here for seven days straight. Are you ready to give up yet?" I mock, crossing my arms in front of my body.

He gives me a bored look before the corner of his mouth lifts in a tiny smile, his eyes lighting up for just a second in a knowing way.

"I don't know, pretty girl. I'm feeling lucky today."

I narrow my eyes at him, giving him a playful glare.

"I thought you didn't believe in luck." I return, referring to one of our earlier conversations at the beginning of the week.

'Luck is for fools who refuse to put in the hard work. There is no such thing as luck,' were his literal words.

He gifts me with one of his full smiles that I've learned are as rare as an eclipse considering the man barely smiles about anything. He's always kind and friendly, but his face is free of expression ninety percent of the time, so making him smile every now and then makes me feel like I can achieve the impossible.

I realize I'm beaming at him, appreciating how incredibly handsome he is when he smiles. Don't get me wrong, he is fucking handsome all the time. He's a man who takes over a room with his presence, without saying a word. He's an authority that you can't deny, and his real secret weapon? He makes you not even want to deny it. He has this way of making you want to agree with anything he says.

Like a fucking magician, messing with your head without you even knowing it.

"True, but sometimes the days roll by with ease. Today is one of those days," he explains with a wink while my face mirrors his in a wide grin.

I'm about to open my mouth when I notice someone

walking through the door, looking up to greet my new customer.

"Good evening, Matt," I drawl with a friendly smile, since he's one of our regulars. His shaggy blond hair is covered in snow, and his face looks stern and troubled. I feel my brows lift while I wait for him to say something. Dread coils in my stomach when I notice the gun hanging loosely in his hand as his fury filled eyes focus on Franklin. Franklin follows my gaze to Matt, who slowly takes two steps forward, bringing up the gun to aim it at Franklin's head.

"Matt!" I call out with uncertainty in my voice while Franklin moves his focus back to me, his face unaffected, as if a gun being pointed at him is the most normal thing in the world.

"Lucky day, huh?" I mumble sarcastically while I try to swallow my panic away.

"The day isn't over yet, pretty girl." He shrugs, the whole situation leaving him unaffected as if he's blind to the man pointing a gun at his head.

I focus my attention towards Matt, who is practically foaming at the mouth.

"What are you doing, Matt?" I ask him carefully. My palms are pressed against the bar to keep my wobbling legs up while I take shallow breaths to calm my flushed face.

"He killed my boy," he growls, cocking his head like a madman.

I glance at Franklin, looking for any denial or confirmation, but all I meet is a blank expression.

How does this not affect him at all?

"Put the gun down, Matt," I plead, freaking out at the thought of watching someone get shot.

"He killed my boy," he repeats while the rest of the bar

watches in silence. The delirious look on his face scares the shit out of me; not knowing how far this will go. And I hate to admit it, but even though Franklin's the leader of the Boston Wolfes, I'm starting to like him. The thought of him getting hurt forms a big rock in my stomach that I can't deny.

Why did Franklin have to pick today as one of the days he would come in alone?

"If you have back-up lurking around, this is the time to make them do something," I hiss.

"I don't."

I look at Franklin with wide eyes, silently asking him for I don't know what, but all I get is a reassuring wink. Clearly he thinks I'm doing a good job so far. His lack of action is replacing my fear with annoyance, wondering if I should be flattered by his trust in a simple bartender or pissed off by the pressure he's putting on me. I'm leaning towards the latter, but the man holding the gun gives me no time to express it.

"Matt, just put the gun down." I press once more, the entire room now silent, everyone focusing on Matt and his gun.

"I can't. He killed my boy."

"How did he kill your boy?" I ask, thinking about him once telling me he has four young kids. Call me naïve, maybe even a bit biased after the nights I've spent with him so far, but I can't see this man killing a boy in cold blood.

"Arthur got shot in a gang fight an hour ago. Ghosts and Wolfes shooting on the street. My boy got hit by a stray bullet."

My eyes widen at his explanation while I feel my heart weep, feeling for this poor man. I also realize he's not thinking clearly at this moment, still overwhelmed by his loss. I shake my head, starting to understand what he's saying.

"He's been sitting here the entire night, Matt." I try to reason with him softly, showing him a friendly smile, hoping it's enough to make him listen. "How can it be his fault?"

"Those Ghosts were looking for him!" he shouts suddenly, startling me.

"It should be him in the morgue with a bullet in his head. Him! Not my boy!" His eyes are starting to well up, and I have to take a deep breath to keep my own emotions in check.

"I know you're hurting. I get it. But you can't blame him. He didn't pull the trigger."

"But he may as well have!" he shouts with force. "It's his fault!"

I can keep trying to reason with him, telling him that it can't be Franklin's fault since he hasn't left his damn chair once in the last few hours. But one look at the grief-filled man tells me that would be a waste of energy.

"How many kids do you have, Matt?" I ask him, trying to use a different approach while Franklin lights another cigarette. I throw an angry glare his way before I put my focus back on Matt.

"Three b-boys. T-two boys and a girl." He corrects himself while a tear runs down his pale cheek.

I close my eyes for a second, trying to keep it together before I open my mouth again.

"Do you want them to live without a dad?" I ask.

My hands are starting to feel sweaty as the pressure is rising, and my heart feels like it's slapping against my rib cage while adrenaline keeps my head as clear as possible.

His eyes widen, confused by my words.

"W-what d-do you mean?" he stammers, clearly not able to keep his emotions in check anymore.

"What do you think will happen?" I try to keep a poker face while being as friendly and direct as I can. "You shoot Franklin Wolfe in the head, and your sorrows are over? Your sorrows would only be beginning, Matt. Because the second you walk out that door, you'd be screwed." I watch him swallow hard as he keeps listening to my words. "The second you cross that line, you'd better go home, grab your wife and kids, and run as fast as you can. Because in about ten minutes, every single Wolfe in this city would be looking for you. Every single one of them would be aiming for your head." I see the moment the realization hits him, lowering the gun before covering his mouth with his hand.

"In fact, standing here now, threatening him while pointing a gun in his face, you've basically signed your own death sentence."

He gasps for air, terror entering his bloodshot eyes.

"I can't die, Kendall," he cries desperately. "Who will take care of my family?"

My heart breaks for him, knowing he's not a bad guy. He got dealt a shit hand and will be forced to live with that. Even though he's not to blame. But that's the thing with life. It's not fair.

"Put the gun down, Matt." My voice is a demand this time, knowing Franklin probably won't tolerate being threatened much longer, even though he's still smoking his cigarette, as if he's oblivious to the entire situation. "Put the gun down and leave. Leave if you want to fucking stay alive." I slam my hand on the top of the bar to spur him into action as tears stream down his face like a waterfall.

"K … Kendall," he pleads, probably wondering if he's still safe living in Boston.

"Just go, Matt. Go before it's too late. Maybe I can

convince Mr. Wolfe here to keep you alive." My words bring a hint of hope to his eyes. Then he turns around and rushes out of the bar. When the door closes behind him, I let out a deep sigh, closing my eyes while I let my head hang, trying to comprehend what just happened.

I'm lost in my own thoughts, the adrenaline still high as it rushes through my veins when the murmur of the rest of the guests has my head raising to look around the bar.

Not wanting to deal with any more people tonight, I open my mouth, impatience clear in my voice.

"Everybody out!" I shout. "Right now!"

I would've expected more resistance, but thankfully, everyone gets up without arguing, throwing some bills on their tables before walking out the door. When the last customer exits, I reach for the bottle of tequila and pour myself a glass before throwing it down my throat at once, causing me to shiver as the liquor flows down my gullet.

Disgusted by the taste, I grab a lemon wedge and sink my teeth in before swallowing the juice down. The acid of the lemon has my eyes squeezing shut while I pull a face. When I finally I open my eyes again, I'm looking straight into the eyes of an amused Franklin.

"Impressive," he remarks softly, taking another drag from his cigarette. He looks at me with approval in his eyes, and I'm not sure how to react to it.

"Thanks for the help," I snarl, shaking my head at him.

"You didn't need my help, Kenny," he retorts with the same look of approval on his face.

I bite my lip in annoyance, even though it's overshadowed by a sense of pride, realizing I did handle that situation pretty well.

"You know I have rules, right?" He puts his cigarette out in the ashtray. "About people who point guns at me?"

"I can imagine."

"Right." He nods as he gets up, throwing a few bills on the bar. "Well, have a nice evening, pretty girl." He walks towards the door, leaving me confused about his next move. Wondering if he'll just go home and leave Matt and his family alone.

Surely it can't be that simple.

"Franklin?" I call out to his back, causing him to turn around with a questioning look on his face.

"Yes, Kendall?"

"Please don't kill him," I plead softly, my chest filled with hope as I wait for his answer.

A small smile flashes on his face before it goes back to being apathetic.

"I will see you in my office, Monday at eight. Don't be late."

I feel my eyebrows furrow as I look at him, not knowing what he means.

"I told you I felt lucky today." He winks, and I suddenly realize what I silently agreed with.

"Good night, pretty girl." He walks out the door, leaving me stunned and shaking my head at what just happened, realizing Josie was right.

I guess I've got myself another job.

Fuck.

7

I close the door of The Library behind me before I set foot onto the street, starting my walk home. It's been three days since Matt walked into The Library, gun raised and shit, and also three days since Franklin sat at my bar. I guess he got what he wanted, so no need to keep me company anymore. The thought alone pisses me off. I feel stupid. I'd thought maybe he'd also been sitting there because he'd felt the same connection I did.

Now all I feel is tricked.

Josie was right when she'd told me Franklin Wolfe always gets what he wants without even having to use force. I thought about bailing, just not showing up. I mean, if he really wants me to work for him he can come get me, right? But then Matt and his kids crossed my mind, not knowing if they would be safe if I didn't start working for the Wolfes. I wouldn't be able to live with myself if that was the case. Part of me feels excited to see his face every day, but there is also a big part telling me one of these days I'm walking into a pile of pig shit.

A pile of pig shit just waiting to swallow me whole.

I shake my head at my own thoughts as I reach into the pocket of my coat to pull out the keys to unlock my front door. Before I get the key in the lock, a warm hand encloses my mouth from behind. I cry out a muffled scream while I'm being pulled into the dark alley next to my house. My heart starts to beat out of my chest, and my eyes widen in horror as a familiar voice enters my ears. A voice that once was part of my dreams yet now only exists in the occasional nightmare.

"Hey, sweetheart." He places a kiss on my cheek, still walking us backwards before he pushes my back against the red brick wall, placing his hands beside my head so it's impossible for me to leave.

I try to settle my racing heart, looking into his amber eyes that almost looking orange in the night, illuminous as fuck. Like looking at the devil himself.

"Jesus, Emerson. Why do you have to scare me like that? You could just say 'hi' like a normal person." I scowl, the dryness in my mouth making me swallow hard. His military haircut is hidden under his hoodie, and his dark eyes are making the hairs on the back of my neck stand up.

I've just spent the last week with a Wolfe sitting at my bar, the leader of the crew everyone says is the most dangerous in this town, but standing here surrendering to Emerson Jones makes me believe that's a lie. Years caught up in his grip, and counting, tell me otherwise.

"What's the fun in that?" He brushes his lips against my cheek, making me shiver in the process. I push him off, trying to create some distance between us.

"Fuck off." I glare at him, only to be met by an arrogant smirk. "What do you want, Emerson?"

"Heard you got a job with Franklin Wolfe."

I narrow my eyes at him, knowing he's up to something. After sharing my life with him for seven years, I've learned that he's always up to something. Love should be unconditional, but nothing is unconditional with Emerson Jones. I learned that the hard way, more than once.

"Why do you ask?"

"Because I need an insider," he clarifies with an evil smirk on his face, telling me exactly where this is going.

Meet the pile of shit I was just referring to.

I huff in response, not willing to do his dirty work. Whatever scheme he's got planned, I'm pretty sure I'd be the one who'd get into a shit ton of trouble when any of the Wolfes find out.

"Nice try," I reply, boldly holding his gaze. It falls within seconds, the smirk replaced with an angry scowl. I swallow hard to hide my unease while I do my best to not crumble under his piercing looks like I used to.

I should've known it wasn't that easy. Emerson might've agreed to breaking up, but he will never truly let me walk away. I was sixteen when he told me he was taking me on a date, forcing me without me realizing it. Telling me that a girl like me deserved to be walking beside a guy like him.

That should've been my first hint.

The first sign I should've run the other way as fast as I could. But the sixteen-year-old me had swooned over his words, wanting to be possessed by a man like him. It wasn't until a few years later that I really understood what exactly that meant.

He grabs my face with force, brushing his lips against

mine. I can smell the rum on his breath, bringing back memories I don't want to recall.

Not now, not ever.

"It's cute, that sassy mouth on you. But it's best you don't forget who you're talking to here, sweetheart."

The pain in my chin increases as he tightens his grip just enough to make me groan in agony.

"Emerson, please, you're hurting me."

"No, *sweetheart*," he bites out with the same southern twang as Josie and me before slamming my head against the concrete wall. "You are hurting *me*. Treating me as if I mean shit to you? Who do you think has been keeping you safe all these years? Or better yet, do I need to remind you who got you and Josie this house? Don't make me take it all away, *little girl*. You will gather all the information I want, giving me the perfect advantage to finally kill that Irish fucker. You got it?"

"He'll kill me if he finds out," I whine, my cheek still painfully pressed against the wall.

A smile appears on his face that doesn't reach his eyes.

"Better you than your brother, right?"

I suck in a shocked breath at what he's implying. The thought of anything happening to my brother tightens my heart in agony.

"No," I whisper, the fear clearly perceptible in my voice.

"Yeah, I heard he's back home. I'm so happy he survived his deployment. We wouldn't want anything bad to happen now that he's finally home, right?"

I clench my hurting jaw while my palms get sweatier. Emerson still has his connections back home, and I know he wouldn't hesitate to use my brother to show me just who's in charge. I'm literally and figuratively up against a wall.

"What if he finds out?"

"Oh, sweetheart." He brings his lips to my neck, pressing gentle kisses on it before he softly bites my earlobe, knowing that's the spot that turns me on more than anything. I feel the hairs on the back of my neck stand up, but this time it's not from excitement.

It's from horror. There were times when he could've brought his lips right under my ear, and I would have turned to mush in his arms. But right now, feeling his lips on my skin, all I feel is disgust.

Finally, he places his lips flush to my ear.

"I guess you'll just have to make sure that he won't." His hot breaths penetrate my ear before he brings his head back and presses a bruising kiss to my lips.

Hard, rough, and demanding.

Just like our entire relationship.

"Bye, sweetheart. I'll see you soon." He winks, finally letting go of me, then walks out of the alley, leaving me alone in the dark.

Once he walks around the corner, I squat down, keeping my back connected with the cold wall, before burying my head in my hands. My lungs are heaving in fear, and my head spins as adrenaline rushes through my body. I bring my head between my knees, taking deep breaths to calm myself down before I look up again, met by the quiet, dark alley. Any other moment, this would be just one of the alleys in Boston that I would avoid, just to be sure. But after looking into Emerson's evil eyes, there is nothing in this dark corner that can scare me more than the thought of not complying with his wishes. A single tear escapes the rim of my eye as I realize once more that I'm still not released of the demon that occupied my life for years.

I worry he will forever hold me in his grasp.

8

Franklin

I'm sitting at my desk, looking at her through the open door of my office. She's sorting papers while standing in front of the reception desk outside of my office, trying to make sense out of the shithole that David left behind as a legacy. Apparently, he wasn't just jumping ship; he hadn't even bothered to dock it before I blew his brains out.

Shithead.

She looks up as if she can feel my eyes on her. Instantly, a glare appears on her face before she turns her focus back on the papers.

I keep a straight face, but I can feel the corner of my mouth twitch in amusement. Her black jeans enclose her legs perfectly, and her white button down is tucked in at the waist, highlighting all her sexy curves. I crane my neck a little to assess her ass some more as she struts around the desk in her high black boots, her brown hair bouncing with her movements. Her eyes find mine again, and she sighs in annoyance, shooting me another vicious glare that makes my dick become wide awake, making me wonder what kind of faces she would make while laying underneath me.

She walked in like that.

Glaring, I mean.

She pushed out a '*good morning*' with effort, but it was clear as day that she was upset. Still is. She's been scowling at me the entire time she's been here and practically barked she would '*figure it all out*' when I told her where she could find the coffee.

It's cute.

But it's also fucking distracting. I've been meaning to look at the health results of a few of my horses, but my mind keeps wandering towards the cute brunette who's mad for some fucking unknown reason. Once more, I force my focus down, looking at the pages in front of me as I light another cigarette.

"Oh, well, hello. Who are you, darling?" I hear Reign's voice outside my office. I look up, noticing my baby brother, cocking his head as he shamelessly checks her out.

"I'm the latest girl on the list of people your brother manipulated into working for him, I guess." She gives him a fake smile, waiting for a reply.

"Yeah," he deadpans, "that sounds about right. I'm Reign."

He offers his hand, then gives her one of his famous smiles, making me roll my eyes internally. Reign has this way with women that's effortless. He's the one who can sell any woman shit just by pointing his innocent eyes at her.

Kendall eyes him suspiciously before finally reaching out her hand, shaking it with hesitation.

"Kendall."

"Are you here to replace David?"

"I don't know who David is?" Curiosity washes over her face as she leans back in her chair waiting for clarification.

"Reign," I call out, wanting him to shut the fuck up.

I love my brother, and I trust him with my life, but he and I? We don't always get along, and this is one of those moments where he would do anything to see me squirm. I don't need him to make things even harder with her when she's already mad at me. Telling her we whacked the man she's replacing probably won't get me into her good graces.

"Sorry." He shrugs with a grin. "The boss is calling. I'll see you around."

He enters my office with a big smirk on his face that is met by my frustrated glare.

"She's feisty. I like her. Is she *the* girl?" He flops in the chair in front of my desk, talking way too loud in order to piss me off some more.

"Stop."

"What?! Is she?"

"Lower your goddamn voice, you tool," I snarl while I feel my blood start to boil.

I rub my face, trying to keep breathing as I clench my jaw, when really I want to punch him in the fucking face. I let out a deep sigh, looking at his taunting face, his eyes beaming like saucers. A carbon copy of my own. Yet otherwise, we are nothing alike. At least, he likes to think we aren't, and I've been going along with that for a long time now. Maybe too long, but I couldn't reach him as a teenager, and it seemed like the more years passed, the more distant we became.

Even though I'd give my life for him in a heartbeat.

"Well?" He wiggles his eyebrows, finally speaking with a

lower voice. "That's the girl, right? The one everyone keeps talking about?"

I lay my elbows on my desk, bringing my head closer to his.

"Who keeps talking about *what*, Reign?" I growl, balling my hands into fists.

He shoots me a bored look.

"Sorry, *bro.* You can't go around telling the guys you're going to marry some girl and not expect it to find its way back to me."

"Dammit, that was a joke," I mutter, the tension in my face giving me a headache. "You'd better silence those fucking chatterbox soldiers."

He cocks his head with an irritated glare.

He glowers for a moment, then shrugs.

"You're an asshole, but I'm the only one who can talk shit about you."

"Thanks," I mumble as I lean back in my chair, doing my best to relax a little.

"Anyway, I got a call from Liam."

"Carrillo?" I frown.

We've done some deals with the Carrillos before, but they usually contact me, not Reign.

"Yeah, remember the tech guy I sent them after I declined their offer?"

I nod in response, recalling how they'd wanted Reign to work for them because he's the best hacker around. Which is also the reason I'll never let him leave Boston.

Well, that and the fact that I want my brothers to be in the same city as I am. It makes it easier for me to keep an eye on them.

"He's dead." He rakes a hand through his hair, letting out a deep breath. "And they're in this crisis or something. They need my help."

"How much are they offering?"

"Blank check."

"No shit!"

I chuckle in response, knowing this must be some serious shit if Kane and Liam Carrillo are throwing away money like that.

"Yeah, so I'm gonna go. They're sending a jet." He's looking at me with anticipation, like he's waiting for my agreement even though we both know it would only be for show, anyway. Reign does what he wants. The last time I told him to stay in Boston, he disappeared to New York for a year.

The little shit.

"Yeah, sure. Go. Just keep in touch, okay?" I take my cigarette out of the ashtray and take a long draw, sucking in the nicotine.

"You know that shit kills you, right?" I follow his gaze as he sneers at the butt between my fingers.

"There is a lot of shit that could kill me, Reign. Smoking is not one of them."

"Whatever, grumpy." He gets up and walks towards the door without a second glance.

"Keep in touch, Reign," I bark to his back, knowing he didn't answer my question.

"Whatever, Franky," he answers before walking out the door.

I pinch the bridge of my nose, then turn my focus back to Kendall once again as she waves goodbye to Reign.

When she turns her head towards me with another scowl,

I offer her a genuine smile, hoping to butter her up a little bit. Instead, her lips a thin strip before she turns her attention back to the task in front of her.

I have a feeling this one is going to be a lot of work.

9

Kendall

I'm happy it's Friday because I need a fucking break from this job, which is a lot more intense than I'd thought it would be. I was expecting to be doing the books, like maintaining them because the previous person quit or something. Instead, I have to reorganize everything in order for any of it to make sense. It's a huge mess, and even though I love that I'm using my brain instead of standing behind a bar, I also feel like I've overstretched the gray matter in my head over the last couple of days. It's definitely more challenging than pouring drinks at The Library. Not to mention the nerves that hit me every time Franklin comes within a five-foot radius.

So far, I've been able to keep my distant attitude. For the entire week, I only discussed what was necessary with him and ignored his annoying glances my way. The glances that make my heart jump out of my chest. And there are a lot of them. Every now and then, he wants to 'show' me something about the books, or 'ask' me for clarification about something else. Obviously there is nothing wrong with that, you know, him being my boss and all, but he does it grazing my back with the tip of his fingers or I can feel his breath on my neck when he points to something on my desk while he's standing behind me.

It's those moments that turn my brain into mush, making it hard for me to concentrate or think at all. Each day, it's getting harder to maintain my defiant stance and not give in to the urging pull I have towards him. Not to mention that I still hear Emerson's voice rumbling through my head, threatening my brother if I don't act as his little spy.

I'm so screwed.

So yeah, I need a fucking break. A break to regroup and take some deep breaths, to make sure I keep my distance. To make sure I keep my head in the game, maintaining my distance from Franklin while gaining enough of his trust so I can find something to get Emerson off my back without any of the Wolfes finding out. The more I think about it, the more unrealistic it sounds that I can actually pull that off.

When I walked out of the house yesterday to go to the office, Nigel, one of Franklin's boys, was waiting for me at the curb.

'Franklin won't be coming in today. He'll be back tomorrow. Here are the keys to the office. I'll text you the code.' I'd just blinked in response, stunned that he would give me the keys to his office after only three days, but I eagerly took them.

My heart beat against my chest as I was snooping around the office an hour later, looking into the archives, searching through Franklin's desk, hoping to find something that would satisfy Emerson. But after three hours, I came up empty-handed. There was nothing accessible to me that would incriminate Franklin or the Wolfes in any way.

Of course not, Kenny. Like he would hide his secrets in plain sight.

I look at the clock, seeing the time ticking away. It's eleven in the morning, and he still hasn't walked through the door. As if the devil is playing a game with me, the door opens, and the subject of my daydreams walks through it. His hair is a bit messy, and fatigue is clear on his face, as if he hadn't slept all night. Regardless, he's still as handsome as ever. He takes off his coat before his eyes focus on me while walking to his office. With a scowl in place, I'm patiently waiting for a flirty comment like he's been constantly making. Obviously, I keep pretending I don't, but secretly, I enjoy his double entendre.

"Morning, Kenny," he greets me. When he doesn't say anything else, my mouth falls open a bit as a feeling of disappointment trickles down my spine.

I get back to work, feeling as irritated as I had been the entire week, determined to not let him get close to me in any fucking way.

AROUND FOUR O'CLOCK, I walk into his office holding some papers I need for him to sign.

He's sitting behind his desk, his head leaning against the back of his chair, and his eyes are closed. I frown at the sight of him, wondering if he's actually asleep.

I clear my throat, watching him carefully, hoping to get his attention.

Instantly, he opens his eyes, then blinks a few times to regain his focus.

"Sorry, I have some papers for you to sign," I explain

while he rubs his hands over his face, looking at me like I'm speaking another language. "It's just papers that confirm I'm authorized to sign off on your taxes and stuff."

"Yeah, okay." He gestures his hand to summon me closer. Then I place the papers in front of him, making sure I keep the desk between us while he assesses the documents in front of him.

"Long night?" I ask.

It's not my place, obviously, but I can't help my curiosity. Wondering what kept him up all night.

Or who.

He lifts his eyes towards mine, and instantly I regret my nosy ass as he keeps staring me down. I'm waiting for his face to display some kind of emotion, but instead, he keeps looking at me with a blank look. I fold my arms in front of my body while I bite my lip, doing my best to hide the nervous feeling that is growing in my stomach.

"More like never ending," he replies before his eyes move back down to the papers in front of him.

Quickly, I let out a deep but quiet breath, feeling relieved the moment his intense gaze left me.

He grabs a pen before his hand hovers above the papers, but then he jerks his head up.

I force a tight smile, trying hard not to let him see my discomfort.

"Are you going to fuck me over once I sign these, Kendall Ryan?" With amusement in his eyes, he waits for my answer. All I can think of are Emerson's devilish eyes.

A tightness forms around my chest while I run a hand through my hair.

"What? No," I huff out, barely convincing myself.

Clearly, he believes me because he turns his focus back to

the papers in front of him, giving me the opportunity to take a deep breath when his eyes are no longer concentrated on me.

When I walked through this door for the first time on Monday, I was pissed at Franklin because, apparently, I'm still a needy little brat.

At least, that's what Emerson used to call me.

We broke up two years ago after the twentieth time, but who's counting?

Right, I am. Because I had tried to leave him nineteen times, knowing I would be better off without him, but not feeling confident enough to leave him behind.

Not feeling confident enough to fight for my freedom. Believing I deserved every punch he ever gave me.

When he finally did let me go, it was only because he'd met some other girl, which made me feel even more worthless. I'd been crying for weeks, wondering what was wrong with me until Josie found me passed out with a bottle of tequila, doing my best to drink my pain away.

I had hit the ultimate low.

When I woke up the next day, I'd looked in the mirror, refusing to believe what I saw was me.

Refusing to accept this was what I'd become.

I looked myself in the eye and promised myself I would never be controlled by anyone again.

Ever.

And I hadn't.

For the last eighteen months, I had felt like me. Happy.

But after Emerson cornered me, demanding my cooperation, I realized I'd been lying to myself. I'm not in control at all. I'm still here, trying to stay alive in a world that's ruled by animals.

Eat or be eaten.

The only control I have now is getting to choose who will be the better option? Who will be the one who keeps me alive. Which one will leave the least amount of scars on my soul? Emerson Jones or Franklin Wolfe?

10

She looks worried, like she thinks I may devour her any second now.

Trust me, I want to.

But the insecure look in her eyes tells me she's not thinking about me the same way I am about her, leaving me wondering what the hell is going on in that pretty little head of hers. She clears her throat, straightening her back before she gives me a sassy look.

"Do I have to remind you that you *forced* me to work for you?" she sasses after I hear her let out a deep breath, clearly feeling nervous with my eyes locked with hers.

I hold her glare, the corner of my mouth slightly rising.

"I didn't *force* you, Kenny."

"You may as well have. You practically put me in a headlock." She shrugs.

I can't fight the smirk that appears on my face before I look back down again.

"I didn't, but don't give me any ideas," I murmur while I sign the papers.

When I bring my head back up, she's blinking at me, looking slightly shocked. A chuckle escapes my mouth before I hand her back the papers. Then she quickly looks through them to avoid eye contact.

"R-right. It's Friday, so I was hoping I could leave a little early."

"Sure." I lean back in my chair, shamelessly gawking at the girl who has been running through my mind this entire week. She's wearing light jeans today with a cream sweater that shows off her slender neck.

God, how I want to explore that neck while she's squirming beneath my palms.

"Thank you." She shoots me a quick smile before she turns around on her brown booties that have just enough heel to make her calves pop as she sways her hips from left to right while walking towards the door of my office.

I clench my jaw, frustrated as I watch her leave, because I don't want to wait until Monday to see her again. I bite my lip, considering my options for a second, before I let out a low growl.

"Kenny," I bark out with more force than I'd intended to.

"Yes, sir?" She spins on her heel.

"Have drinks with me." It's a statement because I rarely ask for what I want.

She blinks, her plump lips forming an amused stripe before she sucks in a deep breath.

I lift my chin, waiting for her to say yes while I feel the muscles in my face relax one by one. My gaze stays locked with hers until she finally opens her mouth.

"No, thank you." She gives me a blushing smile while I feel my face fall. A furious scowl pops up on my face when she quickly turns around, thinking that's the end of this conversation.

I let out a determined grunt as I get up, pushing my chair back before I make my way towards my bundle of annoyance. I can feel my nostrils flare and my cheeks heat the closer I get to her.

I storm through the door, grabbing her upper arm to yank her towards me. Her body is flush against mine, her face mere inches away. My eyes go back and forth over her now frightened face, looking for the same pull I've been feeling all week. Her lips part before she takes some shallow breaths.

"What is up your ass? You've been a cranky little thing the entire fucking week. I've had an exhausting twenty-four hours, and I really just want to have a drink and relax."

"Excuse me?" Her eyes widen with anger before she narrows her eyes at me and tries to push me away from her. Without effort, I hold her arm, making it impossible for her to move as I shoot her a bored look.

I'm too tired to fight her, but that also means I have zero patience for whatever fit she's about to throw.

"You're an asshole," she spits, her eyes now shooting daggers, making me smile with amusement.

"Never said I wasn't, pretty girl."

"Well, I don't really feel like having drinks with an asshole," she snarls, making me roll my eyes before I let out a big sigh, realizing she's really going to deny whatever it is that we have. Maybe it's the best thing to do, since technically she's working for me now, but I don't care. Ever since I felt her pulse racing just for me, she is who I think about at night.

She's the one I'm eager to see when I get into the office each morning.

I want her.

And I'm not going to pretend I don't.

I roughly shove her to the side, pushing her back against the wall, caging her in with my hands before I brush my lips against hers.

"That was your first lie," I muse, as my lips migrate down to the delicate surface under her ear. Gently, I press my lips against her skin while I breathe in her sweet scent, reminding me of honey. I hear a gasp escape her lips when I reach up my hand to softly grab her chin.

I smile in satisfaction when I see that the defiant look in her eyes has completely vanished.

"Why are you pissed at me, pretty girl?" I ask, thinking about the dozens of glares she's given me over the last couple of days.

"What makes you think I'm pissed?"

I arch an eyebrow, calling her out on her bullshit without saying a word while I wait for a real answer to my question. The pull I feel towards her grows by the second, and I have to breathe in through my nose to not give in to my desire to fuck her against this wall right now.

"Kenny," I demand, my voice husky and needy as my thumb starts to caress her cheek in soft strokes.

I look into her eyes, seeing the conflict that is going on in her head while she's staring at my chest, hating whatever it is that is making her too insecure to be honest about what she wants. I let go of the tension in my body, hoping it will make her more at ease while I patiently wait for her answer.

Finally, she lets out a deep breath before she looks at me through her thick eyelashes.

"You didn't come back to The Library," she whispers, her cheeks looking flushed while shame washes across her face as soon as the words leave her lips.

My eyes gleam in surprise, not expecting that answer at all.

I stopped going to The Library because I'd thought I made her uncomfortable. I'd thought she'd be more at ease when it was just the two of us working together, giving me an easier way to get to know her.

"Did you miss me?" I smile.

A slight grin appears on her face, her shame fading away as she lazily leans her head against the wall, giving me easy access to her mouth.

"Maybe."

I like her like this. When she feels comfortable enough to flirt with me, confident enough to tell me what's going on in that gorgeous head of hers.

"I didn't want to stay away," I explain, brushing my nose against hers.

"Then why did you?" Her voice is hoarse, stirring my dick to life, so it's now pressing against my pants.

"How about you have drinks with me, and maybe I'll tell you."

"Franklin Wolfe, is anything free when it comes to you?" she taunts.

"Yes," I admit, ready to push her out of her comfort zone a little further. "Sex."

I chuckle when her eyes widen in shock.

"Don't ask if you don't want the answer, pretty girl." I push off the wall, creating distance between us before I walk towards the coat rack to grab her jacket. When I turn around with her long, black trench coat in my hand, she is still plastered against the wall, frozen to the spot. She looks at me with a bewildered look, finally telling me she feels the lust between us just as much as I do.

"Are you coming, pretty girl?" I ask while I hold out my hand to her with a beaming smile.

11

I*'m fucked.*

No matter how much I try, there is just no denying it.

I'm fucked.

The second he brought his lips to my most sensitive spot, as if he'd been there his entire life, I knew I was fucked. I've been trying to keep my distance all week, yet in just five minutes, he managed to break down every wall I've built. The sexual tension climbed between us as he pushed his body against mine, making my head foggy as if I was stuck in a big cloud that's named Franklin Wolfe. And I enjoyed every fucking second of it. He barely touched my lips with his own, but already I'm craving more, feeling the desperate need to stay physically connected to him.

So much for having a backbone, Kendall.

Now he's escorting me down the clean streets of Boston while I suck in the fresh air, his arm linked through mine as if we've been doing this for years instead of minutes. I have no clue where we're going, but to be honest, I couldn't give a shit right now. Any time he'll give me, I will gladly take.

"Are you sure you want drinks? Shouldn't you go to bed?" I look up to him while we keep the same pace, thinking back to how I found him with his eyes closed back at the office.

"Will you be joining me in my bed, Kenny?" he replies, blunt as always.

Rapidly, I feel my face starting to heat, embarrassed by my question.

"No." *I think.*

"That's what I thought, so I'm postponing sleep to spend time with you."

I smile at his answer, a small flutter swirling through my belly. We continue walking in a comfortable silence for a few more minutes until he leads me into a dark alley, reminding me of Emerson. I hold on tight to his arm, my eyes anxiously looking around me until he stops in front of a black door. He knocks three times, and within two seconds, the peephole opens, displaying a dark set of eyes. They quickly assess Franklin before the small window shuts again, followed by the sound of a deadbolt turning on the other side.

"Evening, boss." The door is opened by a huge guy, tall as a skyscraper, broad like a wall. With his long, scruffy beard, he reminds me of a yeti. I'm looking at him with bulging eyes when Franklin grabs my hand, entwining his fingers with mine before softly tugging me behind him.

"Evening, bear."

"Bear? His name is bear?" I hiss incredulously, looking behind me in hopes that he didn't hear me.

Franklin gives me an amused smile as he nods his head in confirmation.

"I wonder why that is," I murmur sarcastically while we

walk through a hallway that is poorly lit, leading to a burgundy velvet curtain. The sounds of noise and music get louder with every step we take. Finally, he pushes the curtain aside, exposing me to a bar completely hidden from the outside. The area is long but narrow, decorated in the same burgundy color. On the right side is a bar as long as the entire space, while the other side holds a row of tables. A small podium is in the middle where a girl is currently playing guitar, singing some jazzy tune with her eyes closed, completely lost in her song. Almost every seat in the bar is filled, and instantly, all eyes seem to be on us when they notice Franklin entering the room.

"Didn't the prohibition end like a hundred years ago?" I joke while I try to hide my discomfort with a tight smile as I keep strutting next to him.

"Eighty-eight, but yeah." He winks, catching me off guard with his accurate knowledge of American history. He leads us to the back of the bar, towards a huge booth. It's big enough to fit at least eight people, and his brother Reign is sitting in the middle of it. Next to him sits a man with short brown hair, looking slicker than Reign in his leather jacket, yet sharing the same hypnotizing green eyes as him and Franklin.

"Well, if it isn't the feisty accountant my brother forced to work for us," Reign taunts with a boyish grin, making me blush a little.

He taps the empty spot next to him as Franklin softly pushes me in front of him.

"Come sit," Reign offers while I scooch in next to him.

"Kendall, this is Killian. The manwhore of the pack," Reign tells me before he takes a sip of his whiskey while Franklin takes the seat next to me.

I give Killian a friendly smile and offer him my hand. He eagerly grabs it, pinning me down with a barely detectable glare, but I can see suspicion in his eyes before a charming grin appears on his face. An unsettling feeling bubbles inside me while I mirror his expression to try to relieve the tension.

"Pleasure," he mutters before he lets go of my hand. "And don't listen to Prince Charming over here. He's full of shit."

"They're both full of shit," Franklin booms across the table, glaring them both into silence.

They keep their mouths shut as Franklin lifts a hand in the air, waiting for a bartender to take his order. When the waiter arrives, he turns his head towards me, his hand landing on my thigh. I bite my lip at the warmth of his palm radiating through my jeans.

"What do you want, pretty girl?"

I flutter my lashes at him while finding my voice, the small gesture of affection startling me for a second.

"Uh, yeah. Right. A vodka lime, please," I tell the waiter with a smile while secretly glancing at Franklin from the corner of my eye, still highly aware of his hand on my leg.

"So." Reign leans his elbows on the table, bringing his attention towards me. "Did my brother *force* you to come here? Because if you need saving, just say the word."

I chuckle at his choice of words, remembering our conversation from a few days ago.

"Yeah, Reign here likes to play the knight in shining armor. Saving every damsel in distress." I can hear annoyance in Franklin's voice that has my head panning back and forth between the two of them.

"Not every damsel, *Franky*," Reign scolds.

I give both of them a confused look, definitely feeling some kind of tension between them.

"Don't mind my brother here. He didn't sleep much last night," Reign mutters while he bumps his shoulder against mine.

"Who's fault was that?" Franklin glares.

"Your own, because you could've just said no."

"Like I ever say no to you."

I watch how Reign rolls his eyes at Franklin's response while the waiter sets down our drinks.

"Has he been this grumpy to you the whole week? Or am I the only one getting the honors?" Reign says charmingly, ignoring the scowl on his brother's face while I look at him from above the rim of my glass. I let out a soft chuckle before I take a sip of my drink, the clear liquor warming me inside while I enjoy the freshness of the lime.

"He's been nice."

"Just nice, huh?" Franklin muses next to me while he leans back against the bench, draping his arm behind me.

"Hmm." I shoot him a daring smile, meeting his perfectly straight face.

If I didn't have that very clear memory of his body pressed against mine just now, I would've thought he hated me. His typically blank look would be the spark to set off my fire of insecurity. But after the last half hour, I know his whole act of indifference is nothing more than that: an act. An image, an exterior he keeps up for the rest of the world, making sure everyone thinks Franklin Wolfe is nothing more than a heartless criminal. But I remember the passion in his eyes when he pushed me against that wall.

Franklin Wolfe is anything but heartless.

"Well, enjoy it, darling. He's normally not nice to anyone." Reign clinks his glass against mine before lifting it in the air. "Cheers."

"Cheers," I repeat with a pleased grin, looking between the three brothers.

They all have the same green, mesmerizing eyes and a clear resemblance in their faces, yet they are completely different.

Reign really is the charmer, with his boyish grin and his brown hair flopping in front of his forehead every time he speaks. There is a kindness in his eyes that makes it impossible to not like him, even though I'm sure he has his flaws.

Killian is a whole different story.

His appearance is more refined, yet he's equally compelling. He's well-dressed with the sleeves of his dress shirt rolled up, bringing out the muscles in his forearms, and his dark brown hair is perfectly groomed on his head. He looks like a preppy straight-A student or the perfect son-in-law, though I'm pretty sure he's neither.

My heart drops when Killian's eyes find mine, glaring at me without shame. I run my hand through my hair and breathe in through my nose, doing my best not to cower under his intimidating gaze. I smile at him, hoping to warm him up a little while Reign looks between his brother and me. When he realizes he's devouring me with just a look, he kicks him underneath the table, Franklin completely oblivious while he leans in to whisper something in my ear.

"How about I show you just how *nice* I can be later tonight?" Franklin rumbles in my ear. His breath fanning the skin under my ear, opening the box of butterflies I've been trying to keep locked.

Reign gives me an apologetic look, and I give him a tight smile while Franklin trails his fingertips up my leg, slowly moving his hand higher before he presses a kiss to my neck, practically burning me with his touch.

A gasp escapes my lips before I force my focus back on Reign.

"So there's one more Wolfe, right?" I blurt out, hoping to shift the attention in any direction but mine. Franklin straightens his body, a smug smile on his face as he leans back.

"Yeah, Connor. But we call him the ruffian," Reign responds.

"Correction, *you* call him the ruffian," Killian chuckles.

"Why is that?"

"See for yourself," Franklin replies as he pushes a strand of my hair over my shoulder. I follow his observations towards the door, my eyes instantly locking on the massive beast of a man walking our way. He's huge, not only in height but also in muscle. The fabric of his army green t-shirt is wrapped tightly around his upper arms, and I can almost feel the ground shake with every step he takes. Unlike the other three Wolfe men, he has a military haircut, but he possesses the same piercing green eyes.

"Hey, ruffian," Reign bellows through the bar before Connor reaches the booth.

"Shut up, Reign." He glances at his two other brothers before he lifts his chin, nudging it towards me.

"Is she the new accountant?" His focus moves to Franklin, barely acknowledging the fact that I'm actually sitting right here, clearly not amused by my presence.

Franklin nods his head in confirmation before he opens his mouth.

"Connor, this is Kendall. Kendall, this is Connor."

Unexpectedly, a pleased grin splits his face, then he reaches out his hand over the table.

"Sorry, just needed to make sure you weren't some kind of booty call. I don't mingle with his nightly conquests."

"Okay," Franklin exclaims with annoyance. "Don't the three of you have shit to do?" He glares at the three of them with a silent command. Reign and Killian get up, both rolling their eyes in protest.

"Make sure you don't forget one," Franklin adds, pointing his finger in a reprimanding way while still holding his tumbler in his hand.

"Whatever, tool." Reign flips him the bird before turning to me, giving me a sweet smile. "I'll see you around, darling."

"Yeah, see you." I'm surprised Killian even says goodbye to me, though he does it with that same glare, leaving me with an unsettled feeling as he and Reign walk towards the exit.

"You want me to check in on the paddock?" Connor asks Franklin, who gives him a quick nod before he follows his brothers out of the bar.

"Paddock?"

He just takes a sip of his drink, ignoring my question while he starts playing with my hair.

"What are you doing, Franklin?" I ask with a husky voice, feeling the sexual tension between us rise again, like a big blanket covering us up in our own little bubble.

"I have no fucking idea, pretty girl."

I keep staring at him while my breathing speeds up and my fingers start to tingle in nervousness. His hand migrates from my hair to the nape of my neck, then he starts to slowly massage my tense muscles. It feels amazing, so I can't help my hooded eyes. Suddenly totally consumed by his overwhelming energy while his other hand reaches for his pack of cigarettes.

"You know those will kill you," I chide.

He stares at me for a few seconds, the tips of his fingers frozen in place.

"You sound like Reign."

"Reign is right."

"You have a problem with me smoking?"

"No." I swallow nervously. "But I'm not a fan of it either."

It's nerve wracking how much I'm pulled into his energy, drowning in this intriguing man.

"Do I still make you nervous?" His deep voice makes me turn my head to look into his green eyes.

He does.

He fucking makes me very nervous, but I can't seem to stay away. It's like he has my feet concreted into cement, making it impossible to walk away. Fortunately, I don't want to.

"I don't know. You confuse me," I admit honestly, smiling inside when his hand moves away from the pack of cigarettes.

"Why is that?"

I sigh, trying to find the words to describe whatever the fuck I'm feeling right now.

"Because I know you're the most feared man in this city. I should fear you. I should walk away, keeping this professional." His eyes are boring into mine, as if he's looking into the deepest and darkest parts of my soul. The tainted parts, the parts that are hurt, the parts that contain secrets, and the parts that are filled with desire. Desire to feel him closer.

"Do you want to keep this professional, Ms. Ryan?" A hint of disappointment shows on his face, and it's like a tight grip on my heart.

"No." I shake my head. "No, I don't. But you?" I point my finger at him before I move it back and forth between the two of us. "This thing between you and me? It scares the shit out of me."

The faintest smile appears on his face, barely discernible, but I see it.

"What can I do to take that fear away?" he asks with a soft voice that melts my heart.

"Well, you could start by giving this girl something to eat because I'm starving."

A chuckle escapes his lips.

"Fair enough," he replies before he turns to find the waiter.

THREE HOURS LATER, my stomach is full, my muscles are relaxed, and I haven't enjoyed myself so much since God knows when.

"Have you ever been in love?" I ask, not sure where my bravery comes from.

"No."

"What, you can't be serious?" I exclaim, popping another cold fry in my mouth. "Not even puppy love? Middle school, high school, a college kinda thing?"

We've been talking the entire time, and though his intimidating gaze causes goosebumps to trickle along my skin every time he stops talking and stares me down like I'm the most gorgeous thing he's ever seen, it's the moments in between that kickstart the flutters in my stomach.

It's the small smiles, the soft touches as he brushes my hair out of my face, and the interest he so clearly has in me. Emerson never asked me anything. He'd always wanted to talk about him because I was just a silly student, still trying to graduate at twenty-five.

But Franklin? He keeps his attention fully focused on me, as if he needs to know everything about me, inside and out.

"I've never been to college." He shrugs as if that answers my question.

"High school?"

He stays quiet, assessing my face before he pushes a strand of my hair behind my ears like he's been doing all night, the soft brush of his fingers making me blush in response.

"I had to take care of my brothers, I didn't have time for girls." I look at him, waiting for a troubled expression to change his face. But it never comes.

"I'm sorry to hear that," I finally say.

"Don't be, I wouldn't change a thing."

I smile in response, loving how fiercely he speaks about his brothers as my eyes catch someone sitting at the bar. When I recognize the arctic blue eyes that belong to one of Emerson's guys, my stomach drops. Cary still has spiked hair that looks hard as rock with an angular jawline that used to remind me of that Night's King from *Game of Thrones*. He's also staring at me with that same cold look he used to.

Dead and scary as fuck.

Anxiety surges through my veins like a shot of heroin as I force myself to take a deep breath. My hands are starting to feel clammy the longer he stares at me, making me pray the ground will swallow me whole.

"Hey." Franklin's deep voice graces my ears before he follows my gaze, Cary turning his attention elsewhere just in time. "Are you okay?"

His brows are bunched together when he turns back

towards me, his eyes narrowing as they move back and forth, looking for some kind of answer.

I plaster a smile on my face, trying to push my nervousness away while I lay my hand on his arm, hoping to distract him.

"Yeah, I'm fine. I'm just a bit dizzy. Must be the alcohol," I joke.

A smirk appears on his face, helping my muscles loosen up even further, relieved that what I'm doing is working. Still, I can't help glancing at Cary every now and then.

Franklin's hand cups my cheek while he brings his lips to my ear, chills peppering my skin when his breath fans my most sensitive spot.

"This will be your last then," he announces, "because I need you to be completely aware of all the things I plan to do to you."

My eyes widen at his words as I clench my thighs together.

"What does that mean?" I ask, both intrigued and scared to hear him talk to me like that. Ever since I lost my virginity, sex has been a duty. A task that every boyfriend has demanded, and I, as his girl, have needed to fulfill. A duty they threw in my face many times.

Something tells me it won't be like that with Franklin.

The way he looks at me … his eyes are filled with promise, a promise to cherish me, to play my body like a piano, pressing every key with care and patience so we create the perfect melody.

I want to give in to him, but there is also a part of me that holds back, a part that remembers the past, a part that is scared to walk into the arms of another demon.

"How many men have you slept with, Ms. Ryan?"

I pull my head back, confused by his question.

"How many, Kenny?" he repeats, a little more demanding now, yet the flirtation in his eyes remains intact.

"Three," I admit as I push out the breath I hadn't realized I was holding.

It's something that I normally say with pride, being completely content with the fact that I've only ever slept with men I was serious with, even though they might not have been on the same page. But right now, assuming this man must have had hundreds of women, all capable of pleasing him to his full content, it feels like a monumental lack of experience.

He smiles as he bites on his bottom lip.

"You really are a good girl, aren't you?"

"Is that a bad thing?" I raise my chin and square my shoulders, no longer willing to be mocked by men for being a '*good girl.*' If Franklin Wolfe thinks I'll be one of those girls who does everything because he's not just a Wolfe but *the* Wolfe, well, he's fucking wrong.

"Your innocence makes you even more beautiful." He doesn't wait for my reply before he lifts me onto his lap, his arms pressing me against his body while I look down at his face.. "It also makes me want you more."

His hand threads into the hair at the back of my head, pulling me close until our lips connect. His kiss is slow, thoughtful, but clearly filled with desire. Without hesitation, I part my lips, deepening the kiss as he tugs me closer against his chest. The tips of my fingers gracing his broad shoulders with care. It seems like he's letting me take control, but in reality, he guides me with his entire body, making me lose all reason the longer our mouths connect. His hand brushes my back while our lips stay connected. Small kisses full of craving but never sloppy, causing me to forget everything around me.

I've always liked kissing, loved that passionate connection between two people, and I've never complained about the way any of my previous boyfriends kissed. Not even Emerson; he's a good kisser. But nothing compares to Franklin Wolfe. He controls my body with a simple kiss, like he holds the key to unlock every secret nerve in my body, making my body react in a way I've never felt before. I feel so good just from kissing him. My body is screaming for more, imagining his mouth all over my skin.

I break the kiss and bury my face in the crook of his neck, my lips close to his neck as I try to catch my breath.

His hand moves up under my shirt, softly caressing my back in an affectionate way.

"You still want to know my plan?" he questions against my hair.

I hum in agreement, trying to pull myself together as I breathe in his fresh scent.

"I'm going to explore every inch of your body, leaving no piece of skin untouched until I find your most responsive spots. The spots that make you come undone with just a single touch, a single kiss, a single stroke of my tongue. I will push your buttons, every single one of them until it feels like torture, and then, only then, will I make you combust in my hands, erasing from your memory every man who came before me."

I gasp at his words, literally feeling my clitoris throb inside my jeans. It takes everything in me to not start grinding against the bulge in his pants after hearing those words, so I take a deep breath to keep it together.

"You don't seem like the type of guy who settles with one

girl." I bring my head back up, looking into his mesmerizing green eyes, which are now filled with lust. Like a Wolfe stuck in a crate, desperate to get out.

"I'm not," he admits, his lips brushing against mine.

"Well, let me ask you again, then. What are you doing, Franklin?"

"I don't know, pretty girl," he answers, then licks his lips before pressing his forehead against mine. "That's the truth. All I know is that I want to take you upstairs and devour you like you've never been devoured before. And I know you want me to." He presses another kiss on my lips.

"Don't fight it. Don't fight *me*," he adds, pulling a soft chuckle from me, knowing there is no use in fighting him. The pull is too heavy, the desire too intense.

I couldn't truly fight this, even if I wanted to. He kisses me again, his thumb drawing circles on my lower back like the most delightful torture. My resistance grows smaller with every circle until finally I can't take it anymore.

"What's upstairs?" My voice is husky and scratchy. I'm barely keeping it together.

"My apartment."

"Take me upstairs."

12

FRANKLIN

It's true.

I have no fucking idea what I'm doing.

There is something about this girl that's different from the random women I occasionally take home to release tension. Those women are nothing more than an outlet, a fuck and run.

In fact, most of the time I don't even bother to ask their names. They're nothing more than a transaction, a release. I haven't set my eyes on a woman as anything other than a means to an end for years now, not willing to risk getting distracted. But this woman?

Yeah, I don't know.

For some unknown reason, I keep wanting to touch her. To feel the softness of her skin, her silk hair between my fingers. I was joking the first night we met, telling the boys I was going to marry her, but right now, I'm not sure I was.

"Take me upstairs," she rasps against my neck.

I suck in a deep breath, trying to ignore my twitching dick

as I pull her closer, feeling the desperate need to have her melt against my body.

My lips move to her neck, where I smell her honey-flavored skin.

"Are you ready, Kenny? Really ready? Because I want you. I want you, and once we go there, there is no way back." I hear her gasp as I whisper the words against her skin, then press a soft kiss below her ear, my other hand cupping her cheek to keep her still. I expect her to pull away any second now, but instead, she leans into my touch, giving me more access to her slender neck.

"What do you want to do to me?"

"I want to kiss your entire body," I say, kissing her in between every word I voice, "until all of your skin is on fire. Until you're begging me to make you explode. Until you scream my name."

"Hmm, that's an ambitious list, isn't it?" There is a laziness in her voice that turns me on even more, and I move my head back up, grabbing her chin to direct her gaze towards mine. And that's when I see it. The resolve that had previously been sewn into her soul is completely gone now.

She's mine.

"Remember how I told you I always get what I want?" I ask, brushing my lips against hers.

"You shouldn't say stuff like that."

"Hmm, and why is that?" I ask her before softly pressing my lips against hers again.

"Because it makes me want to tell you that you can't have it all."

"See, that's where you're wrong, pretty girl. Because I *can* have it all." Before she can respond, I push my lips against her with urgency, showing her that I'm not going to hold back anymore. My hand reaches up to fist her hair so I can tilt her head and deepen the kiss as my tongue sweeps the seam of her lip, demanding her to open up. When her lips part and she breathes against my mouth, I waste no time and start exploring her mouth with my tongue. Sweet and soft, but demanding. Our tongues twirl around each other in a perfect balance of slow and sensual. At first, she lets me have control, but then I feel her hands grip my shirt, pulling me tighter to her. With a moan from her, I break our connection as I gently push her off me and climb out of the booth. After she grabs her bag and stands, I press my chest against her back, and my arm wraps around her body. My mouth finds her neck as we stumble to the kitchen.

"Where are we going?" She laughs while she bends her neck some more, giving me full access. I grab her hips, and rapidly spin her to face me before I push her against the wall, pressing my body against hers.

"I'm a gentleman. I'm giving you one last chance to back out." My nose brushes against hers while I ignore her question.

"I thought you always get what you want?"

"I do. I'm having you in my bed tonight. There is no denying that. Me giving you an out is just a courtesy. Don't think I won't be able to convince you if you tell me no. *I will.* And you will say yes."

"Franklin?" she whispers softly, her breath gracing my lips.

"Hmm?"

"Take me upstairs."

The corner of my mouth curls up in a pleased grin.

"Good girl," I muse before I link my fingers with hers and tug her behind me. We move to the door in the corner of the kitchen that's locked with a code. After I enter the code, I lead her into the small corridor leading to the elevator. My ears register her panting beside me as I press the button, locking my jaw as I fight to keep myself from fucking her right here and now. The loud ping of the elevator is a relief, knowing I won't have to wait much longer. I let go of her hand, then lead her inside the elevator before I push in the code to the penthouse apartment. I can't stop looking at her, so when the elevator doors close behind us and she turns around, her eyes widen as if she's the prey that's being cornered by a Wolfe.

She is.

"No way back now, pretty girl." With one step, I close the distance between us. I cup her ass and lift her up against the wall, groaning when her legs wrap around my waist. My lips crash into hers, and she lets out a moan when our tongues meet. I can still taste the lemon of her vodka lime on her tongue, and it's the sweetest thing I've ever tasted. Her pussy is grinding against the bulge in my pants, every movement leaving me burning with more desire.

When I hear the elevator doors open up, I turn her around, carrying her into my penthouse while her hands run through my hair. She never breaks our connection, so I take long strides to my bedroom. When I reach the bed, I carefully lay her on it before I migrate down, my chin close to her body as my fingers travel inside the waistband of her jeans. With as much care as I can muster, I peel both her jeans as her thong off her hips, not stopping until they both hit the floor. I straighten my body again to take off my shirt before I unbuckle my pants and let them drop to the floor. My feet step out of them, looking down at the stunning woman in front of me, draped on my bed like it's exactly where she belongs. My jaw drops, admiring the luscious curves of her naked body, waiting for me to slide inside of her. The desire in her eyes makes my dick push even harder against the fabric of my boxers while I drag my body over her soft legs. I push my arm under her to straighten her back, then I pull her sweater over her head. She's completely naked now other than her black lace bra, so I take a moment to move back and soak her in while she bites her lip in anticipation.

"You're gorgeous, Kendall." My fingers grace her flawless skin, moving up and down her upper body until they linger around her breasts. Slowly I push her bra down, exposing her perky nipples, then I lean in and take one in my mouth while my hand starts massaging the other. She moans loudly when I suck on the soft skin. I'm thrilled when she arches her back and unclasps her bra, throwing it across the room. My hand migrates down to cup her between her legs, where I softly rub my finger through her folds.

I hear her gasp when I start exploring her body with my mouth, my lips gracing her fair skin, just like I promised her. I start at her neck, slowly moving down, not letting an inch remain untouched while I continue rubbing gently around her clit. Just around it, never actually touching it directly.

Her moans become more demanding, and I smile against her skin, pleased to have her melting under my touch.

"Franklin, please."

"Hmm, what's wrong, pretty girl?" I murmur against her skin when my mouth reaches the area between her legs. She huffs when I kiss the inside of her thighs, her pants growing even more frantic as I get closer to her center.

"Please," she begs, squirming under my touch, "please touch me."

"I am touching you."

"I want you t-to—" Her words halt when I dip my finger into her wetness. She sucks in a deep breath, arching her back to give me more access.

"You want me to what?"

"Kiss me," she pleads, her hands pulling my hair, leaving a burning feeling on my skull.

"Kiss you where?" I tease, kissing her only an inch from her center.

"Fucking *kiss* me, Franklin," she growls with force, making me chuckle against her skin before I blow lightly between her legs.

"Kiss you here?" My fingers dip in again before I coat her pussy with her wetness.

"YES!" she yells, demanding as fuck, turning me on even more.

I press my hands against her thighs, opening her up wider before my tongue dives into her hole, desperate to taste her. Her saltiness coats my tongue as I swirl it through her folds, and she tries to twist in my hands. I growl while I use my forearms to push her deeper into the mattress, making it impossible for her to move before I start sucking her clit.

"Oh God," she whines. "I can't take it. Please! Please!" Her cries become more desperate as my finger continues pushing in and out of her pussy while I lick up and down her sweet folds. I start tracing the skin just below her clit with the tip of my tongue, small brushes with each stroke, flicking her sensitive nub until finally she tenses and her pussy clenches around my fingers.

"Fuck, fuck, fuck, FUCK!" she cries out while she reaches the high she's been chasing before her body goes limp and her head falls back in gratification. I keep softly kissing her pussy in an affectionate way, not ready to relinquish her taste while she recovers from her release. My eyes glance up when she pushes up a bit, leaning on her elbows as she looks at me with dazed eyes.

"Holy hell." Her southern accent shapes her words, pulling a chuckle from me before I lick my lips. Slowly, I lift myself up, pushing my boxers down before placing my body on top of hers, my dick eagerly pressing against her entrance while I kiss her neck.

"I'm not done yet, pretty girl," I whisper, my mouth flush with her ear while I reach above her head to grab a condom from my nightstand. With a quick move, I tear the wrapper off with my teeth before I swiftly push the rubber over my cock.

"You'll kill me, Franklin."

"I know," I agree, "but I will also bring you back, baby." Without waiting another second, I push inside of her, immediately greeted by the warmth of her pussy wrapping around my dick.

"Fuck," I mutter, "you feel amazing, Kenny."

She moans in response while I start thrusting inside her, my lips still gracing the sweet skin on her neck. Her hands run through my hair before she grabs it tight, forcing my head back so I'm looking at her. I bit my lip in excitement when I see the desperation in her eyes, not sure if she's begging me to stop or to keep going.

"You like that, pretty girl?"

I thrust deeper with every pump when she frantically nods her head, presumably unable to voice anything. With intent, I slowly grind along her clit with every move, making sure she feels me everywhere with every push. When her lips part while she gasps for air, I can't stop myself from dragging my thumb over her plump lower lip before I dip it against her tongue, which she eagerly sucks on. I close my eyes at the sensation, wondering how my cock would feel in her mouth instead. The tips of her fingers trail down my back, then her fingernails dig deep into my skin, tearing at it while she drags them down, causing me to growl against her lips. When she reaches the curve of my ass, she grips my cheeks and pushes me in deeper, huffing against my lips.

"Faster," she begs, her eyes closed while she throws her head back, arching her back to bring more friction against her clit. I pick up the pace, my face tensing as I chase my release.

"Oh God. Yes! Franklin, yes!"

The feeling coursing through me gets more intense every second, even stronger as I feel her hands travel back up before she digs in her nails once more, dragging them down like she owns me, leaving her mark on me like she wants to make sure it will stay there forever. Finally, her nails reach the swell of my ass before she lets out a feral screech and her entire body goes rigid, her eyes rolling to the back of her head. I feel her walls tighten around me, pushing me over the edge while I explode inside her.

"Fuck!" I roar while I thrust inside of her a few more times before I rest my head in her hair while we both heave in exhaustion.

"Holy hell," she croaks out.

"Yeah," I huff while I wrap my arms around her and lay her on top of me. My fingers slowly stroke her back while she buries her face against my neck, her breath warming my skin in a soothing way. We lay like this for a few minutes before I hear her breathing even out. I turn her a bit to get full access to her neck. While I gingerly brush the skin on her hips, I leave soft kisses against her collarbone, eventually migrating back to the skin beneath her ear.

"Mmm, what are you doing, Franklin?"

"I want more, pretty girl. A lot more," I murmur against her skin, ready to do it all over again.

13

Kendall

I suck in the fresh air, my heels tapping on the red cobblestone street as I make my way home. Franklin wanted to let his chauffeur—I didn't even know he had one—drive me home, but I insisted I wanted to walk home. I wanted a minute to let last night sink in.

Last night was fucking incredible. I can't describe it in any other way.

Once Emerson finally had his eyes set on someone new, I'd had no desire to expand my experience when it came to sex. Josie gave me a vibrator for my birthday last year, and even though it felt awkward at first, pleasuring myself like that … I was hooked the second I had my first orgasm. It felt so damn good. I'd never believed a man was capable of making me feel that good, so I sure as fuck never thought one would. Emerson hadn't cared about my pleasure; he barely took the time to warm me up, shoving inside me like I was his to take whenever he wanted. Making me feel cheap, like a slut.

But Franklin Wolfe … sweet mother of Jesus.

He found nerves I didn't know I had, pushed buttons I didn't know were meant to be pushed, and licked places I didn't know wanted to be licked. Franklin shattered my body, only to glue it back together and make me beg for more.

Just like he'd said he would.

Is this what I've been missing out on?

Is this what everyone keeps talking about?

A smile stretches my face the entire walk home. I feel light as a feather until I notice the familiar figure sitting on my doorstep, clearly waiting for me to get home.

My heart practically stops when his glaring eyes meet mine, his mouth curling into an evil grin.

"Hey, sweetheart," he quips.

"E-Emerson, good morning." I offer him a tight smile, reaching into my bag to look for my keys while trying to avoid eye contact.

I know what he said. It's not like I've forgotten how he cornered me in that alley seven days ago, scaring the living shit out of me. But part of me had hoped that he would realize I'm not cut out for these kinds of things. I'm not some seductive con artist who can pull information out of the most dangerous crime lord in the city. Hell, up until last night, I could barely talk to him. But I should've known doing nothing wasn't going to fly. When I saw Cary last night, creeping from a distance, I should've known Emerson would be right behind him.

Emerson gets what he wants when he wants. Even if he has to risk my life to do it, not that it has ever been of value to him, anyway.

"How was your night, sweetheart?"

Before I can find my keys, he softly pulls my bag out of

my hands and fishes out my keys himself, dangling them in front of my face.

I can't prevent the scowl tugging at my lips before I reach out to grab them, only to grab a bunch of air as he turns around and walks towards my front door. He pushes the key in the lock and opens it, not even waiting for me while he makes his way up the stairs, and I follow him like a beaten puppy.

I'm no match for Emerson.

I'm well aware of that.

"Em, Josie is home." I can hear the plea in my voice. I certainly don't want him in our house either, but Josie will definitely throw a fit if he's the first face she sees on a Saturday morning.

"So?" He shrugs as he leans against the doorpost, watching me as I take the last steps until I'm right in front of him.

"Please."

He folds his arms in front of his body as his eyes roam my face, traveling all the way down to my feet before he brings them back up.

"I heard you had fun last night, sweetheart. Did he find your special spot?" Before I can respond, he grabs the back of my neck and tugs me into his body, then his tongue starts licking the skin below my ears.

Goosebumps scatter across my body while a stone forms in my stomach. He has always used that small piece of skin as an easy way to turn me on, making me wet even when I wasn't in the mood. But right now, I feel nothing but disgust, hating how his mouth is on the very same spot where Franklin's lips were less than an hour ago.

I roughly push away from him, giving him a dirty look

while my heart thrashes in my chest. I hate that he can still make me feel like I'm his little toy he can touch whenever he wants. A damn broken toy.

"Stop it, Em."

"Why?" There's a hint of annoyance visible in his eyes, making me think he's jealous, even though he is the one who dumped me for the next best thing.

"What do you want?" I counter boldly, as if I wasn't impacted by the threats he made against my brother yesterday.

"Do you have anything for me?"

"What does that even mean?" I roll my eyes.

Within a split second, he morphs into the vicious man I remember him to be, and in one fast move, he grabs my throat, making it hard for me to breathe. He spins us both then throws me against the door. When his smoky breath fans my face, instantly regretting my gutsy remark.

I could push my knee up and kick him in the balls, but my muscles always feel paralyzed when it comes to defending myself against Emerson, scared of what will happen if I actually defy him. Never have I been able to stand up for myself, always freezing under his touch, just hoping it will pass if I comply with what he says.

I thought I'd grown in the last year, feeling more confident, better able to stick up for myself.

But today is no exception. Like always, I still cower under the wrath of Emerson Jones.

"You should know by now, sweetheart. I don't play games. When I said I wanted information, I meant right now. Not tomorrow, not yesterday. Now." He softly bites my lower lip, causing bile to form in the back of my throat.

"I don't have anything. He doesn't share that part of the

business with me. I've only been working there for a week, and he wasn't even in town the last two days."

"Is it true he's been in Montana? I heard some shit about the Carrillo brothers."

"I don't know. I swear." I shake my head while a single tear escapes the corner of my eye.

He examines my face as if he's looking for the truth.

"Are you falling for him?" He frowns.

Fuck.

"No," I lie, frantically shaking my head again. "He's just a job. If I knew more, I would've told you. You know that, Emerson. I would never betray you."

Sadly, it's true. I would never betray him. Not because I don't want to or haven't thought about it, but because I simply don't know how. No matter how many times I've tried to cut ties with him, he holds me in his grasp like I'm his pet rabbit. A pet for him to play with or torture whenever and however he pleases.

"I believe you, sweetheart," he coos as he brushes his lips over my cheek, then squeezes my neck in a dominating way, knowing he can do whatever he wants with me. "But Cary told me Mr. Wolfe was pretty fond of you last night. So I have a new plan. Gain his trust. Make him fall in love with you. You got it?"

I nod my head, willing to comply with anything in this moment just to be able to get to the safety of my home. To escape his grasp and wash his scent off my body.

"Good girl," he says, while the back of his hand strokes my cheek. "Just seduce him like you seduced me, and you'll be fine."

He places another kiss on my cheek before he releases my neck and pushes off, shooting me a wink.

"Do that, and your brother will be safe. Oh, and there's a package coming tonight. Keep it safe, someone will pick it up tomorrow. Bye, sweetheart."

My mouth is so dry it's hard to swallow as I watch him walk down the stairs, feeling like it takes forever. Carefully, I take two steps to peek over the railing, letting out a sigh of relief when I see that the hallway's empty.

"What are you doing?" I jump, grabbing my heart as I turn around to find Josie staring at me with a puzzled look. "Did I hear Emerson?" She stretches her neck to glance at the stairs.

I take a deep breath and shake my nerves away before I put on a straight face.

"No, it was just the guy living on the fourth floor," I lie, walking right past her, giving her no time to ask me anything else.

14

FRANKLIN

I let out a deep yawn, feeling it flowing through my entire body, stretching the muscles in my back while I lift my arms in the air. I haven't slept much in a few days. Staying out late, dealing with business, but not sleeping last night, was worth it. My feet bring me to the kitchen of my apartment in Beacon Hill, looking out over the public garden through my kitchen window. I reach up to grab a cup out of the cabinet, then I hear the front door open as I place the cup under the machine and press the button. My nose is greeted with the sweet aroma of fresh coffee when I hear the heavy footsteps of one of my brothers walking over the hardwood floor. All three of them have keys, but at this time of day, there's only one possible option since the other two are not early birds.

"Morning, Kill," I grunt, still watching my cup fill.

"Morning."

When the machine stops, I pick up my cup and turn around, greeted by the troubled face of my brother. Resting my back against the counter, I take a sip of my coffee while I look at him over the rim of my cup.

Something is on his mind.

I know my brothers better than anyone. I know how they act; I know how they think, and I know when something is eating them inside. Reign is the one who doesn't like to talk about his feelings, Connor is the one you have to drag it out of, but Killian? He's an open book. He's also the one who has no trouble calling me out on my bullshit, expressing his doubts about business choices, or letting me know when he flat-out doesn't agree with what I'm doing. He's my partner in the biggest decisions I make for our businesses because he challenges me, and he knows what the fuck he's talking about 90 percent of the time.

He keeps me sharp when the whole world wants to kiss the feet I walk on.

Right now, he's looking at me with suspicious eyes, like he's worried and insecure even though he's never been afraid to blurt out whatever is on his mind.

"What is it?" I growl, wondering what it is that's bothering him this morning.

His lips flatten in displeasure, as if he's picking his words wisely, making me even more curious.

"Did she sleep over?"

"Why are you asking?" My brother never interferes with my choices of women, so why he has a sudden interest in my latest sleepover makes no sense.

"I don't know, Franky." He shrugs.

I straighten my back, and my jaw tenses in annoyance.

"You know, or you wouldn't be here at ten in the morning on a Saturday to see if there is a girl in my bed."

"Not *a* girl. *That* girl. I have a feeling."

"You have a feeling?" I keep a straight face, but there's no doubt he can hear the irritation in my tone. He shakes his head slightly, obviously uncomfortable with this conversation. Seeing him like this should give me a reason to take his feelings seriously, but to be honest, he's just pissing me off. Making me feel like I have to defend her, even though I've known her for two minutes.

"I don't trust her," he states with finality, as if he knows more about her than I do.

"Why?" I clench my teeth as my eyes demand that he spill whatever information he has that I don't.

"Like I said, it's just a feeling. What do we even know about her? Why is she around all of a sudden?"

I huff in response, amazed by his ridiculous reasoning.

"Kill, you do realize I pursued her, right? I forced her to work for me. I took her out for drinks. I took her to my bed last night."

"So? She could've set it all up. Who knows?"

I look at him, examining his face. I must be missing something here. I've always thought I could read people pretty well, yet not once did I have the feeling Kendall wasn't genuine. If anything, she needs convincing to spend time with me, which gets on my nerves most of the time.

"What do you know that I don't?" I scrutinize my brother as he drags his hand over his face, looking tired as fuck. He's the one we use to manipulate people; he has the skill to get people to trust him and can read body language like no other. I've always trusted his judgment, but something inside me doesn't want to believe him this time.

"Nothing." He rolls his eyes. "I can't explain it, okay? I just have a feeling she isn't really who she says she is. That she's hiding something. Let me do some background checks.

If I can't find anything, I'll shut up about her." He throws his hands up in the air in surrender, giving me a look that is washed with sympathy.

I know he wouldn't bring this to me if it was just a hunch, but everything I've learned about Kendall Ryan so far tells me she's the good girl she claims to be. That the girl intriguing me with her insecure yet defiant stance who gives me nervous glances that are quickly replaced by bold glares is genuine. She is the perfect contradiction, and she's fucking with my head.

In the best possible way.

I don't believe she's not who she says she is, but I have to give my brother the trust that he needs. The trust that makes our bond the strong one that it is.

"Fine, look into her. But if you come up empty-handed, I don't want to hear anything about it again. You got it?" I point my finger at him, showing him I'm serious.

If his feelings are right, we have to know. But if Kendall turns out to be the girl I think she is, I want her to stick around.

"I got it." He grabs his phone and keys from the counter before he knocks his knuckles on the marble, looking at me as if there's still something on the tip of his tongue.

"You really like this girl, don't you?" he finally asks.

"What do you mean?"

"I don't know. You're different with her."

His words have me reminiscing about last night. I can't deny she's stirring something to life in my body that was never there before, and I have no clue what it is.

"We'll see, Kill," I respond, not answering his question.

"Fine. I'll see you at the races. Is she coming?"

The races have always been a great way to gain new business connections and an even better way to maintain the ones we already have. Not to mention the fact that we own half of the horses that are racing, winning us a shit ton of money. Many of our associates bring their spouses or their girlfriends, but I've never brought anyone. For some reason, the thought of Kendall beside me seems like a damn good idea.

"Yeah, she's coming."

15

The door slams shut behind us, then I speed walk to my bedroom, trying to avoid Josie. I know she'll want to know where I was last night. It's not that I don't want to tell her, but after having my ex up in my personal space thirty seconds ago, I want to shower.

"Where the hell are you going, missy?" she bellows behind me, her footsteps telling me she is following in my tracks. "You can't stay out all night and not even bring me food."

"To shower." Before she can walk into my bedroom, I slam the door shut and lock it before letting out a relieved sigh.

"What the hell, Kenny! Are you seriously going to deny me whatever hot shit happened to you last night? I know you've been with Franklin. I've heard the whispers going around town."

I roll my eyes to the empty room, my back pressed against the door.

This damn town.

"I'll tell you, just let me shower first," I reply, hoping she'll let me be for five minutes.

She stays quiet for a while, as if she's contemplating if she is going to push some more or wait until I'm ready.

"Please," I call out, waiting for her answer.

"Fine. But if you're not out in the next hour, I'm using my key."

"Thank you." I chuckle before I hear her footsteps move away from the door.

I take a deep breath and rub my face in desperation, then I pull my phone out of my pocket.

My brother is a soldier, so I know he can hold his own. In fact, I wish I had his strength and confidence.

Still, I shouldn't have doubted Emerson when he said he'd hurt my family if I don't give him what he wants. He's threatened me with that many times, and knowing his track record of hurting people who don't comply with his wishes, I believe him.

I press the button to FaceTime, then wait while the dial tone echoes through the room.

"Hey, Kenny." I smile when I'm met by the bubbly face of my big brother, my eyes welling up in relief.

"Hey, Jameson."

"You okay?" He frowns with suspicion, probably seeing the emotion on my face.

"Yeah, I'm good. Just missing you." I run a hand through my hair to give myself a second to force my tears away, sucking in air through my nose before shooting him a comforting look.

"I miss you too, sis. Maybe you can come home for a few days at the end of this semester?"

"Yeah, I'll do that. Have you run into any people from high school since you've been home?" I ask casually, hoping he doesn't see right through me.

"Not really, to be honest. Except I saw Mrs. Williams the other day."

"Oh, really? How is she?" I ask him, even though I honestly don't give a shit about our old history teacher. But I led him down this road. Have to stick with it now.

"She's good. Kept me occupied for ten minutes telling me about her grandchild." He pulls a face that makes me laugh as I feel my body relax some more. "Oh, and that old friend of Emerson's. Ran into him when I went for drinks the other night."

"What old friend?" I do my best to keep a straight face, but my ears prick up as my heart rate speeds up in anticipation.

"The one with the curls. He's a bit goofy. He never went to Boston with you guys because he's running the hardware store. I forget his name."

"You mean Leo?"

"Yeah! That's him."

I sigh in relief, knowing Emerson hasn't talked to Leo in years. At least, as far as I know.

"Oh, yeah, he's nice. How's Mom?"

"She's good. Like always." He smiles. "I have to go now. I'm going for a run. Call me later?"

"Yeah, of course."

"Alright, talk soon. Love you."

"Love you." I hang up and close my eyes, leaning my head back against the door while I hold my phone to my chest, happy to know my brother is safe. Leo has never been close to Emerson, so when most of us followed Em to Boston, he stayed behind to help his dad with his store. I'm pretty sure Jameson seeing Leo was just a coincidence.

Right?

I push those thoughts to the back of my head as I walk into my small bathroom and take my clothes off. My hand reaches out to turn on the faucet before I step under the warm stream, letting the water run through my hair. I feel like I can finally breathe, feeling comfortable in the safety of my small shower with nobody getting into my personal space, making me nervous as fuck.

How the hell did I end up here?

Two weeks ago, I was finally feeling free of Emerson, working at the bar to pay my bills and studying my ass off so I could graduate this summer. Life was finally calm, boring, and uneventful, leaving me to live my life in peace until I move back home after graduation.

I press my head against the wet tiles, closing my eyes, thinking about the mess I'm in.

Yet here I am, two weeks later, caught between two notorious criminals.

One demanding my attention, the other demanding me to give him the information he needs to bring the other down.

Franklin will kill me if he finds out I'm part of Emerson's plan.

Emerson will kill my brother if I don't do what he asks.

Either way, this doesn't end well for me. Not to mention the fact that Franklin ignites something inside me that makes it hard for me to keep my distance from him.

Especially after last night.

THIRTY MINUTES LATER, I've calmed down a bit and am walking into the living room. My hair's still wet, and I'm wearing some jeans and a sweater, feeling the need to wear something comfortable because life refuses to give any to me.

Josie's feet are tucked under her ass while she's sitting on the couch reading a magazine with a cup of tea in her hand and a bag of Hershey's on her lap. She glances at me when I flop onto the couch next to her before her eyes move back to the pages in front of her, as if she isn't dying to know what I was up to last night. Even though I'm sure my walk of shame told her enough.

"Really, J?"

"Ssh, I need to finish this first."

I roll my eyes at her, letting out a small grunt.

She's such a drama queen at times.

She makes me wait another minute before she closes the magazine and throws it on the table. Then she faces me, getting more comfortable on the couch before she takes a sip of her tea.

"Spill it, woman." The stern look she gives me makes me snicker.

"What do you wanna hear?" I shrug, not sure where to start.

"Every-fucking-thing. Did you sleep with him?"

"Yes." I avoid eye contact, feeling a bit slutty for admitting that, even though I'm hardly a slut compared to her escapades.

"I knew it!" she screeches in joy, almost jumping off the couch in excitement. Her eyes are sparkling in mirth when she starts the cross-examination she's been waiting for.

"Did he take you home?"

"Yes," I admit with a small voice, burrowing a little deeper into the couch while I hide my face behind my hands.

"After work?"

"No."

"No? He fucked you in the office?"

"Jesus, Josie!" I exclaim incredulously at her bluntness. "Of course he didn't fuck me in the office. You make me sound cheap."

"Oh, please. There is nothing wrong with a good fuck in the office." The way she states this in her thick Southern accent makes me giddy just thinking about it.

"He took me for drinks first," I explain, resulting in Josie clapping like a seal, "after he cornered me in the office and kissed me."

"WHAT!" She bounces on the couch, and I let out a full belly laugh at how ridiculous she looks. Though to be honest, I probably would've done the same if it was her telling me she slept with Franklin Wolfe. And I haven't even mentioned that it was the best sex in my life.

"I knew it! I knew that guy had a thing for you! Told you, you were on his radar."

I hold my face in my hands, listening to her and realizing she's probably right.

"So, how was it?" she continues, her lashes fluttering in anticipation.

I let out a satisfied grunt while I sink deeper into the cushions.

"Fuck, J. It was incredible." I close my eyes and bite my lip, getting all turned on again while I think about his hands on my body.

"Dear Lord," she drawls. "Rate it for me on a scale from one to ten."

"Hell, twelve," I blurt without hesitation.

"A twelve?!" she screeches, her mouth gaping.

"A twelve. That man knows his way around a woman's body. Clearly he's had some practice."

"Well, yeah, obviously. He's slept with almost every woman in South Boston."

My smile wilts when I realize what she's saying. I know he isn't a saint. I mean, rumors about how the Wolfes lure women into their beds have been going around town for as long as I've lived here. I know this. It's nothing new. But after spending last night with him, I can't deny that there is a part of me that's hoping things will maybe be different between us.

That he actually likes me.

"Oh God, I didn't mean it like that." Josie's looking at me with sympathy, slightly shaking her head.

I wave my hand in the air, brushing her words away.

"It's fine. I know who he is. I don't expect to be anything special." I push the words out without a second thought, though my heart takes a beating when they leave my tongue, making me feel stupid. Why would I think I would be any different to him than any other girl he's slept with? Hell, why would I even want to be special to the most powerful criminal in Boston? My ex is only a small fish compared to Franklin Wolfe, and look where dating him got me? Basically, fucking nowhere other than under Emerson Jones's thumb until he decides he no longer needs me. I need to get through this, graduate, and get the hell out of dodge. Move back home, start over, and live a nice, boring life.

She stays quiet for a few beats, then cries out, "Oh, crap! You like him!"

"What? No!"

"Yeah, you do. I can see it in your eyes. You like him."

"I do not." I fold my arms in front of my body, like a three-year-old, hoping she'll let this pass.

"Kenny, don't lie to me. I can see it in those sparkling eyes when you mention his name or when you got all giggly when you admitted that you slept with him. Plus, your head almost exploded when I mentioned him fucking other women. Just admit it. *You like him.*"

I bury my face in my hands, shaking my head at her remarks.

"*You like him,*" she repeats, this time more demanding, telling me she's not going to let this one pass.

"I like him," I confess against the palms of my hands, muffling my words. I hate admitting it, but there is no denying what's written all over my face.

I like Franklin Wolfe.

Even though I shouldn't.

"What was that?" She brings her hand behind her ear, demanding me to say it again, louder, like the bitch that she is.

"I like him!" I exclaim before I push out a frustrated breath. "I like him, okay? There! Happy now?"

"Now what? When are you seeing him again?"

"Monday, probably." I shrug. This morning, part of me was hoping he would ask me to go to dinner with him tonight or something, but after getting cornered by Emerson, I just want to call in sick and hide from him. How am I going to look Franklin in the eye, knowing I have to screw him over in order to keep my brother safe? I need to find a way to detach myself from him, yet still get him to trust me, preferably in a way that I can still live with myself.

This is impossible.

My thoughts are interrupted by the ringing of my phone, and I glance at the screen, noticing an unknown number. My eyes move towards Josie, shrugging my shoulders when she looks at me, silently asking me who it is.

"Hello?"

"Pretty girl." When his deep voice meets my ear, a wide smile instantly appears on my face.

Stop that, Kendall.

"Mr. Wolfe."

"Are we back to that?"

"I don't know," I answer softly. Josie is hanging on my every word, her head resting in her hands as if this is the best story she's ever heard.

"Call me Franky, Kenny. I want to take you to the races this afternoon."

"The races?" Josie's eyes widen in surprise when she hears the words leave my lips. Then starts to quietly clap like a seal, making me chuckle.

"Yes. I'll pick you up at four. Bring a coat, it will be cold." His tone leaves no room for anything other than agreement, but my conscience is protesting heavily. I want to comply and spend time with him, but I'm scared to face him now that Emerson paid me another visit. I'm worried he'll see right through me the minute he lays his eyes on me.

"Okay," I respond, knowing he won't take no for an answer anyway.

"Good. See you in a bit, Kenny. " He hangs up, and I look at Josie, unable to hide my concern from my face.

A grin splits her face from ear to ear until she notices my unease.

"What am I going to do, Josie? He's a criminal! Emerson was enough for me. I don't think I can do this."

"Kenny, one of the hottest guys in this city, wants your attention. So what if he's a criminal? That's nothing new to you, doesn't mean he's anything like Emerson. Just enjoy the ride."

I press my lips together while a nervous ball forms in my stomach, making it hard for me to breathe. My hands are fumbling with my sweater, not knowing what I should do while Josie keeps her eyes focused on me.

"What's going on, Kendall?" She stares at me until I look up and rub my hands over my face.

My mind keeps switching back and forth between Emerson's devilish brown eyes, haunting my nightmares, and Franklin's green eyes chasing me in my dreams. Both men are capable of things that are not meant to see the daylight, both ruthless when people betray them, making it impossible for me to determine who's the bigger evil.

"I need to tell you something," I blurt out, already regretting the words that are about to leave my lips but realizing I can't do this by myself.

"Okay," she says, dragging the word out so that it lasts at least two seconds.

I shift my body towards her before I suck in a deep breath, trying to calm my nerves.

"You can't tell anyone." She chuckles at my serious expression, to which I scowl in response. "I mean it, J. This is serious. If this gets out, I'm in serious shit."

She raises her hands up in surrender, waiting for me to continue.

"Okay, okay. I won't tell anyone." I push out the air in my lungs, trying to push my anxiety out with it. Which works for shit, obviously.

"Emerson cornered me last week. Actually, he jumped me

in the alley beside our building." Josie's eyes grow bigger by the second.

"He did what?" Her tone is furious. "Why would he do that?"

"He found out I was going to work for The Wolfes. He forced me to spy on them for him. To give him any information about them that I can find."

"That son of a bitch. Kenny, this is bad." Josie voices this in a reprimanding tone as if I didn't know this already.

"I know!" I yelp in frustration, knowing how bad this sounds.

"You don't fuck with the Wolfes, Kenny. Or Emerson."

Yeah, as if I don't know that too.

As if I don't know how fucked I am.

"He threatened Jameson, Josie!"

"Who? Emerson?"

"Yeah." I nod with a sigh. "If I don't give him what he wants, he will hurt Jameson."

She blanches as she processes the words, her eyes widening in shock.

"Dear Lord, Kenny. That bastard can never let you go, always ready to fuck up your life and make you do whatever he wants."

Her comment hurts, but she's right.

"I know! I'm in so much shit." I jump up and start pacing around the room, my heart racing. The panic entering my body is making it hard to breathe.

"What is it exactly that he wants?" she asks carefully.

"At first, it was information, but now that he knows I slept with him he wants me to gain his trust."

"How the fuck does he know you slept with him?" she shrieks, shaking her head in confusion.

"He's tracking me."

"He's tracking you?"

I nod my head in confirmation.

"I saw Cary while I was having drinks with Franklin yesterday."

"Dear Lord, Kenny. This is bad. This is really bad."

"I know! What the hell am I going to do?"

"As much as I want you to tell Emerson to go fuck himself, we all know he'll beat the crap out of you if you defy him. It wouldn't be the first time," she mutters. "So you're going to have to gain Franklin's trust and give Emerson what he wants. This is Emerson we are talking about. You know what he's capable of."

"What if Franklin finds out?" I hiss, running my hands through my hair.

I knew this was a fucked-up situation, but hearing Josie confirm it heightens the panic in my body, making me want to run and hide.

"Emerson on a mission is far more dangerous than Franklin Wolfe. You know Emerson. He gets what he wants. If he wants to bring the Wolfes down, he won't stop until he succeeds. I don't know for sure, but I've never heard stories of Franklin Wolfe torturing anyone, yet I sure as fuck have seen Emerson doing it."

"Fucking hell," I mutter, freaking out some more, knowing she's right. "I can't do this, Josie. I can't handle Emerson, and I sure as hell can't handle Franklin Wolfe. I'm not the kind of girl who can stand up for herself, let alone seduce the biggest criminal in the whole of fucking Boston. What am I going to do?"

She takes a deep breath before giving me a knowing look.

I already know I'm not going to like whatever is about to roll off her lips.

"The fact that he just called you means he's already interested. So you are going to put on the show of your life and make Franklin Wolfe fall in love with you."

Holy hell.

16

Kendall

Franklin picked me up right on time, so we arrived at Killimore Down just before four thirty. He looks incredibly handsome with his gray dress shirt and black pullover, looking like the epitome of a successful man. He was waiting for me outside, leaning casually against the car when I walked out the door, feeling nervous as fuck. My hands were sweaty, my heart was pounding in my chest, and I felt like my feet would stumble underneath me with every step I took.

But he changed that pretty quickly.

His eyes sparked with lust as his eyes drifted over my body, my nervous feeling instantly fleeing, making me feel sexy and conscious at the same time. For a second, I felt like my tweed skirt was too short, worried that my black sweater was too plain, my gray woolen coat too boring, and my black fedora not classy enough for an event like this. But when his eyes flashed with approval and the corner of his mouth curled up, my worries melted away, giving me the courage to press myself against his body to press a kiss against his lips. When I pulled back, I wanted to get lost in his gorgeous green eyes, but then he glanced up, and I turned around to follow his gaze. Josie was waving from our front window, the stern look on her face reminding me I should shut my feelings off. I sighed deeply before I put on my game face and internally cautioned myself that this can't be real.

Put on the show of your life, Kendall.

The heels of my black, knee-high boots click against the floor as he escorts me to one of the private boxes. Inside is a large table, and because it's surrounded by higher rows of stands. It's like we have our own space, separating us from the regular audience and shielding us from the boxes on either side. When I see the perfectly set table containing more cutlery than I've ever learned to remember in my life, I suddenly feel extremely out of place. As if he can feel my unease, Franklin places his hand on the small of my back and brings his lips close to my ear.

"It's what money buys, but you can't buy class. Which you have in spades. You're fine, pretty girl. Go take a seat. I have to talk to the hospitality manager." He presses a chaste kiss on my cheek, making me feel better within a second. When I look down on the racetrack in front of me, I feel a sense of excitement I've never experienced before. A smile stretches my face when I hear the familiar voice of Reign walking down the steps.

"Well, well, look at you." His eyes are taking me in as I turn around to greet him.

"You look great, Kenny." Before I can reply, he grabs my hand, brings it in the air, and starts spinning me around.

I like Reign.

He's fun, sweet, easy on the eyes, and definitely one of the

Wolfe brothers who is on my side, making me like him even more.

"And you even put knee-high boots on. How the hell did you get past him?" He looks down at my new boots before nodding his head towards Franklin. I thank Josie in my head for putting my outfit together.

"Oh, stop it."

"I mean it, girl. You look great."

"Thank you," I reply before I take a seat in one of the chairs. Reign takes the seat on my right as I examine his outfit. Unlike his brother, he isn't wearing a pullover. No, Reign stopped at the dress shirt with a tie combined with a long black coat. The ensemble is capped off with Adidas shoes and a scally cap.

"I thought men didn't have to wear hats to the races?"

"Oh, we don't. But it's my only opportunity to wear this cool thing." He winks as Franklin takes his place on my left, placing his hand on my leg. It feels familiar, as if I belong to him, and I can't help but smile at the sight of it while I fight to ignore the flutter in my belly.

"So when do the races start?" I ask.

Franklin softly squeezes my leg so I look at him.

"Not for another hour."

"An hour? Why are we here already then?"

"To make an appearance," Reign mumbles beside me.

Before I can ask why, Connor walks down the steps towards us. His huge body is covered in a sweater and a leather jacket, clearly not interested in following racing day etiquette but looking nice, nonetheless.

"Hell will freeze over before you'll see him in a three-piece suit. Makes sense, though. Have you ever seen a ruffian in a suit?" Reign whispers this in my ear when he sees me checking out Connor.

"Where's your suit, Connor?" Reign bellows for the sake of it.

"Shut up, tool," he snarls before he turns his troubled face to Franklin. "I need to talk to you about your girl. Something's wrong."

Franklin jumps up then turns towards Reign, pointing his finger at him with a reprimanding look.

"Stay with her!" Without giving me a second glance, he follows Connor back up and out the door, leaving me behind with Reign and a lot of confusion. An aggravated ball forms in my gut when I consider Connor's words.

Your girl.

Flashbacks of Emerson telling me about his side chick run through my mind, and I can't help but feel stupid. How could I have been stupid enough to think I'd be the only girl in his life after one night? The thought that I had made me feel even more stupid because even though I'd tried to keep him away the last few days, what happened last night definitely made me feel something. Made me realize it's impossible for me to pretend otherwise. It's a little too late to *keep my feelings out of it*, and even though I don't want to like him, I do. I hear Josie's voice booming through my head ... '*make him fall in love with you.*'

But what if I fall for him first?

I brush the thought away, knowing my feelings don't matter. I just need to gain his trust and keep him interested. My track record may not be the best with men, but I do know one thing: they all want to be challenged. I'd vowed to myself that I would never let someone treat me like a side piece ever again, and I'm sticking to that. Right now, all I need to do is focus on keeping his attention long enough to please Emerson.

Deciding to be brave, I turn my head to Reign.

"His girl?" I ask.

He has a relaxed grin on his face until he sees my expression. His face falls before he considers my question and lets out a chuckle, pissing me off even more.

"Honestly, if I'm one of many girls on a list, I'd like to know. I have no illusions. I mean, I realize that he's Franklin *fucking* Wolfe, but if he's sleeping around with multiple women, I would appreciate a heads up. Don't get me wrong, I'm not expecting him to be exclusive with me, but I don't want to be confronted with other women who share his bed. I don't normally share, but I may consider it because something about your brother keeps my attention. But I'd like to have all the facts first. I think that's the least I deserve." I finally stop rambling, trying to hide the insecurity I just spewed while simultaneously feeling brave as fuck at the same time.

Tell 'em, Kenny.

Reign smiles at me with sympathy before he gets up and holds out his hand. I huff in response, my aggravation now replaced by anger over his lack of an answer.

"Come on," he commands as I cross my arms over my chest.

"Not until you answer me."

"I'll show you."

I roll my eyes at him. Is he for real? As if I want to be watching Franklin with *his girl* right now, whoever the bitch may be. I can't believe I let Josie talk me into thinking I could actually do this. How do you keep the attention of a man who has an entire city at his disposal?

"Come on, silly. You can trust me." He's looking down at me with a devilish gleam in his eyes. I try to keep my face straight, but I can't help feeling the corner of my mouth tilt up slightly. Finally, I place my hand in his before he pulls me on my feet and ushers me outside of the box.

My arm is hooked in his and his free hand is resting on mine as he leads me through the corridors until we reach the paddock; the late afternoon sun instantly warming my face. The track is filled with women wearing heels and big hats, escorted by men wearing three-piece suits like Franklin and Reign.

"Where are we going, Reign?" I finally ask when we come closer to the stables, near the groomsmen taking care of the horses.

I glance around me, looking for Franklin, even though I'm scared of what I may find. Not that I expect Reign to confront me with one of his brother's *girls*. I know I should focus on the main goal—gaining Franklin's trust—not worrying about who he fucks and when, but after spending the night with him, I can't help what I feel for the man. It's strong enough to not want to see him wrapped around someone else.

"Kenny, really. You can trust me." Reign offers me a smile while we keep walking. "My brother is an asshole. But he's not the kind of asshole you think he is."

"Aren't they all?" I mutter loud enough for Reign to hear.

"Who made you believe that?" His voice sounds concerned, making it hard for me to keep my distance, even though I know I should.

Without answering, I let out a deep sigh, hoping he'll let my comment pass.

"Spill it, girl," he commands in a jovial tone, even though I can tell he's serious.

"My ex."

He stops us in the middle of the path, horses either side of us, as he looks at me in concern.

"Is that why you don't trust men? Did he cheat on you?"

I avert my eyes in shame before I offer him a silent nod. It's not my fault, I know that. Many people have told me that a hundred times, but whether it was my fault or not doesn't take away the shame of it. Embarrassment that I let him toy with me, let him do whatever he wanted. That I still do now.

"Did he hurt you?" He nudges up my chin, forcing me to look at him as my eyes well up.

I hate the concern I see in his eyes, the genuine interest that makes me want to tell him everything about Emerson Jones and how he haunts my past. And my present now too. How I was breaking loose, finally finding myself and the confidence to hold my own. Thinking I'd grown to the point where I would not let him waltz all over me. Who was I kidding?

I can't stand myself standing here in front of Reign, acting like that's all in the past when really, having Emerson in my life has never weighed heavier on my heart than it does right now. For a split second, I contemplate telling Reign everything, hoping the Wolfes can save me from my demons and keep my brother safe at the same time. But the thought is quickly pushed away by memories of Emerson's dark eyes, his cruel grip, and his history of brutality.

I take a deep breath.

"Yes, he did."

"I'm sorry that happened to you, Kenny. But my brother will never hurt you like that." He cups my cheek before he tugs me into his chest, giving me a warm hug. I smile at how affectionate Reign is, reminding me of my own brother. When he pulls back, he wraps his arm around my shoulder, moving us forward again.

"Come on, it's right there." He nods towards the last stable on the right where Connor is draped over the stable door, a stableboy standing next to him.

I frown in confusion, wondering what's going on when Connor sees us approaching, mirroring the puzzled look on my face.

"What are you doing here?" he booms before we reach the stable.

"Kenny wanted to meet Franky's *girl*," he emphasizes.

Connor's brows shoot up in realization before he lets out a chuckle.

"Yeah, okay, fair enough."

I crane my head to look into the stable, seeing Franklin crouched down in front of a gorgeous, auburn-brown horse while holding one of the hoofs in his hand. Its mane and tail are light blonde, in bright contrast to the rest of the brown fur, giving it a royal appearance.

Franklin looks up when he hears Reign's voice, his eyes meeting mine before he lets go of the horse's leg and straightens his body.

His impassive face makes me wonder if he's unhappy to see me here. His eyes meet Reign's with a questioning look, then he glances at me with a smile that is barely detectable.

"Kenny here is dying to meet *your girl*." Reign wears a mocking grin.

Franklin shoots me an apologetic look then moves closer, reaching out his hand towards me in silence. I grab it without hesitation before he tugs me closer and curls his hand around my neck. As his eyes roam over my face, I enjoy how close we are, even though the stable door is still between us.

"Are you jealous, pretty girl?" he taunts with a smug grin.

"Maybe." I shrug, telling myself it's just an act.

"Don't be. Come on, meet my girl." He lets go of me, grabbing one of my hands before he opens the bolt with his free hand, ushering me inside the stable.

17

Franklin

"She's my lucky charm," I explain as Kendall reaches out to pet my girl's velvet nose. "This girl has never lost a race."

"Is that really her name? Lucky Charm?"

"No, her name is Posey." I move closer, invading her personal space, my breath fanning her face while we both stroke the soft fur of my horse. "And that's her sister, Inka." My finger points to the black horse standing in the stable next to us before I quickly glance at Reign and Connor, who are watching us with interested expressions on their faces. My jaw flexes in annoyance, not liking being a part of their entertainment, which I communicate to them with my eyes. They never take an interest in the female company I keep, but apparently, all of my asshole brothers have a feeling this one is different because they keep butting their big heads up in my business.

"Right," Connor finally says when he sees the look on my face. "We'll see you back in the box." He claps Reign on the back as a sign for them to leave, but my youngest brother doesn't move, displaying that mocking grin of his that pushes all of my buttons.

"What?" he drawls, as if he's oblivious to my wishes.

He's not.

In fact, Reign and I may not see eye to eye, but we can have an entire conversation without voicing one word, the looks on our faces speaking for us.

I pinch the bridge of my nose, trying to stay calm.

"Leave, Reign."

"Fine," he chuckles as Kendall turns to give him a sweet smile that heals my fucked up heart yet irritates me at the same time. I like that she gets along with Reign, knowing that out of all four of us brothers, he's the one who deserves every kind smile that he receives. But I don't need anyone on Reign's team. He already makes life harder for me every chance he gets. I growl when he shoots her a wink, laying his ridiculously boyish charm on her before he finally walks off with Connor.

Asshole.

When they are out of sight, I bring my eyes back to Kendall and brush a strand of hair off her face, the tips of my fingers caressing her fair skin.

"You guys don't really get along, do you?" she asks carefully. She avoids making eye contact with me, telling me she's unsure of how I will respond to her question. It's none of her business, and I can't help but hear Killian's words in the back of my head, asking me to be careful. But for reasons I can't explain, I want this girl to open up to me, and I'm smart enough to realize that won't happen if I don't do the same.

"It's not that we don't get along. We used to get along better than any of us." Her eyes find mine again as she looks up from beneath her thick lashes. I let the corner of my mouth rise up a little, showing her she doesn't have to be wary of me.

"What happened?"

"Life happened. I did things Reign didn't agree with." I softly push her back, crowding her space until her back hits the cold concrete of the stable. "Are you the jealous type?"

She huffs in response while I brush my nose against hers, needing to taste this girl like I did last night. To sate the craving that I thought I'd satisfied yesterday when really all it did was make me long for more. Wanting to corrupt her more until there is no way back for her.

"No, yes. I don't know." Desperation reshapes her face, and she wrings her hands, making me want to fix whatever issues are going through her pretty little head. My mind is dying to know what made her so insecure that she's scared to answer a simple question.

"Who hurt you, Kendall?" My question surprises her because she jerks her head back and her eyes widen. It's like I can see the cogs turning in her brain. First, she starts chewing the inside of her cheek, but then I watch her grow almost an inch after she squares her shoulders.

"Who says anyone hurt me?" Her defiance turns me on, even though I just watched her scrape the bottom of her internal barrel to find the strength to challenge me, making her even more of a turn on. I don't feel the need to scare women, especially not this one, but I can appreciate anyone who can overcome their fears, and standing up for herself is clearly a fear of Kendall Ryan's.

"You got insecure when you heard Connor refer to my horse as 'my girl', you are scared to tell anyone what you want, yet you try your hardest to change that, and you become smaller and look like you're scared I will lash out when you ask me personal questions." She just blinks while the back of my hand strokes the soft skin on her cheek. "Who hurt you, pretty girl?" I ask again.

"My ex," she admits, looking off in the distance as she rubs the back of her neck.

"The ancient one?" I growl, looking into her deep blue eyes. My fingers dig into her sides while I try to curb my frustration, thinking about some asshole treating her like shit.

She gives a single, decisive dip of the chin, looking at the floor before I bring one of my hands up to nudge her chin, forcing her to look at me.

"Is he from Boston?"

She shakes her head, a hint of panic in her eyes.

"Does he live in Boston?"

She closes her eyes as if she's hoping I will go away and stop asking questions, that's never going to happen.

I'm a Wolfe, after all.

"Just leave it, Franklin. It's in the past. Yes, he hurt me. But I'm trying to work on myself, to do a better job of sticking up for myself. Let's not talk about my ex." I can see fatigue creeping into her features, and all I want to do is take her worries away, to kiss it all better while I look for the son of a bitch so I can teach him a lesson on how to treat a woman. My eyes assess her face while my thumb softly strokes her jaw.

"Okay, Kenny. But let me make one thing clear," I say while my eyes peer down at her troubled face. "Never be scared to ask me anything. Don't hold anything back. You can trust me. I *want* you to trust me. Be honest with me. About *anything*."

Her eyes darken a bit as her hands reach out to my coat.

She starts fumbling with the buttons; her face fixated on my chest.

"Hey." I run my hand through her hair before I fist it and tilt her head back so I'm peering down at her with a more demanding look this time. "I mean it. Trust is key to me."

I lean in to press a soft kiss to her lips, doing my best to convince her of what I'm saying.

I'm not as ruthless as most people paint me to be. I value people; I value relationships. Relationships are built on trust and loyalty. Give me that, and I'll give it back.

"Okay," she finally whispers, though I'm not sure she really believes me. I tug her to my chest before I kiss her soft lips again. "Come on, pretty girl. The races start in twenty minutes."

"She won't be racing?" She looks back at Posey with a confused look on her face.

"No. Today is the junior league. Posey was supposed to race tomorrow."

"But she can't now?"

"No." I shake my head. "She won't."

"What's wrong with her?"

"Someone put a nail in her hoof."

Her expression turns horrified.

"Who would do that? Is she gonna be okay?"

"She will be in a week or so. The person who is responsible won't be."

I carefully grab her arm to escort her out of the stable, then close the door behind me, turning the deadbolt to prevent Posey from running off on her own. Just as I place my hand on Kenny's back to encourage her to start walking, we're approached by a little girl in pigtails who is beaming up at Kendall.

"Hey, little girl," Kendall greets her as she crouches down to eye level. The girl doesn't say a thing, just hands her a piece of paper that's folded into the shape of a butterfly.

"Is this for me?" Kendall opens her hands to accept the paper, gifting the little girl with a smile that sparks a warm feeling inside of me.

The girl nods and places it in the palms of Kendall's hands.

"Thank you so much," Kendall tells the girl who is now studying me with an intimidated look on her cute little face. "Did you make this?" I hear Kendall ask while I look around to see who she belongs to. Without replying, the little girl turns around and runs off.

"What was that? Do you know her?"

"No clue, Kenny." I offer my hand, helping her to straighten her body. I then offer her my arm, and she hooks her hand in there.

I walk us back to the main building while she holds up the butterfly in her hand.

"It's Origami. A Chinese folding technique. My grandma used to make these with me when I was younger," she explains, pulling a grin from me. For no reason at all, I press a kiss on her hair while I breathe in the sweet smell of her vanilla shampoo. The act surprises me since I've never been touchy feely with any other women. I've always been distant with people, and I rarely grant any kind of affection outside of the bedroom, but this woman fucks with my head, and frankly, I don't give a damn.

We enter the box five minutes later, and she takes a seat next to Reign. I stand beside them, my back pressed against the railing.

"Satisfied?" He softly bumps his shoulder, giving her another friendly wink.

Her cheeks redden as she glances at me before turning back to Reign.

"That was embarrassing. But yes."

"Hey, what's that?" He frowns as he looks down at the Origami butterfly in her hands.

"It's a butterfly. This little girl gave it to me down at the stables."

The blood leaves his troubled face, growing paler by the second.

"Can I see that?"

She hands him the piece of paper, and he twirls it in his hand, his lips pressed in a thin line before he gives it back and continues perusing the track.

"What is it, Reign?" I fix him with a stern look, demanding an explanation for his pained expression.

His eyes find mine before he softly shakes his head, forcing a smile onto his face.

"Nothing. Just reminded me of someone."

"You sure?" I know my brother. He's fun and easygoing most of the time, but he has a heavy heart and more empathy in his pinky than I have in my entire soul. It's what broke our relationship all those years ago, and I know he doesn't turn quiet unless something is eating him up inside.

"Really, Franklin. It's cool." He gives me a harsh look, telling me to let it go as his eyes darken. "Just a memory. Don't worry, it has nothing to do with you." His sneer telling me that's the end of this conversation, even though it has barely begun.

Like every conversation we've had the last decade.

18

Franklin

She jumps with excitement, a huge grin on her face while the crowd around us cheers for number eight, the winning horse.

"Did you bet on number eight?" Her hands are pressed against my chest as I wrap my arms around her waist.

"No, pretty girl. I don't gamble." I dip my chin, dropping a kiss against her lips.

"You don't?" She frowns in surprise then crinkles her nose a little, making her look cute as hell. "So it's just a rumor that you run the biggest illegal gambling circuit in Boston?"

I smile at her boldness as I adjust my cufflinks.

"What do you know about illegal gambling, Ms. Ryan?"

"Nothing. Other than you are, apparently, the one leading it all. But maybe I need to check my sources."

"Oh, you should definitely check your sources," I taunt, gripping her hips a little tighter. "But I didn't confirm or deny anything, so who knows?"

She tilts her head.

"So you can't teach me the ropes of the underworld?"

"I can teach you a lot. Making you part of the gutter of Boston ain't something I'm willing to teach you, though."

"What? The king doesn't want a queen?"

The thought alone makes my heart stop for a second, and actually it likes what she's saying. Yet I keep my reaction off my face, and instead examine hers for any motive.

"Do you want to be queen, pretty girl?"

"No," she says resolutely, the look on her face growing sterner as the moments pass. "I'd rather just live my life in peace."

"Peace is not always an option."

"I know, but if it is an option, I'll take it." Her focus moves to the floor, her thoughts clearly forcing her happy mood to disappear.

My hand reaches up to grab her chin, forcing her to look me in the eye.

"Hey, where did you go?"

"Nowhere," her perfect mouth lifts into a small smile, "still here."

I'm about to lower my head to drop another kiss onto her soft, plump lips when a voice behind me calls out my name.

"Franklin! You need to come!" There's urgency in his voice, so I turn my head while keeping Kendall in my arms. With a scowl fixed to his face, Nigel is hurrying down the steps of the box entrance, followed by one of the stable boys. The stable boy's face is flushed red, and he's panting as if he ran up here.

"It's Inka. She's dead," Nigel proclaims.

I gnash my teeth together as I feel a ball of fury rush through my body.

"What did you just say?" I growl before bringing my focus to the stable boy who shrinks a little under my gaze.

"What are you talking about, Nigel?" Connor chimes in as he takes a step forward, wearing an angry look on his face that I'm sure mirrors mine.

"Tell them," Nigel barks as he gives the boy a nudge forward. The boy looks older than twenty-one-year-old Nigel, but being aware of the kind of men he's surrounded by, he looks like he's about to break out in tears any second now.

"W-we found her. Just now. I was going to get the ointment for Posey's leg, but I had to go to the Killimore shop because we were all out. I couldn't have gone longer than fifteen minutes, but when I got back, she was laying down. She wasn't breathing."

"How?!" I roar with more force than the boy deserves. "We were just there twenty minutes ago." I feel Reign set his hand on my shoulder to try and calm me down, but I shrug it off and let go of Kendall.

"I-I d-don't know, sir." The stable boy is noticeably flustered, looking like he may pass out any minute now.

"Bring Kendall home," I yell to Connor, then squeeze Kendall's hand. Without giving her another glance, I storm up the stairs on my way to the stables.

I hear Reign trailing behind me while I ball my fists, ready to punch anything. This isn't the first time he messed with my horses. Ever since I found out David told Emerson the names of my horses, something I've tried to keep quiet for years now, weird shit has been going on in the stables. Custom equipment switched with standard shit that doesn't suit my horses, special cereals getting mixed up, supplements gone missing. Last week, Posey got the wrong food, giving her a form of colic. Luckily, it was a mild case, but it can be deadly for horses. It made me realize Emerson wouldn't hesitate to hurt innocent animals to hurt me. I've been testing my patience, waiting for the right moment to retaliate. I can be a very patient man, but touch my family or my horses, and my patience becomes non-existent.

My feet rapidly move over the concrete, and I reach the stables within a minute. I peek my head over the wooden door, looking at the black horse laying in the straw like she's peacefully sleeping. I don't have to check her pulse; I know the stable boy wouldn't have delivered me bad news if he wasn't sure he needed to.

"Did you call the vet?" Reign asks the stable boy, looking over my shoulder into the stable. I know that the vet will tell me it was a heart attack, that these things happen to the healthiest of horses. But I know Emerson killed her. Twenty minutes ago, I left a perfectly healthy horse. She wasn't as fast as her sister, but she was a good horse, winning me enough to make her valuable.

"I did." The stable boy confirms as I rub a hand over my face. With a heavy sigh, I open the door, walk in, and crouch down next to her. My fingers softly stroke the fur on her head, her skin still warm even though she doesn't respond to anything.

I breathe out angrily through my nose before I scowl up at Reign.

"What was with that Origami thing?"

He gives me a bored look.

"What does that have to do with this?"

"I saw the look on your face, Reign." I get back up and walk out of the stable. "What are you not telling me?"

He takes a deep breath through his nose, his nostrils flaring in anger.

"I've been asking you the same question for years. How about I answer when you do?"

This again.

It always comes back to this.

"We are not talking about the past, Reign." I rarely lose my cool, controlling my emotions and expressions, but Reign is one of the few people who gets on my nerves within a second. Not because he rubs me the wrong way, but because we can't fucking communicate as adults.

"You're right, we're not. So let's not bring up things that don't matter right now. Your horse is dead. You're pissed, I get it. But whatever Kendall got had nothing to do with that. It was just something that reminded me of my days in foster care. You remember those days, don't you?"

I huff in response, annoyed he even brought that up.

"Yeah, *Reign*," I emphasize, "I remember."

They're the bane of my existence.

He has fucked up memories of his time in foster care; I get that. And I hope one day he'll tell me about them. But to be honest, whether he tells me or not, I don't think I could possibly feel worse than I already do. Living with the guilt of not being able to protect him from whatever happened in foster care fucks with my head every single day. I couldn't forget that time even if I wanted to because I'm confronted with it every fucking time I look at my brothers. Reminding me how I failed them and how I have to do better to secure their future in every way possible. Reign particularly, since he was the one who was in the longest.

"Good." He glares before his face softens a fraction. "You know Emerson is behind this, right?" He points back at the stable, his jaw tight.

"Yeah, I know," I groan, running a hand through my hair

in frustration when I notice Nigel standing next to the stable boy. Narrowing my eyes, I glance from Nigel to the boy, telling Nigel with a single look that he needs to keep an eye on him. "I want all the footage of the security cameras around the stables within the hour. If anyone gives you a hard time, tell Connor to help you."

Nigel nods his head, grabbing the boy by his neck before yanking him forward and storming off.

"What are we going to do about it, Franklin?" Reign asks, looking pissed off. "You keep saying he's a small fish, but he's becoming a real threat, fucking with us like that."

He's right. When Emerson Jones started provoking us a few months ago, I was hardly concerned. Just another coke-head with a big mouth, or that's what I thought. All the smaller gangs try overthrowing us at some point, and I can't even be angry about it because I would do the same. But while they've all been straightened out by us threatening to fuck with their businesses or by having the authorities mess with their shell companies, Emerson Jones showed that he's not planning on backing down anytime soon. My main priority is keeping the peace in town, making sure everyone benefits from their side of the law, but it appears that Emerson Jones needs a bit more persuasion.

"Find out why he's so cocky. There is no way in hell he'd have the guts to go against us if all he does is push around drugs. There must be more."

Reign nods in agreement. The glower on his face softening minutely, but there's still judgment in his eyes.

"What, Reign?" I sigh loudly.

He jams his hands into the pockets of his pants while he just stares at me, and I wait for him to say whatever is on the tip of his tongue.

"You like this girl, don't you?" he finally asks.

"Oh, no. Not you too." I huff, throwing my hands up in the air. "Save it, Reign. Kill already beat you to it."

I appreciate my brother's concerns, but I'm the one taking care of them. Not the other way around. After always having to provide for myself and my brothers, I've met and worked with a lot of people. In that time, I've learned to read people, to easily figure out who is friend and who is foe. Not to mention my gut; it's always been the main tool I rely on to help me decide on whatever choice there is to make. It's rarely been wrong or let me down.

And my gut tells me I can trust her.

She barely dares to stick up for herself. I can't even imagine her going against a Wolfe.

"Beat me to what?" He raises an eyebrow in questioning.

"Warning me to be careful with Kendall."

"Kill warned you to be careful with her?"

I nod in agreement, waiting for him to finish the speech Killian started earlier today.

"Why?"

I'm surprised by his question, expecting Reign to be aware of our brother's suspicion.

"He doesn't trust her. Says he has a bad feeling about her. Don't you?"

He shakes his head.

"No. I was going to say that if you want to keep her around, you should apologize for being a dick to her just now. I like the girl. I think she's good for you."

"Don't get ahead of yourself. When was I a dick to her?"

"When you ordered Connor to take her home without so much as a second glance," he deadpans like the smartass that he is.

Fuck, he's right.

Again.

Regret fills my stomach as I pinch the bridge of my nose, groaning when I think back on how I stormed off like a maniac, hoping I didn't fuck everything up.

"You really like her, don't you?" he chuckles, clearly enjoying the irritation I feel at my behavior.

"Shut up, Reign."

"Fuck me, you really do like her." He lets out a deep laugh that pisses me off even more. I'm about to lay into him when I see the vet heading towards the stables.

"Unless you want my foot in your ass in the next minute, I suggest you shut up."

He laughs even harder before he raises his hands in surrender, covering his mouth to muffle the rest of his chuckles. I roll my eyes before I nod to the vet in greeting.

"Evening, Mr. Wolfe."

"Evening," I respond, watching him walk inside the stable as I give my little brother another reprimanding look.

19

I get home, a disappointed feeling running through my gut while I pull off my boots by the front door. I stumble to the living room as I pull off the other.

"Josie, where are you?"

I know I'm not Franklin's family or his friend or anything, for that matter, but after the sweet words he said this afternoon, I'd kinda hoped I was at least *something*. That he would share his frustrations with me or show me how much his horses meant to him.

Instead, he sent me home like I was a nuisance.

"Hi, sweetheart." My heart stops when I notice Emerson sitting on the couch, as if he never left. Josie is sitting in the window, looking apologetic as she sinks her teeth into a donut. I'm surprised she doesn't look annoyed by his presence like she normally is.

"Emerson!" I exclaim. "What are you doing here?"

Before he came to advise me of his latest plan, I hadn't

seen him in weeks. Now here he is, visiting me twice in the same day.

I have a severely deficient amount of luck.

"I came to check on my girl. See if we're still on the same page. Still on the same team, you know?" His arms are draped over the back of the couch, a glass of whiskey in one hand. He shoots a glance at Josie, who is now glaring at him from across the room. We all came to Boston together, all looking for some adventure after we graduated high school in Clover, Alabama.

Emerson had always been the bad boy in town, my boyfriend throughout junior and senior years, yet somehow my best friend's worst enemy. She's never liked him. They never saw eye to eye, and they got into each other's faces more often than they got along. When we all moved up north, following Emerson on his new adventure, they became civil. But they've never hid their annoyance for one another.

"Didn't you already do that this morning?" I scowl, my hands pressed into my sides. Having Josie around gives me a bit more confidence to maintain my backbone and not cower under his gaze.

"Josie here tells me you may need a little more persuasion."

"That's not what I said, dickhead."

I scowl at her, my jaw already hurting from grinding my teeth.

Thanks a lot, friend.

"Okay, that's true. She didn't say that exactly. But she did tell me she hated me for fucking things up for you. You see," he continues while I continue staring at my best friend, "that gave me the feeling there's more going on between you and Franklin Wolfe than I'd realized. Is that true, Kenny?"

My eyes move back to Emerson.

"What is more, Em? I slept with him, you already know that because your little spy followed me around last night. He asked me to come to the races with him, so I did. You wanted me to gain his trust. I'm gaining his trust."

"So, it's all an act?"

I huff in response, annoyed with this conversation. I'm doing what he wants me to do. I'm getting Franklin Wolfe to trust me, even though it's killing me inside. I'm putting on a show like Josie told me to. I'm putting myself on the line here, though there is a big chance my heart will be shattered after this. Not to mention my brain. But I'm doing it, anyway.

"Yes, Em. It's all an act." I may be able to trick my head into thinking I'm being honest, but my heart is calling me a stone-cold liar.

He gets up, sauntering towards me with a grin on his face that used to turn me on, before he links his fingers with mine and guides me to the breakfast bar as if I'm still his girl. I let him because even though I feel more confident after feeding off of Franklin's interest in me and having Josie here as a backup, I also know how incredibly unpredictable of a character Emerson Jones is. That knowledge is what has kept me on edge for many years now. He grabs my hips and guides me onto one of the bar stools before he kisses my neck. I have to close my eyes and take a deep breath to hide my discomfort.

"It's okay, sweetheart. I get it. You're alone now; any attention is tempting to give in to." The way he talks to me makes my blood boil. This is what he's always done, talking down to me as if I'm some naïve little girl, unaware of how the world works. I know how the world works. I know it's a world full of assholes and people trying to take advantage of you. Making you feel smaller with their words so they will feel bigger. I'm not stupid, even though he likes to pretend I am. There are a bunch of words sitting on the tip of my tongue that I want to voice right now, but my brother's smile, still fresh in my memory, keeps my lips sealed.

He reaches into the pocket of his jacket and pulls out a set of photos, placing them in front of me.

"I just wanted to remind you that the Wolfes are the enemy. Explain to you what kind of people they are. The kind of person Franklin Wolfe is."

The moment I peer down at the images in front of me, I gasp for air and press my palm against the cold surface of the bar to prevent myself from falling off the stool. The images show a dead man with a bullet hole in the middle of his forehead, sitting in a desk chair, the rest of his face covered in blood. His eyes are wide open, staring at me, his soul undoubtedly long gone from his body. I try to take shallow breaths to keep myself from gagging, even though I'm nauseous as fuck.

I am not cut out for this shit.

"Do you know who this is?" he asks, pushing back a strand of my hair behind my ear.

I hate that he's mimicking the act of affection Franklin gave me last night and today, tainting a wonderful memory with his appalling touch.

I shake my head, barely capable of voicing anything right now, while I look at Emerson. Anything to stop looking at the photos of the dead body in front of me.

"This is David Callahan." Em looks sympathetic, but I know him well enough to know he's full of shit. He feeds off of my fear, knowing he can scare me with stuff like this. I've seen more than one dead body, countless people who'd been beaten. I've even watched Emerson torture his men when they were disobedient. More than once. You would think I'd have gotten used to it by now, but I definitely haven't. It made me feel horrible every single time it happened. It still makes me sick to my stomach just thinking about what I've seen. A few years ago, he skinned one of his men because he suspected him of talking to the police. I can still recall his excruciating screams, bringing goosebumps all over my skin just thinking about it. He made me watch, telling me he needed me close 'for support', but really he just wanted to scare me, to make sure I would never betray him.

It worked.

"W-who is that?" I push out, my voice cracking.

"David was the latest accountant for the Wolfes." My eyes widen in horror, immediately understanding why Emerson is showing me this. "That's right, sweetheart. They aren't any different than I am. If anything, they're worse. They don't hesitate to eliminate anyone who gets in their way. Women, men, *children,*" he emphasizes, "it's all one and the same for them. Don't get too comfortable behind that desk, because before you know it, you may end up like David."

My mind goes back to Matt and how his little boy was killed just a week ago, blaming the Wolfes for his death. Franklin in particular.

"Why are you telling me this, Emerson?" I whisper, confused about the last twenty-four hours. Not knowing what to believe.

I know Emerson is not flat out lying about the Wolfes being dangerous. I've heard about their reputation. The entire city has, but after the last twenty-four hours, it's hard to believe Franklin is more ruthless than my abusive ex-boyfriend.

He turns my stool so I'm facing him, then cups my neck and leans in before pressing his forehead against mine.

"Don't fall for his sweet words, Kenny." It's like the asshole can read my mind, unsettling me even more.

"Uh, guys?" Josie chimes in from behind us, causing us both to turn our heads towards her. She's looking outside the window with a troubled look on her face. "He's here."

"What do you mean 'he's here'?" I squeak in disbelief, grateful that Emerson lets go of my neck.

"Franklin!" she hisses. "His car just pulled up."

"Oh, my God." The panic is engraved into my words as I look at Emerson, who's currently looking at Josie with a tight face. "You have to go. You have to go now before he sees you."

"Leave, Emerson," Josie agrees, her fear as loud as mine as she pushes out the words. I start pushing Emerson towards the door, wanting him out of the house, while my heart starts to race like it's going to tear through my chest.

"Move, Emerson. GO!" I keep pushing him towards the door, even though he's obviously in no hurry to leave.

"Relax, sweetheart. I'll hide out in your room until he's gone," he says with a smirk I wish I could tear off his face.

"Are you trying to get us killed?" I hiss before I frantically look around, glancing at Josie, hoping for an answer.

Her eyes widen before she quickly walks towards us. "The fire escape beside my bedroom window. Come on, let's go."

"Oh, your bedroom? I've always wanted to see that, Josie," he taunts her in a husky voice that makes my skin crawl.

"Shut up, Em." She grabs his arms and leads him out,

leaving me alone in the hallway while they disappear inside her bedroom. My heart is pounding against my rib cage and my hands are shaking while I press my forehead against the cold wood of the door, trying to give myself a moment to calm down and put on a straight face. I suck in a few deep breaths and am wiping my sweaty hands on my sleeves when I'm startled by a knock on the door.

When I look through the peephole, I find the man who just ordered me to go home. The man who makes me feel worthy but thinks very little of human life if I'm to believe Emerson Jones. I glance at Josie's bedroom, unsure if Emerson is already out, waiting for her to come back. It feels like forever until she peeks her head around her bedroom door, giving me a thumbs up. After she shuts it again, I open the door to Franklin with his head hanging, one arm pressed against the doorpost. When he hears the door opening, he brings his head up and gifts me a sweet smile. It melts my heart, even though I know it shouldn't after what Emerson just showed me. His face is laced with fatigue, and my hands want to reach out to cup his face, to kiss it all better. Since I'm still not sure why he's here, I keep my hands to myself.

"Hey, pretty girl. Can I come in?" His smile leaves as quickly as it appears, leaving me with the expressionless face he's known for.

"Of course." I open the door wider, and he immediately wraps his arm around me, pressing me against my hallway wall. He's totally crowding my space, like Emerson did just minutes before, but when it comes to Franklin Wolfe, there isn't a hair on my head that doesn't want him to be there. He lowers his lips to mine. Without a second thought, I bring my arms up to his neck and slowly part my lips before my tongue meets his, and he deepens the kiss. The fluttering feeling inside my stomach gets heavier the moment he lightly massages my tongue with his in a tender way. His kisses are sweet and full of intention, but never demanding, as if he's asking me if he can continue with every move he makes. When he grabs my butt and lifts me up, I instinctively wrap my legs around his waist. I moan against his lips, the traumatizing photos completely forgotten when the bulge in his pants is pressed against me in just the right spot.

"Where is your room?" he murmurs while he nibbles my lower lip.

"Second door on the right."

We don't stop kissing as he walks us through the open door of my bedroom. I literally bounce when he tosses me on the bed, making me screech. I watch as he walks back, closes my door, then locks it. The lustful look on his face has me gasping for air.

Holy hell.

He saunters back towards the bed while taking off his coat before he drags his pullover over his head. He throws it across the room, then starts unbuttoning his shirt. I get on my knees, kneeling on the mattress, and softly push his hands away so I can finish undressing him. He leans in, placing small kisses on my neck while I slowly unbutton his shirt. My fingers intentionally grace his hard chest with every button I undo, making him grunt with every touch. I'm at the last button when he can't handle it anymore and pushes me back on the bed, making me chuckle as I stare up at this intimidating man. When I was with Emerson, there was always fear. Fear of what he could do to me if I upset him, fear of what he would do to me if I didn't do whatever he wanted. Even though Franklin Wolfe is supposedly more dangerous than Emerson is, there is not an ounce of fear in my body when this man looks at me as if he's about to devour me.

As if I'm the most delicious thing he's ever seen.

I'm ready for him to take me in whatever way he wants.

I gnaw on my lip, watching as he rips his shirt off before removing his pants and dropping them to the floor. I lick my lips at the sight of his hard dick pressing against the fabric of his boxers. He crawls over the mattress, his weight making me sink deeper with every move, before he tugs his fingers between the waistband of my skirt and tights. With his eyes pinning me to the bed, he softly starts rolling the fabric down my legs. He does it excruciatingly slowly, ensuring that I relish the sensation of every light touch, making me wetter with every second that passes.

"Take off the rest," he growls as he removes my skirt, adding it to the pile on the floor.

I comply without any reluctance and pull my sweater over my head before unclasping my bra and throwing it at him in a seductive way. He catches it with a gorgeous smirk before dropping it on the floor in front of him. He grabs my ankle and tugs my body towards him, my legs now hanging between his legs. Forcefully yet not painfully, he pushes them open, then reaches out to pull me up by grabbing the back of my neck. I look up at him as he grabs my hair and fists it in a dominant way, turning me on even more.

"Have I told you how beautiful you are?" His eyes stay locked on mine.

"Well, you do call me pretty girl." I smirk in response, feeling completely surrendered to him.

"True." He leans in softly, pressing his lips against mine while his fingers rub the fabric between my legs. He smiles against my lips. "Your panties are wet."

"I blame you," I tell him as I lick his lower lip, resulting in a groan from him.

"You better."

He straightens his body, standing in front of the bed. Eager to taste him, I drag his boxers down his hips, exposing his throbbing cock as it bobs against his stomach. My confidence rises sky high when I see the way he's looking down at me with hunger clear in his eyes, biting his lower lip as he cups my face.

The mix of pure lust and affection saturating my system makes me want to please him like he pleased me. I want to bring him to the edge and make him come undone. With a seductive smile I get up, getting comfortable on my knees, sitting on the bed. I lean in, taking the tip of his cock into my mouth, tasting him before I drag my lips along his shaft, all the way down to his balls. When he growls, I look up and see him throw his head back at the sensation, a sense of pride forming inside me. I do this a few more times, and each time his growls become more feral. I then take one of his balls into my mouth and swirl my tongue around it.

"Jesus Christ," he rasps while he starts pulling my hair.

I hated giving head to my ex-boyfriends. It always felt degrading, as if they saw me as nothing more than someone meant to please them. This time it's different. Feeling, hearing, and tasting how this man loses control from every move I make makes me feel empowered and confident. Plus, it makes me hot as hell. I take him into my mouth again, and he slowly starts fucking my mouth, finding his rhythm. My left hand massages his balls while my right reaches down to touch my folds, desperate to reach the same high.

His moans become more frantic as he starts thrusting into my mouth faster, while I do my best to relax every time he touches the back of my throat. My eyes start to well up, my climax racing towards me when his face goes rigid. He looks incredible when he lets out a ferocious roar just before the first spurt of his cum touches my tongue. I eagerly swallow his salty sweetness while his eyes find mine. He pants, his chest heaving as he cups my face, brushing off a tear that runs down my cheek.

"That. Was. Phenomenal," he whispers while he examines my face. "You're gorgeous."

The look on his face makes me want him to fuck me more than anything, yet his words and the way he says them make me want to take him in my mouth all over again.

Anything to keep him looking at me like that.

"Turn around. On your knees," he orders, the controlling man I've gotten used to over the last few weeks returning.

I obey without hesitation, my ass up in the air. I lift my legs to help him as he pulls my thong off. He throws the piece of fabric across the room, before his hand starts to caress my ass in small circles, slowly migrating closer to my entrance. With every brush of his hand, I feel my excitement build. When he's almost there, he roughly slaps my ass, making me screech, my eyes widening in shock.

"You like that, Kenny?"

I clear my throat, ready to scold him when I realize that I do. I've been slapped more than once in my life, but never in a way I enjoyed. It's insane how everything with Franklin Wolfe feels different.

Better.

I nod in agreement and close my eyes, waiting for more.

"Good," he replies as he grabs my hair from behind, pulling my hair back as he starts to rub a finger through my wet heat. I gasp for air; the amazing sensation of his finger entering my body combined with his burning grip on my scalp makes it hard to think. He continues dipping his finger in and out, brushing my clit every time he goes back, leaving me whimpering. When I feel like I can't take it anymore, his lips latch onto my clit, and I let out a desperate moan.

"Oh, God."

He kisses my most sensitive part, switching between sucking it to flicking it with his tongue while he pushes two fingers inside me. I can feel my orgasm building, and when he lets go of my hair, my head falls down, no longer able to hold it up while I climb higher and higher. When I'm almost at the top, he removes his mouth, rubbing me one last time with his full hand before pushing his cock inside me. My lips part as I feel him stretching me wide, touching every nerve that's hidden inside my walls.

He moans when he's completely buried inside of me, then he leans over, pressing his chest against my back, his lips flush with my ear.

"I want it rough, pretty girl. I want to own you. Can you handle that?" My heart jumps in fear and excitement, thinking about how I want to be owned by this man. How I long to be his and how I want him to tear me apart.

"Take me however you want, Franklin," I concede. I give him my cheek, and he softly bites the skin before he straightens and again fists my hair from behind. I'm thinking about how the scorching feeling of his tight pull somehow heightens the throbbing in my core when he starts to drive into me. Each thrust is harder and harsher than the one before it, unleashing a side of him I haven't seen before. A side I adore right away. The burn inside me becomes all-consuming as he continues plowing in and out of me. All I can think about is wanting more.

Wanting it rougher.

Wanting it deeper.

Wanting him to destroy me.

"Harder, Franklin, harder," I cry as I get closer to the edge.

"My girl likes it hard. Good." The tone of his voice is ominous, but before I can think about that, he slams his cock violently inside of me, making me gasp for air before I scream in pleasure. Clearly taking my request as his cue to do however he pleases, he plunges his cock in and out with force, until he pushes me off the mountain I've been dying to jump off.

"Yes! Yes! YES!" He lets go of my hair and grabs my hips as my body starts to shake. His fingers dig deep into my skin, making me whimper under his touch as he keeps thrusting until he finally lets out a primal cry. Finally he stills, dropping his chest against my back so I fall down to the bed with him on top of me, his cock still stretching me wide.

God, I love feeling him inside of me.

His lips brush the back of my neck after he pushes my hair to the side.

"I think I'm addicted to you, Kendall Ryan." His confession makes me smile, glad to hear I'm not the only one because I'm not sure I can ever come back from this.

"I'm not going to stop you, Franky," I reply, my cheek still pressed against the bed.

"You couldn't stop me if you wanted to, baby," he tells me before he kisses the sensitive skin beneath my ear. "I'm sorry for earlier. I was an asshole."

"It's okay."

I mean it. It is okay. After the photos Emerson just

showed me, I should take every opportunity I get to break this off, but I can't.

I trust him.

I believe him.

And fuck me, I care about him.

20

FRANKLIN

It's a Tuesday evening when I get out of the car in a back alley in Seaport, a shiver going through me when I'm met by the cold breeze. I enjoy the cold, the blistering sharpness keeping me alert and more alive than I do during the constant heat of summer. Before I can open the door to the garage, it pops open, and Nigel gives me a slight nod.

"Evening, boss."

"Evening, Nigel. How are you?" I walk past him into the garage, then turn around to face him as he locks the door behind us.

"I'm good." He smiles with a genuine look on his face, like he appreciates my question.

Connor found him on the street three years ago, a scrawny little junior fighting a group of seniors from the local high school he attended. He knocked them out with ease after they'd cornered him, even though he was greatly outnumbered. Impressed by his boldness, Connor took him to the local gym, providing him a place to train after school and keeping him off the street. By the time he turned eighteen, Nigel wasn't scrawny anymore, and Connor had developed a bond with the kid. I gave him a job with us after Nigel confessed he couldn't go to college because he needed to take care of his mother and siblings.

Like I did once upon a time.

"Good." I nod before I turn on my heel and walk farther into the garage. The space is stuffy and dark, the result of no additional windows, and the hollow space means my footsteps echo through it. In the middle sits the stable boy, tied up to a chair with a scowl. I'm sure he's doing his best to ignore the pain of his split lip and his swollen face.

Connor is practically fuming as he looks down at him, his arms crossed in front of his chest, only quickly glancing at me when he notices my arrival.

"Anything?" I ask as I move to the wall, where I let my back rest against the hard concrete.

"No," Connor growls. When Nigel walks in with a hammer, I notice the blood on his knuckles. He gives the hammer to my brother, who playfully throws it up in the air, then catches it with ease. He repeats the move, the boy's eyes widening more every time Connor throws it up, putting on a small show.

"You did that?" I ask Nigel, nodding at the boy in the chair. He nods as he comes to stand next to me.

"This is Connor," I tell the stable boy, who quickly glances at me before his focus goes back to Connor and his hammer. "If you thought getting a beating from Nigel was bad, I'm afraid I have some disappointing news for you." I pause, enjoying the panic in his eyes. "Nigel is a walk in the park compared to what Connor will do to you."

The boy's eyes briefly flash to me, but he's focused on the hammer.

"Do yourself a favor and talk, Roger."

The blood drains from his face, terror entering his eyes when he hears his name roll off my lips.

"You didn't really think I wouldn't find out who you are, did you? Roger Lowell, suspect in a hit and run in Lafayette, Indiana. Missing since January of last year, which just happens to be when Richard Kemp turned up looking for a job as a stable boy at Killimore Down."

I'm interrupted when Connor unexpectedly punches him in the face, his other hand still gripping the hammer.

"Talk!" he roars. "Or the next one will be with my other hand."

Roger cries out, hunched over in pain.

"Connor, I was in the middle of something," I deadpan, while Connor turns his head to me in annoyance.

"I don't care," he snarls. "I don't have all fucking day."

"As I was saying." I glare at my brother before I turn my focus back to Roger. "I know who you are. I know where you're from, and I know why you're in Boston. You're fucked either way. So I highly suggest you—"

"Start fucking talking!" Connor slams the hammer down on Roger's tied up hand, sending the sharp sound of his painful cry echoing through the garage. I let out an irritated sigh, reaching into my pocket to grab my pack of cigarettes before I put one in my mouth and light it.

Without waiting for an answer from Roger, Connor slams the hammer against his knee. Roger throws his head back in agony, another yelp leaving his lips.

I take a deep drag of my cigarette, enjoying the smoke

entering my lungs as I look at my brother, who is practically foaming at the mouth.

Connor's the *'punch-now-talk-later'* kinda guy, and even though he can be a bit drastic, it saves me from the annoyance of having to convince assholes like Roger to give me what I want.

"Please, Mr. Wolfe. Please." Roger is squirming on the chair, discomfort dripping from his face.

"Did you kill my horse?" I ask before taking another toke of my cigarette.

"No. No, I swear I did not kill her. Someone just offered me a grand to leave her out of my sight for ten minutes."

"Emerson Jones?" Connor grunts, still holding the hammer up in a threatening way.

Roger frantically shakes his head.

"No, a girl."

"A girl?" I repeat, pushing off the wall, slowly moving towards him. "What girl?"

My mind goes to Josie and the weird feeling I had about her. She may be Kenny's best friend, but I have a feeling she has a shitload of secrets Kendall doesn't know about.

Connor gives me a confused look before folding his arms in front of his body, the hammer still in sight.

"A girl. She didn't tell me her name."

"Black hair?"

"No, she was short. Like 5'1", long, straight blonde hair, but it could've easily been a wig." His voice sounds hoarse and scratchy from screaming. "She had a little girl with her, in pigtails, and a dog. A husky dog with bright blue eyes. It scared the crap out of me."

"Are you making this shit up?" Connor takes another

threatening step towards him, causing him to flinch back in his chair.

"No, I swear. Check the cameras! I'm telling the truth, I swear." I take him in, a mix of sweat, tears and blood streaming down his face. I believe him. He's not smart enough to be one of Emerson's guys, and considering his past life choices, it's easy to believe he'd be enticed by money.

I turn towards Nigel behind me.

"Check the cameras. I want to know who she is. Tonight." I wait until Nigel walks out of the garage before facing Roger again. "You know, lying will make this worse, right?"

"I swear." He looks me straight in the eye for a beat before he lets his head drop to his chest, and he starts sobbing like a big baby. I bring my cigarette towards my lips, then suck in a deep breath before blowing out the smoke in his face.

"Now what?" Connor scowls, probably disappointed he can't kill the guy.

I look at my brother, contemplating my next move, before I turn my head back to Roger.

"What am I supposed to do with you, Roger?"

"Please," he begs, his voice a raspy whisper.

"You fucked up, Roger. You gave someone access to my stables, making it easy for them to hurt my horses. I don't like people fucking with my horses. That fucks with my livelihood, and I can't have that."

"Please—" he begins again, but I raise up a finger to interrupt him.

"Luckily, I'm in a good mood," I explain while I hear Connor grunting behind me, displeased as fuck. "I'm gonna let you go."

"Oh, for fuck's sake, Franky," Connor huffs.

"I'm gonna let you go," I continue, ignoring my brother. "You're going to pack your bags and take the first flight back to Indiana. I don't want to see or hear anything from you ever again, and I will have someone keeping tabs on you to make sure you do what I say." I give him a sinister smile.

"B-but they'll arrest me as soon as I cross the border."

"Connor here will gladly make you cross a more permanent border, if that's what you prefer?" At my threat, his eyes bulge.

"No. I'll leave," he promises, his Adam's apple visibly moving. "I'll leave."

"You'll leave, turn yourself in to the Lafayette police, and never set foot in Boston again." I take a final pull from my cigarette before I throw it on his lap. He shrieks like a bitch and jerks in his seat.

"I'll leave!" he pleads, panic coating his voice.

"You'll leave, and?" I cross my arms in front of my body, a dull look on my face.

"I'll leave, turn myself in, and I'll never come back to Boston ever again." The words rush from his mouth in rapid speed before he starts to let out desperate cries from the cigarette butt that's now between his legs. "Please, I'll do whatever you say! I'll leave! Just let me go! Please let me go! I'll keep my mouth shut, just let me go!"

"Franky." Connor shoots me a reprimanding look.

"I'm feeling generous, Connor."

"It's that girl. She's making you soft." He slowly shakes his head, though I can see a hint of amusement in his eyes.

"Shut up."

"What if he starts talking?" Connor tilts his head towards Roger.

"Nah, Roger here wants to live. Don't you, Roger?"

"Yes! I won't say a thing. I swear!" His eyes are wide, doing his best to look as sincere as possible. It's sad, really. This guy is a pussy. At this point, I could tell him to eat shit, and he'd happily do it.

"See, we're all good." A sigh of relief leaves Roger's lips before Connor gives him another punch on his nose. I silently chuckle as blood spatters fly through the garage.

"What was that for?" Roger cries.

"My own personal entertainment," Connor answers with a grin on his face before his gaze finds mine.

"What?" He shrugs when I give him a questioning look. "An innocent animal died because of him. He's lucky to be able to walk out of here."

I turn around, making my way towards the door.

"Just put him on a Greyhound back to Indiana before midnight."

"Where are you going?" Connor bellows to my back.

"To see my soft spot, apparently."

21

FRANKLIN

I walk inside the bar with my phone pressed against my ear. After two rings, I'm greeted by a long moan.

"Morning, pretty girl." I smile.

"What time is it?" she croaks, her voice still sleepy, making me wish I was laying next to her with my arms wrapped around her luscious body.

"Ten."

"Ten?" she shrieks, sounding more awake now. "It's Saturday. I need to study."

"I know, that's why I'm calling you."

A tired yawn meets my ears before she responds.

"You should've woken me up."

"Technically, I just did. But I didn't do it earlier because I felt bad for keeping you up all night." My words have me thinking back to how she rode me like a fucking rodeo queen. We've spent every night together since the day of the races, and even though it has been only two weeks, it feels like she's always been a part of my life. She fits in perfectly. Well, aside from Killian's skepticism. She's been working in the office in the mornings, then she goes home to study until I pick her up to have supper. Most of the time we don't even make it to the restaurant, ordering takeout after we've stripped each other naked and temporarily sated our need for one another.

"You should feel bad." I can tell by her voice that she's joking. "I'm exhausted. You're killing me."

"Sorry, pretty girl. Told you there's no stopping me."

"I never realized the true meaning of those words."

"Well." I smirk. "Now you know."

She hums in agreement before letting out another yawn.

"I'll see you tonight, okay?"

"Are we ordering in, Mr. Wolfe?" Her voice is filled with lust, and I can feel my dick twitch in my pants.

"Probably." I chuckle, loving that I can hear the smile in her voice.

"See you tonight, Franky."

I hang up the phone and am pushing it back in my pocket when I hear the door behind me opening.

"Weird place to meet, *Franky*." Reign's voice is filled with disdain, and though that's nothing new after all these years, his derision still punches me in the gut every time it reaches my ears. I turn around, watching my youngest brother walk into the bar in engineering boots matching his brown leather jacket. Since his hair falls in front of his face with every step he makes, he runs a hand through it to keep it in place.

He's the whole package. Handsome, sweet, smart as fuck. He was ten when I first realized the computer skills he had. At that young age, he'd hacked into the local police station to get rid of some incriminating records, resulting in me being released. He'd done that to protect his big brother, even though it should've been the other way around. If you have a heart in your body, it's hard to resist anything Reign suggests. At least that's how it goes for me. I can rarely deny him.

Not a problem since he never asks for anything. Reign decided a long time ago that he didn't need me. He sticks around out of loyalty, but he'd do anything to avoid me.

"Well, look around. Do you like it?" I open my arms and spin around, my eyes roaming the area.

It's nothing special, really. A walnut hardwood floor that matches the bar, some red bar stools in front of it. The paint on the walls is blistering, and the glass shelves behind the bar are covered in a thick layer of dust. But it has potential.

I can see that.

"I prefer my bars to contain a bartender and to serve me alcohol, but yeah, looks fine. Why?"

"It's yours."

His brows shoot up in surprise and his mouth falls open for a few seconds before he asks, "What's the catch?"

"No catch." I shake my head as I walk towards the bar to grab the bottle of whiskey I brought. "I know you and Killian want to start a bar. This place was listed for a cheap price." I grab two of the dusty tumblers from the workstation and hold them under the tap, quickly washing the thick layer of dust off of them before I pour us each a glass.

"Anything to keep me in Boston, right?" His shoulders sag after he takes the glass from my hand, walking farther into the bar to check things out.

"Is it so bad that I want to keep my brother's close?" I ask his back, following him with my gaze as he walks around.

"The only reason you want me close is to make sure I'm still here to do your dirty work. Let's not make this prettier than it is."

My eyes find his, the same green, hypnotizing color as mine, it's like looking into a mirror.

In a way, I am.

He likes to paint me as the bad guy, and truth be told, I am most of the time. But he fails to see how alike we are, how we fight for the same causes. How we would both go through hell to protect our family.

It's not worth voicing though. Somewhere along the road, I lost my baby brother and all that we were. Now all I can do is keep him in my sight, keeping him safe until one day he hopefully sees the truth.

"You're not even going to deny it?" he questions me with an arrogant smirk on his face when I don't reply.

"What's the use, Reign? You won't believe me, anyway."

I meet his unblinking stare, his lips firm stripes of annoyance.

"Hey, what are we doing here?" Killian walks through the door, giving us both a chin lift.

"Oh, you know, Franklin is buying us a bar," Reign deadpans, before taking another sip. His eyes never leave mine, and his attitude is pissing me off.

"Hold up, what?" Killian stops in the middle of the bar and looks around, his lips parted in awe. "You bought a bar?"

I turn my head towards him and nod.

"No shit!" he exclaims before taking the seat next to me. "Since when are we in the bar business?"

"Since he figures it's a good way to keep me around," Reign answers before I can respond.

Killian looks at him for a moment before turning his focus on me. Killian and Reign are two peas in a pod, but Killian has always been more on my side when it comes to the differences between Reign and me. There have been multiple times when he's begged me to tell Reign the truth, but I've forbidden him from bringing it up. I want my youngest brother to come to me, to ask me what happened that day instead of listening to the people around him, to talk to me like we used to before shit hit the fan. He's my brother, and I miss him more every day, but I'm not going to try to convince anyone of my intentions.

"You know, Reign," I mock, bringing my glass to my lips. "He's always figuring shit out."

I hear him huff beside me as Killian ignores my comment and looks at both of us with a wide grin, used to our banter over the years.

"Where's my glass?" he asks.

"Here, take mine. I've got shit to do, anyway." Reign moves in between us then slams his glass on the bar while giving me a glare. "Thanks, *Franky*. And congratulations. You found a way to keep me in Boston."

Without another word, Killian and I watch him walk out the door. Once he's gone, I let out a loud sigh as I pinch the bridge of my nose.

"You bought him a bar?"

I look up at Killian, who has a wide smile on his charming face.

"No, I bought both of you a bar. It's time to start making money legally, and this seemed like a good opportunity. Now I'm not so sure." I let out another deep breath before finishing my whiskey.

"You know he loves it. He's just giving you a hard time like always."

"Yeah, I know."

He examines my face as I look around the decaying bar.

It's going to need a lot of work, but I do believe this is our future. One bar at a time.

"Why don't you just tell him, man?" Killian pleads with sadness in his eyes.

"Not going to happen, Kill." I shake my head.

"This is stupid. He's mad at you for something that isn't even true."

"Yeah, it is. I did kill that boy," I counter.

"But not for the reason he thinks. He doesn't even know the truth."

"He never asked." I shrug. "And you're not telling him." I point my whiskey glass at him with a scowl. "I don't want his pity or regret unless he finds it out himself."

"How will he ever find out if no one tells him?"

"I will tell him if he wants to know, but he has to ask. Not just jump to conclusions."

"You know he wasn't going to leave Boston anyway, right?" A knowing smile stretches his face, making me chuckle in response.

"Yeah, I know."

"So why the bar, Franklin?"

I look at my brother as he waits for my answer. He's the only one I discuss business with, simply because he's as cunning as I am. He sees the bigger picture in everything I do. In fact, he's my primary confidant when it comes to our businesses.

"It's time, Kill." He frowns. "We need more money."

"We have a shitload of money. Buying a bar isn't going to make us the big bucks." He tilts his head skeptically before taking a sip of his drink.

"We have a shitload of money stashed around the city, but it's black. It's time to turn that around. I want out. I want your children, Reign's children, and Connor's children, to never have to worry about money. I want to build a legacy. This," I wave my hand in the air, "is the first stone in that plan."

"What about *your* children?"

The corner of my mouth curls into a slight smile at his comment.

"I'm not ever having children," I state with finality, even though Kendall's face flashes in front of my eyes for a split second. Growing up as the eldest in the Wolfe family gave me enough reason to never want to father any children. I'm a selfish bastard, but not that selfish.

"Not even with Kendall?"

"Not even with Kendall," I retort.

"Don't let her hear that," Killian suggests, bringing his glass to his lips once more.

"Why?"

"You know women," he scoffs. "Once they know they're more than a fuck buddy, they start thinking about the next step."

His words make me frown while processing them. Kendall and I haven't talked about what we are, or aren't, but I can't deny she's more than someone to release the tension. She's got me hooked, craving more of her every day. But is there a future for us? I don't know. I've never imagined myself sharing my life with a woman. My life has always been preoccupied with making sure my brothers have everything they need. That's what has been driving me since the day our mom died and our father bailed, and I've never planned on changing that.

"You know I'm right," he continues, while I worry my lower lip.

"We are not serious."

"Right." He dramatically rolls his eyes. "You've been with her every single night for the last few weeks. Not just *sleeping* with her, but actually sleeping with her. Waking up with her every morning. You can tell yourself you're not serious with her, but you are. Is she coming to my party Sunday?"

I nod, my defenses rising when I see annoyance in his eyes.

"You still don't like her?"

He turns his head towards me, a stern look on his face before he softly starts to shake his head.

"I never said I didn't like her. I don't trust her."

"Same thing. But you haven't told me anything to back up your feelings."

"I haven't heard anything from the private investigator yet."

"You hired a PI?" I ask, confused. "Why didn't you ask Reign?"

"He likes her. He's biased. And you know him, he's stubborn as fuck. Like you."

He does like her, that's been clear since the first day he met her.

"Yeah, I guess that's why we are the way we are. We're too much alike."

"You know this could go on until one of you is dead, right?" he points out, referring to the troubled relationship between Reign and me, which bothers him as much as it does me.

I nod in agreement.

I know. Of course, I know. I just hope it won't come to that.

22

My phone rings, and I look up to see my brother's name on the caller ID. With the corner of my lips curling up, I answer as I look at my outfit in the mirror.

"Hey, James."

"Hey, Kenny. How's my little sis?"

"I'm good. Trying to focus on my last exam, but work has been keeping me busier than expected."

"You shouldn't be working nights at that bar anymore now that you're so close to graduating."

"Yeah," I start with hesitation, "I'm not working at The Library anymore."

"You're not?" he asks with surprise in his tone.

"No, I got a new job as an accountant with a local company."

"I thought you didn't want a day job? Said it would screw with your studies?" The disapproval in his voice is indisputable, and I can imagine the worried frown on his forehead I always tease him about.

"Yeah, well, the owner made me an offer I couldn't refuse. Besides, I'm graduating soon. I just have to work a little harder for the next few weeks. It will be fine."

"If you say so. Just don't overwork yourself, okay?"

"I won't." I smile at myself in the mirror. "I've gotta go now. I'm going out with Josie."

I don't want to lie to my brother, but being his little sister, he'd just interrogate me if I told him the truth. And I'm not feeling confident enough to have that conversation.

"Have fun, Kenny. Talk later. I love you."

"Love you too."

I throw my phone on the bed before doing another twirl in front of the mirror.

Around four, Franklin sent me a text telling me to wear something nice and to be ready by seven. I freaked out, texting him back, asking 'how nice?' but the asshole never responded. So here I am, looking in the mirror for the fiftieth time, wondering if this is nice enough. My little black dress hugs my hips, and I've put my hair in a long braid that hangs beside my neck. I'm moving my body around to make sure I look good from all angles when I spot Josie leaning against the doorway of my room.

"You sure seem to care a lot," she says, judgment dripping from her words.

My eyes find hers in the mirror, and seeing the censure in her eyes, my annoyance instantly spikes.

"I'm going out to dinner, I want to look nice."

"You're trying very hard."

"At what?" I snap my head towards her with a glare.

"Making Boston's biggest criminal fall in love with me so my ex-boyfriend won't hurt my family? Wouldn't you, Josie?"

"I'm just saying you should keep your feelings out of it," she says.

What the fuck is she worried about? It's not like it's her family that's on the line.

Or her fucking life.

"I *know*, Josie," I emphasize, while I blow out a frustrated breath.

"Do you? Because you keep swooning over him, you haven't slept at home in the last two weeks, and you're all giddy when you see him."

"What the fuck is your problem? You said, *'put on the show of your life.'* I'm putting on the show of my life, and now you're bitching about my doing what you told me to do?"

"You're falling for him," she states, her fists planted on her hips. "That's bad, Kenny. I'm worried about you. Feelings will cloud your judgment."

Everything about her, the way she's looking at me, the way she's standing, her words … it's all annoying me.

"What are you talking about, Josie? This is *my* brother we are talking about. My family. Nothing is going to cloud my judgment. Why would you even say that?"

As if she knows how I feel.

As if she knows how fucked I am.

She doesn't.

For her this is an easy fix. Not only is one half of her heart made out of ice, the other half is buried behind a stone wall. She vowed to never fall in love, and so far, she has done a bang-up job.

Josie is the type of girl who will easily tell a guy she's done with him after a few fucks, and who will ask a guy to leave once she's squeezed a few orgasms out of him.

I've always loved her brutal honesty, her fearless ability to tell people to fuck off. She will never let anyone take advantage of her, and I admire her for that.

But where her heart protects her from feeling anything, mine has always felt too much. I've struggled my entire life to say no to the people close to me, simply because I sympathize too much. Or empathize. Both, maybe. What I mean is, if you are my family or I consider you my friend, I will move mountains for you. Even if it's at my own expense.

"I'm just saying it for you," she murmurs, her face softening, though I can still see some frustration in her eyes. "This is Emerson we're talking about. We've seen him torture people for fun. I just want to make sure that you're aware of that."

She gets closer and offers me a tight smile while I take a few deep breaths to try to lower my irritation. I know she means well, but I don't like how she's talking to me, as if I don't know Emerson better than anyone.

I do.

She forgets I spent too many years of my life with him. I know him inside and out, the good and the bad and definitely the ugly. Yes, we all grew up together. But while she was the best friend with an opinion, I was always the one by Emerson's side. Witnessing his every move.

I scratch my head as I stare back at her in the mirror.

"I know. Trust me, Josie. I know."

"So you're not falling for him?"

My instant reaction is to snap and say, 'What the fuck does it matter?' But my gut is telling me to not even go there. She probably won't understand and will do her best to talk me out of it. But the truth is … I do. I am falling for him, and it feels like a train wreck waiting to happen. Every moment I spend with him I'm happy, having fun until I go home and realize that no matter what happens, my heart will end up in pieces. My heart is fucked either way, and there is nothing I can do about it.

"I'm not falling for him," I lie, turning around to grab my black clutch off the bed.

"Good. Because I don't want Emerson to hurt you." She purses her lips while softly nodding her head. "You deserve a nice guy giving you a boring and happy life, not being caught in the middle of a criminal war."

Before I can give her words any more thought, my phone starts ringing with Franklin's name on the screen.

"Hey."

"I'm downstairs, pretty girl."

"Alright," I reply with a smile. "I'll be right there." I put my phone in my clutch before turning back to Josie. "I have to go."

"Alright, good luck," she says before she gives me a small smile, which I return with my own. The tension is thick and hanging between us like a curtain, separating us with a wall of courtesy. I hate these kinds of situations. I hate confrontation most of the time, but even though I'm not as fierce or badass as Josie, I'm also sick of being talked to like I'm a little girl. Like I'm still a naïve, seventeen-year-old teenager.

I'm fucking twenty-five years old, and even though my life choices may not always result in me having the best situations or experiences in life, I'm not fucking stupid.

I wish everyone would stop pretending like I am.

"Bye, girl. Don't wait up." Without waiting for her reaction, I walk out of my room, grab my jacket, and head out the front door. When I step outside, I'm greeted by the brisk air of night and the most gorgeous man I've ever seen.

I've been spending the last few weeks with him, so I shouldn't be captivated by his hungry looks anymore, but I still am. He also still has me gasping for air whenever his eyes peruse my body. His smoldering looks burn me now while he shamelessly assesses every single piece of me with his hands tucked into the pockets of his pants.

His brown hair is perfectly styled with his short bangs up, and he's wearing a gray dress shirt covered by a black vest that hugs his hard rock abs.

I freeze a few yards in front of him, hypnotized by the smoldering look on his face, my pulse quickening. I gift him with a tender smile before he closes the distance between us and circles his arms around my waist.

He keeps his lips pressed together as he pushes out a long breath through his nose.

"You look amazing, baby."

"Thank you," I answer before he leans in and sets his warm lips on mine. He softly pushes me back, making me arch my back as he slowly dips me. When I'm completely surrendered in his arms, I let out a playful screech before he straightens my back again.

"Where are we going?" I ask after he grabs my hand and leads me into the car, taking the seat next to me.

"One of my favorite restaurants."

Ten minutes later, we arrive at the Boston Harbor Hotel. When we exit the car, he links his fingers with mine, escorting me into the gorgeous restaurant. The hostess leads us to a private corner of the waterfront deck that is sheltered by a few plants, giving us the perfect view of the luxurious boats yet also giving us the privacy Franklin always craves.

"Wow, this is amazing." I look around in awe as Franklin helps me take a seat at the extravagantly set table before sitting down himself.

It's endearing and both unexpected to know that this man is the most powerful man in this city, yet he's also the one to show me chivalry isn't dead.

Not in Franklin Wolfe's book.

"Glad you like it, pretty girl." Before he can say more, his phone starts ringing. He reaches into his pocket, then answers with a growl that makes me chuckle.

"Not a good time, Connor."

He listens to his brother on the other end of the phone while his meadow green eyes stay focused on mine. I bite my lip while goosebumps shower my body.

"Throw the papers on my desk, and I'll check them out in the morning. Don't call unless it's an emergency, you tool." He ends the call then tucks the phone back in his pocket, the corners of his mouth rising. "Sorry about that."

I incline my head as I take him in with a pleased look on my face.

"What?"

"People say you don't care about anything but the power you have over this city," I explain.

"Is that what they say about me?"

I nod my head.

"Oh, yeah. Franklin Wolfe, the man who rules Boston with his persuasive ways, supposedly fair and just, but don't piss him off or he will bite your head off like the Wolfe he is."

He throws his head back and lets out an amused chuckle before shaking his head.

"Who told you this shit?"

"Josie."

"Josie?"

"And the women in the bakery." I set my napkin on my lap, fighting to keep a straight face.

He narrows his eyes on me and leans forward a bit, pinning me with his eyes while I suppress a grin.

"Do you believe the women at the bakery?"

"Oh, yeah," I admit, "they're not wrong. You can be very persuasive, just, and fair. But I've yet to see you bite someone's head off, and the way you are with your brothers makes me believe you aren't the violent type."

"Why is that?" he asks, his eyebrow creeping towards his hairline in surprise.

"Because you love them more than you love yourself. I see it in the way you talk to them; you bitch at them, but you also cater to them. There is nothing you wouldn't do for your brothers, so I have a hard time believing someone who can love so deeply, sibling or not, is capable of being a ruthless criminal who bites people's heads off."

He lets out a deep breath before he looks at me with satisfaction, as if he's relieved someone finally sees the real him. Hopefully considering letting his walls down for me just a little bit more. But as fast as I see that, he changes his expression and replaces it with a stern gaze.

"Don't get things confused, Kendall. You *are* right. My brothers are the most important thing to me, and there isn't a thing I wouldn't do for them. Period. I try to be an honest man, always trying to give the people around me options, and I do try to prevent violence if I can simply because my upbringing provided me with enough violence for a lifetime. But make no mistake. I'm not a good man. If you push my buttons, I will push back." His pupils dilate, and it's the first time that he causes a hint of fear to enter my body. As if he's showing me the side of him he has been hiding up until now, showing me a glimpse of the man I will be up against if I keep walking the path I'm on.

"I've hurt people," he continues, clearly trying to shock me and surprising me with his honesty. "I've killed people. I've done things that are not worth repeating and things I will never talk about." He gets a little closer as he leans on his forearms, his look softening again, showing me the man I've been spending most of my time with. "I *am* the man you've been seeing for the last few weeks, but that doesn't mean I'm not the man the city says I am, too. I am *both*." He locks me in his stare, unmoving, while he waits for my response. The truth is, I don't know what to say because he just confirmed everything I already felt in my heart. He's right, he really has two sides. Just like I do.

This makes me think about Emerson, leaving me wondering who really is the greater evil.

Franklin Wolfe is not the first man walking on the dark side of life to hold my attention. Emerson introduced me to the other side of the law when I was sixteen, and even though I didn't have the confidence the rest of my friends had, I can't deny that I always loved the thrill. I loved to push boundaries; I think that's what drew me to Emerson. Life was exciting with him, even when the excitement included me being bruised and beaten up. I have a soft spot for men who defy authority, and in a way, I guess I like to defy it too. But where Emerson has always looked at me through a set of eyes provided by the devil himself—glaring, cold, and ominous, always keeping me on edge—Franklin is nothing like that.

Where Emerson scared the living shit out of me, controlling me with his explosive temper, Franklin makes me feel safe, treasured, and confident.

When I look into Franklin's eyes, I see a person who knows what love is, a person who feels that love in the marrow of his bones for his three brothers, a person who will go out of his way to keep them safe.

That's not evil.

That can't be evil.

He can't be evil.

Finally, a grin stretches my face before I grab his hand, craving to be closer to him and to show him I heard him.

"Are you trying to scare me away, Franklin Wolfe?" I ask with fluttering lashes, making him laugh in response.

"Are you scared?"

"Not even a little bit." I smile as relief swims through my veins.

It's true.

Franklin Wolfe raises a lot of feelings inside of me, but fear isn't one of them. Not like the fear I feel for Emerson.

"Good. Because I told you, there's no stopping me. Now, do you want me to order, or do you want to have a look?" He lets go of my hand and offers me the menu while my heart swoons over his sweet words.

"You can order. I trust you." Although the words leave my lips quietly, somewhere deep down inside of me, tucked into a very dark corner, I mean every word.

I trust him.

As if the devil can hear my thoughts, my phone starts to buzz in my clutch. I pull it out of my bag while Franklin studies the menu. My smile is instantaneously wiped off my face when I read the name on the screen.

Emerson.

Shit.

Tension hardens my shoulders as my eyes flicker up to

Franklin, hoping he doesn't notice my unease. Thankfully, Franklin is still focused on the menu in front of him, but my mouth becomes dry, wondering what the fuck to do. Making a rash decision, I decline the call as my heart thrashes in my chest, shoving it back into my clutch.

"You're not going to get that?" He cants his head a bit with a slight frown, and I swear to God, I feel like he sees right through my scam. It's like he can see that I'm hiding something that is killing me inside.

"No, it's okay. I'm sure it can wait."

He keeps his eyes locked with mine for a beat, his face impassive. Finally, he looks around for the waiter, raising his hand when he sees him. I feel like I'm going to puke by the time the waiter arrives. As soon as he finishes placing our order, Franklin offers me a reassuring smile. I wipe my sweaty palms on my napkin, having no clue what he just ordered because the blood was rushing through my ears, making it impossible for me to hear anything.

My stomach drops when my clutch starts vibrating again. I do my best to keep a straight face, sighing in annoyance, as if that's all I'm feeling. It's disgusting how my brain seems to be able to go into lie and deceit mode in just a split second.

"I guess it can't wait." He smirks.

I let out an uncomfortable chuckle while I open my clutch again, declining once more.

"Hey," he leans over the table, his gaze focused on mine, "you can answer that. It's okay."

The corner of my mouth curls into a troubled smile, getting more anxious by the second.

"Are you sure?"

"Of course."

"I'll be right back." I get up, my fingers tightly wrapped

around my clutch, before I do my best to strut away as fast as possible without raising any suspicion. Before I walk inside to find the restroom, I open my clutch and pull my phone out.

"What?!" I bark with more force than I normally dare to give.

"What?" His smoky voice sounds amused, but I know that will quickly be replaced if I'm not careful.

"What do you want, Emerson? This isn't exactly a good time," I hiss into the phone as I walk into the restroom and lock myself in one of the stalls.

"What I want is for you to do what you've been told to do instead of playing millionaire's girlfriend."

"I'm doing what you told me to do! You want him to trust me. I have to spend time with him for that to happen. You can't call me unexpectedly like this. What if he finds out?"

"You better be more careful, then. Not my problem, sweetheart." He's clearly not listening to me. That or he just doesn't give a fuck. "You've always been good at screwing shit up, but you better not screw up this one. You know I care about you, sweetheart, but you better pull this off. I'm not joking, Kenny. Think about your brother."

"The only thing I've been doing for the last few weeks is thinking about my brother, Emerson!"

"Have you? Because I don't think he's the only one you think about."

"God, you sound like Josie." I huff, rolling my eyes.

"Well, Josie is probably right." I frown at his comment before I let out a disheartened breath.

"Don't worry, Em. You know where my loyalty lies."

"It better, sweetheart. It better." Before I can say anything, he hangs up. I press my forehead against the cold door, shutting my eyes in despair. My lungs feel like lead weights as I take a deep breath, trying to calm myself down. With every exhale, tension slowly leaves my body a little more.

"Fuck," I mutter.

If one of the men controlling my life doesn't blow a bullet through my head, I'm pretty sure I will die from a heart attack. I lay my hand on my chest, willing my heart to stop slamming against my rib cage as I suck in another deep breath before releasing it as slowly as possible.

After a few minutes, I walk out and check my flushed face in the mirror. When I walk out of the restroom, I slam into a hard chest, hands instantly steadying me by my arms.

Franklin looks down at me, a concerned look in his eyes, while I push out another deep breath.

God, I really can't catch a break.

It's like the devil and God are tossing me around, wondering who or what will kill me first.

My conscience or the criminals who rule Boston?

"Are you okay?" I can see genuine concern on his face, and once more, it kills me a little more inside.

"Yeah, that was just Josie," I lie while he examines my face.

"You look stressed."

I feel like he's calling me out, so I know I have to give him something.

"Josie doesn't like you," I blurt out.

It's not a complete lie. She made it perfectly clear earlier that she doesn't like to see me with him.

"Because I'm a Wolfe," he states, as if he expected this from the beginning.

"Yeah. She's been giving me a hard time, telling me you're dangerous."

He leans in, brushing his lips against my cheek, making the hairs on the back of my neck stand up.

"Do you think I'm dangerous?"

Automatically, I tilt my head to give him better access to my neck as I close my eyes. His arms snake around my body, and I lean into his touch.

"Hmm, no," I answer in all honesty.

"Then fuck her. Fuck anyone with an opinion about me. Fuck them." He clasps my hand and walks us back to our table while I keep repeating his words in my head.

Fuck her.

Fuck them.

Right.

Easy enough.

23

FRANKLIN

The next morning I'm sitting at my desk while Kendall archives some folders on the other side of the office. I'm focused on her luscious curves. Although I should be looking at the documents in front of me, it's hard to when she's wearing a gray, skin-tight pencil dress. When she gives me a quick glance, I smile in approval, pleased to see I'm not the only one having a hard time concentrating. Eventually, my head does what I want, and I focus on the medical records I need to check for my old and new horses along with a few potential ones I may buy.

"What are you doing?" she asks while she rounds my desk and lays her hand on my shoulder.

"Checking the health records of my horses," I explain as she leans in to get a better look at the papers.

"Hey!" Her finger points at one of the papers on my desk. "Isn't that the one that won the other day? Lord Calypso? Number eight?"

I nod my head in agreement before she gives me a knowing look.

"Wait. That's your horse?"

I hum in confirmation, making her brows jolt up.

"Didn't Reign win a lot of money betting on him?" Her confusion is written on her face, and it's kinda amusing, wondering when it will click.

When I answer by just smiling at her, her eyes widen.

"I thought you didn't gamble?"

"It's not gambling if you know who will win." I shrug with a straight face before I grab her waist and pull her onto my lap.

Her hands circle my neck while I hold her in my arms, my nose brushing against hers as I look into her blue orbs. She cocks her head when she realizes what I said.

"You fix races?"

I keep a straight face, not confirming or denying this. I've always been fascinated by the races, so when I decided I wanted to grow my money that way, I bought Posey, my first horse, ten years ago. Her father was a world champion, and she clearly had his genes. She won her first three races, and it was by then I realized this was a great way to make money. Quickly, I bought another horse.

And another.

And another.

By the time we owned eight horses, there wasn't a race where our horses didn't place in at least the top three. But it wasn't until I realized I could double my earnings by controlling who won that we started making the big bucks. It was a hell of a lot easier than moving around cocaine.

When I turned twenty-five, I bought the family mansion

and started investing in relationships with the people in charge of Massachusetts.

It's amazing what you can do and achieve once you have money. Money literally opens doors and mouths. Now, at thirty-three, there isn't a politician I don't own.

It's a vicious yet fabulous cycle. Politicians control the city, but since I control the politicians, the city is mine.

"You do, don't you?" she asks once more. I hold her frown but keep my mouth shut while a seductive smile appears on her face.

"You own a shitload of horses, and you control who wins. But then what? You can't bet on your own horses, can you?"

My brow quirks up at her unexpected excitement.

"I could, but I rarely do it. I have people betting for me, and I give them a percentage."

"Bookies? Just illegal ones?"

I smile in response, shaking my head in amusement.

"This turns you on?"

Before she can answer, I hear someone clear his throat, and I look up towards the door. Killian is glaring at us, his hands balled into fists beside his rigid body as he clenches his jaw.

"Kill," I call out, acknowledging his arrival. His face looks heated, fury practically dripping down his face. Involuntarily, my eyes close for a second, knowing what will come next.

"Are you serious, Franky?" he questions through gritted teeth.

I purse my lips in aggravation. His eyes widening as he turns his attention on Kendall, giving her a fake smile that has her straightening her back, clearly making her uncomfortable.

"Can you give us a second, *Kenny*?"

Her eyes move back and forth between Killian and me until I give her a soft nod. She gets up and walks towards the door while I keep my eyes focused on my brother.

"And shut the door," he barks behind her back, making my blood boil.

"Don't talk to her like that," I growl with enough force to hopefully make him tone down his attitude.

"You told her about the races? Have you lost your mind?" he hisses. "It's bad enough that you took her there."

His fair skin gets redder with every word he says as he starts pacing the roomy office.

"You barely know this girl. But you'll give her inside info about everything we do?"

"Not everything, just the horses." I shrug.

"That's enough for felony criminal charges, Franklin." He clenches his jaw in frustration while I keep the same bored look on my face.

I trust my brother, he's right about a lot of things. But he's not right about this one. There is something about Kendall that tells me I can trust her.

I don't know everything about her, and it's clear that she's still holding back from me, but she isn't some undercover cop waiting for my destruction.

Whatever we have, it's real.

I can feel it.

She can feel it.

"She's not a cop, Killian."

"Maybe not, but what if she's worse?" he whisper-shouts at me.

"What the fuck do you mean?" I ask, getting really annoyed with his suspiciousness.

"What if she's part of someone's crew? What if she's

looking for your weakness to bring you down? What if she's not, but one of our enemies finds out *she* is your weakness?"

"She's not my weakness," I snap.

"Isn't she?" he growls in exasperation.

I let out a frustrated breath while I rub my face.

"Now you're just getting paranoid. She doesn't work for anyone. Look, I know you've got people skills, but so do I. We can trust her. *You* can trust her."

"Says who? You know nothing about her. You're not thinking straight because she has a pussy." He points his finger at me while he steps closer. The anger is seeping out of his veins, and I have to admit, I haven't seen him this worked up in a while.

But he's wrong.

I slam my fist on my desk to make him shut up before my lips start moving in a vicious tone.

"You're my brother, I love you, and I never take your opinion for granted—"

"Except for now," he interrupts.

"Shut up!" I shout, losing my cool. "I always listen to you, and I'm listening to you now. But I'm telling you we can trust her. And I would appreciate it if you trusted *me*."

He stays quiet, glaring at me before he finally opens his mouth again.

"I've seen her with one of Emerson's guys," he says, a troubled look on his face.

"What are you talking about?"

"I'm shadowing her," he admits. I close my eyes at his words, he's taking this too fucking far. "Tuesday night, I saw one of Emerson's guys walking into her building. I never saw him come out."

"You said *'let me do a check'*. I never gave you permission to shadow her. You're ending that. *Now.*"

"Na-ah! We can't trust her."

My mind wanders back to Tuesday night, even though I already know what I'm looking for.

"She was with me Tuesday night." I sigh.

"What? I thought you said she was going to sleep at home."

"I did, but after I met Connor at the garage, Kendall and I had supper at the bar, and she decided to stay." Confusion clouds his features. "She wasn't with him, Killian. She was with me."

He shakes his head in disbelief.

"I can feel it, Franky. Something is up with this girl. She's not who she says she is."

"Look," I roar with finality in my voice, sick of this back-and-forth bullshit. "You don't like her. I get it. Run her through the system and come back when you have proof, but don't fucking bother me with this bullshit until you have it. You got it?"

He lowers his head while rubbing his temples. He knows I won't accept anything other than acquiescence, and the irritation he feels is clearly visible.

"I'm going to ask Reign to do a background check on her," he informs me as he moves to the door.

Arrogant bastard.

"Do whatever, Killian. I don't care. But don't bother me about it. Just stop tracking her." I focus back on the documents in front of me, silently telling him this conversation is over. Without another word, he walks out of my office.

I look up at the ceiling and blow out a deep breath. I've trusted my gut my entire life, it's got me where I am now. And though I trust Kendall, there was something in Killian's words nagging at me. A niggling in my gut asking me, 'what if he's right?'. What if she is hiding something? I never bother to do background checks on the women I sleep with because they rarely stay longer than a night or two. But I've been with this girl every single day for the last month.

What if she really isn't who she says she is? She's in the perfect position to get close to me, capable of bringing me down when I least expect it.

24

Kendall

Killian's arrival at the office has me anxious for the rest of the day. He glared at me as he stormed out of Franklin's office, his finger pointed at me in a threatening way.

"I'm watching you," he'd said before he slammed the door closed behind him. I blinked at the closed door for probably a full minute, knowing I was playing on a cliff's edge. I could fall down at any moment or be thrown off by Killian Wolfe. Although Reign and Connor seem to really like me, I keep thinking about what the fuck I can do or say to convince Killian he can trust me.

Because he definitely doesn't.

When we get back to Franklin's apartment, I barely let him get through the door before I put him in a corner.

Well, figuratively that is.

"Your brother. He hates me."

"He doesn't hate you."

"Franky." I pull a face, telling him he's full of shit, making him roll his eyes.

I chuckle in surprise. I've never seen him actually roll his eyes since he's usually serious as fuck.

"He doesn't hate you," he presses while his hand cups the front of my neck to softly push me against the wall.

He's so fucking hot.

"He does. I can see it in his eyes." I try to keep a straight face as Franklin uses his other hand to loosen his tie, not letting myself get distracted because I'm serious about this.

I've seen the way Killian looks at me. It's different from Reign who adores me and different from Connor, who doesn't say much but at least gives me a chance.

Killian loathes me.

When he looks at me, I want to run and hide. His piercing green eyes turn ominous, as if he's trying to look through my soul. And to be honest, I can't really blame him.

"He has my eyes," Franklin mocks with a playful grin.

"Maybe, but you don't look at me like that."

"Like what?" He softly brushes his lips against mine, making it hard to concentrate while his other hand strokes my back in a possessive way.

"Like he's about to swallow me whole when I'm not looking." My hands reach up, holding on to his broad shoulders.

A lustful grin appears on his face, and I instantly regret my choice of words.

"Don't worry, the only one who will be swallowing you whole is *me*."

"Franklin!" I push him back, pulling a laugh from him.

"What do you want me to say, pretty girl?" He shrugs while I push myself off the wall and walk towards the bathroom.

"The truth," I call out, looking in the mirror. He follows me into the bathroom and wraps his arms around my stomach, my back pressed against his chest as his lips lean in to kiss the crook of my neck. He places a string of kisses on my flushed skin before he meets my eyes in the mirror.

"He doesn't trust you," he pushes out with a breath, as if he's bothered to even voice this.

I'm not at all surprised, but I am curious.

"Why?"

"He thinks you know Emerson Jones, one of our enemies. Thinks you may be playing me."

My brows shoot to my forehead, and my mouth is suddenly dry. He sees the change in my expression, and the look on his face grows stern as his grip tightens around me.

"Emerson Jones?" My heart is about to race out of my chest. I feel like this moment will determine my future. If I'll be able to keep my heart in one piece, or if I'll have to watch it get shattered alongside Franklin's brain once I give Emerson the chance to shoot Franklin through the head. He notices my discomfort, and the look in his eyes slowly changes him into the ruthless man that everyone warned me about. The wolf who isn't afraid to bite.

"Kendall?" My name rumbles against my cheek, his seductive mood gone, replaced by a threatening one while his eyes turn dark, pinning me down in the mirror.

I take a deep breath, closing my eyes, doing my best to find every ounce of courage tucked inside of me before I open them again and raise my chin.

"I need to tell you something," I confess, hoping and praying I'm making the right choice.

Though at this moment, it feels like the only choice I ever had.

His nostrils flare and a muscle tics in his jaw. There is

disappointment mixed with a shitload of rage in his eyes as he roughly grabs my hips and spins me in his arms, pressing my ass against the bathroom sink, his eyes locking with mine.

The people in this city call him 'the wolf', not only because of his last name, but because he's the leader of the pack. The ultimate alpha, ready to eliminate any kind of threat. The last few weeks, I was lucky enough to see the alpha who cared for his family, his friends, and the people around him. Witnessed that he was fair, far from the cunning man people paint him out to be.

But I see it now.

I see it in his eyes.

It's like the wolf is showing me his true form, ready to rip my throat open if the next words are not the ones he wants to hear.

"Speak," he growls, his tone making my lashes flutter with fear.

It's hard to not cower under his glare right now, but for my own safety, I need to hold my own.

I know that.

They say to never look a wolf in the eyes, to show them you are not a threat. But in this case, I need him to listen to me, whatever it takes, or it will cost me dearly. I need to give him something to fully gain his trust and make sure I survive the next few weeks and keep my brother safe.

"Promise me one thing," I say while I keep my chin raised in defiance, fighting not to give in to the fear piercing my body.

His eyes narrow, clearly losing his patience with me, so I offer him a small smile to comfort him.

"Please."

"What?" he barks. Although he didn't raise his voice, his furious energy almost knocks me out.

"Promise me that whatever I'm about to say, you will listen until I'm *completely* done."

He stays quiet, tilting his head a little before finally he gives me a curt nod in agreement.

I take another deep breath and close my eyes, not able to look him in the eyes until I say everything I need to say.

"I … I d-do know him."

"Goddammit," he snaps through gritted teeth, pushing his fingers into my side so hard that I wince under his touch.

"I do know him," I repeat clearly, ready to blurt it all out. "Better than you think. He's my ex."

"He's your…" he huffs and trails off, looking up to the ceiling in frustration. "Fuck me."

"Emerson Jones is the ex I've been talking about," I continue, looking him straight in the eye with a pleading look when he brings his focus back to me, hoping he'll let me finish. "We came to Boston when we were eighteen. Me, Josie, Emerson, and a few of Emerson's friends. He wanted to leave Alabama, and I followed him here. We broke up about two years ago, even though I tried to leave him many times before that. It took me a while to realize he was abusing me, both mentally and physically, and I didn't have the guts to leave him, fearing what he would do to me. When he found a new girl, I finally saw my chance and left. That's the short story." I wait a few seconds before I finally open my eyes, fearful of what I may see.

"Why the *fuck* didn't you tell me?" he snarls with fury in his voice.

"I don't know? Because I didn't think I needed to give you a list of my ex-boyfriends, maybe," I sass, turning this around on him. It's a bullshit comment, and I hate myself for saying it because it's a lie wrapped up in a blanket of innocence.

A get-out-of-jail-free-card that I'm now waving in front of his face as if I'm completely innocent while I look into his fire filled eyes.

I don't know what I expect him to do, but whatever it is, I expect it to be painful. But instead, his face softens a little, and my heart slows down in relief when he cups my face.

"He's your douchebag ex?"

I nod as I feel my eyes well up, hoping he will see the truth and be willing to give me another shot. He licks his lips before he bites the bottom one.

"He's the one who hurt you?"

I shrug in response, not knowing what to say.

What am I supposed to say, anyway?

"Do you still see him?" I would expect this to be an accusation, but his voice is calm and warm.

I close my eyes for a second, thinking about what I can and can't say, choosing my words wisely.

"He checks in every now and then, reminding me and Josie how we owe him everything. He bought our house for us."

"He bought you a house, and now he holds it against you? Why? What do you do for him in return?"

"He sends packages to our house, and they get picked up by one of his men."

"What kind of packages?"

"I don't know. We never question anything. We did once, and he made us watch when he tortured this courier who stole from him."

"To scare you?"

I nod.

"That's what he does. He likes to see people suffer." I avert my gaze, suddenly fascinated by my cuticles as a tear escapes the corner of my eye. "I'm not as strong as you think I am."

His thumb brushes away my tears before he grabs my chin and forces me to look at him.

"I'm sorry. I'm so sorry," I plead, looking into his gorgeous green eyes, hoping I made the right choice.

"Ssh, it's okay."

"I just want to forget about that part of my life."

"I believe you, Kenny." He pushes a strand of hair out of my face before he leans in and presses a compassionate kiss on my lips. Longing for his touch, I circle his waist and tug him closer to me.

His hand runs through my hair a few times before he rests it on my neck while I look up at him.

"If there is anything else, you should tell me now." He's looking at me with a serious gaze, and my heart starts to race again. It's like the blood is rushing through my body a hundred miles an hour. My heart and my mind wrapped up in a torturous battle.

"Is there anything else you should tell me?" he asks again. "I told you, trust is key to me."

I think about his words, letting them really sink in. I debate with myself over what I should do, what I should tell him, but mostly how *much* I should tell him.

Finally, I shake my head.

"No. No, there's not."

25

Kendall

Franklin turns onto a private driveway that ends in a round with a fountain in the middle. My lips part in awe when I look at the huge home with arches and pillars on the ground level. The brick walls are a soft beige while the windows and doors are a solid white, making it look cozy yet impressive at the same time.

"This is your house?" I blurt out in awe, turning my head his way. His penthouse is spacious, modern, and luxurious. But this?

Holy hell.

He smiles as he rests his hand on my leg, softly squeezing.

"This is the family home. We all live here."

"You grew up here?"

"I grew up in South End. I bought this a few years ago. I wanted to give us a place we could all call home after my brothers had been in foster care."

My heart melts at his words, further proof of how he always does everything with his brothers in mind. He parks the car directly in front of the door, even though there are other cars parked on the side. He gets out and rounds the car while I continue staring up at the enormous mansion. With the sun starting to set and the dim lights surrounding the house, it seems like home out of a fairy tale.

Franklin opens the car door and holds out his hand. I grab it with a smile, enjoying his chivalry.

"Why thank you, sir."

"Pleasure is all mine, pretty girl." I expect him to hook my arm in his, but instead, he holds my hand, linking our fingers as he directs us inside. As soon as we walk over the threshold, I'm greeted by the murmur of voices with an occasional laugh in between. A waiter is standing in the foyer holding a tray filled with champagne, and Franklin lets go of my hand to grab us each a glass. He gives me one before clicking our glasses, then we both sip the sparkling bubbly. As usual, his face is inscrutable, but I can see the satisfied look in his eyes as he gives me a kiss that goes through my veins, my toes curling just from feeling his lips on mine and the hand on my back that tugs me even closer to his body. I'm wishing I could kiss him like this every day for the rest of my life, when I remind myself that will never happen. When I disconnect my lips from his, I'm instantly met by a scowl.

"It's your brother's birthday," I explain to cover up my depressing thoughts.

"I've been with him for his birthday for the last twenty-seven years. I'll be there again next year. Let's go upstairs."

I chuckle at his ridiculous behavior, loving how loose he is with me. He's a man that tries to hide his emotions for the outside world, and there may not be a lot of people who would describe this man as *fun*, but that's exactly what he is with me.

"Your brother already hates me. He'll hate me even more if I make you bail on his birthday."

"You're not making me bail. I am." He sucks my bottom lip between his before I drag my head back, trying to avoid his lips while he leans in once more.

"Baby," he growls, pulling another chuckle from me. Last week we grew closer, and I'm pretty sure that after Friday's confession, he has enough feelings for me to truly trust me. But while I live for our moments together, I also dread them, feeling like a piece of trash for pretending I'm not hiding anything from him.

"Show your face, mingle, then take me upstairs when you're ready. Who knows? Maybe I can even win your brother over first.".

His lower lip juts out, which I find incredibly endearing, as he pushes a strand of my hair out of my face.

"He'll warm up to you, baby."

"I know," I reply with a tight smile as one of Franklin's men clears his throat.

"Everyone is waiting for you in the ballroom, sir," he says with a slight nod.

"Thank you, Nigel." He grabs my hand and leads me into the hallway.

"Ballroom?" I hiss behind him. "You have a freaking ballroom?"

"It's more like a dining room." He shrugs as he leads me into the area filled with at least thirty people, all talking and laughing with drinks in their hands. At the far end of the room is a small bar with a waiter serving drinks, while on the right side of the room is a long table that is set up as a buffet. The hardwood floor is shining like it was freshly oiled, serving as a small dance floor, and in the middle of the room hangs a colossal chandelier, illuminating the entire room.

Everything is gorgeous.

"Yeah, I'll have to go with Nigel on this one," I quip. "This is definitely a ballroom."

"It's not, but you can call it that if you want to." I'm glowing under his teasing tone as he gives me another peck on the lips.

"Evening, brother." Killian comes up behind us, slapping Franklin on the back before his suspicious eyes land on me. "Kenny."

"Happy birthday, Killian." I give him a friendly smile, even though I know he doesn't want me to be here. Franklin convinced me to come with him, even though he never answered my question when I asked him if Killian wanted me to be there.

He doesn't.

He doesn't trust me, and I can't blame him. Every suspicion he has about me is true, and I respect him even more for trying to protect his brother. Too bad it just makes everything that much harder. Not to mention scarier.

"Thanks," he retorts curtly before turning his attention back to his brother. "Can we talk?"

"In private?" Killian eyes me with a look of disdain that causes cold shivers to run down my spine, but I roll my eyes to keep up the appearance of being unaffected.

Franklin looks at me with a pained expression, probably hesitant to leave me by myself in a room full of people I don't know.

"It's alright. I'll keep Kenny company." An arm falls over my shoulder, and I look to my left to find Reign, who is looking at his brothers, wearing a playful grin. Franklin gives his brother a warning glare before turning his attention to me.

"I'm good, really." I encourage with a smile, feeling more confident now that Reign is by my side.

"Are you sure?" He leans in, brushing his nose against mine.

"I'm sure."

"Okay, I'll be right back." He presses a kiss to my forehead before he points his finger towards Reign.

"Make her uncomfortable and I will make you uncomfortable."

Reign, unimpressed, just rolls his eyes.

"Well, that's nothing new. Bye, Franklin." He waves his hand towards his brother before tugging me with him towards the bar, his arm still draped over my shoulder.

"What do you want? A vodka lime?" He taps the bar to grab the attention of the bartender before giving me a questioning look.

I nod in response, examining Franklin's youngest brother as he places our order. His hair is brighter than Franklin's, and Reign as a whole is lighter than Franklin, who carries a heavy energy. Reign seems to always be smiling, while Franklin rarely smiles. They seem to be opposites in everything they do, yet the resemblance between the two is striking. Different from Killian and Connor, who own the same green eyes but are still very different.

"What?" he asks with a grin when he hands me my drink, catching me staring.

He turns around, leaning his back against the bar, taking a sip of his whiskey.

"Nothing." I shrug. "You just look a lot like Franklin."

"I'm nothing like my brother." He huffs, looking slightly offended.

"What happened?" I ask, thinking back to all the banter I've witnessed between the two of them. It's not the same banter they share with their other brothers. No, the banter between Reign and Franklin is filled with emotion, as if there is a lot of unfinished history between the two of them.

"What do you mean?"

"Franklin told me how the two of you used to get along better than any of your brothers. Clearly, that's not the case anymore. What happened?"

He sucks in a deep breath through his nose before taking a sip of his drink, then he exhales loudly.

"Can't believe he told you that."

"He didn't tell me anything else, no details, he just mentioned that."

He runs his hand through his light brown hair, a few strands flopping back onto his forehead while I look at him in anticipation.

"It's complicated," he states, looking at me with a small grin. The look on his face is still open and friendly, but there is a finality in his voice that tells me he doesn't want to talk about it.

This last month, it felt like Reign and I developed some kind of friendship, an understanding that makes us respect the other. Not wanting to ruin that foundation we seem to have, I tilt my head before smiling in understanding.

"Will you tell me one day?"

He nods his head, looking into the room while his elbows lean on the hardwood surface.

"Sure."

"Good," I reply before taking a sip of my vodka,

mirroring his stance.

Franklin is still talking to Killian on the other side of the room, yet his focus remains completely on me. Heat flashes up my face, so I take another sip while I keep my eyes locked with his from above the rim of my glass.

"He's falling for you, you know?"

Confused, I snap my head towards Reign, not sure what he's talking about.

He nods his head towards Franklin before his eyes find mine.

"Don't get ahead of yourself," I huff, rolling my eyes in disbelief.

"That's what he said."

"I mean it."

I glance at him before bringing my attention back to Franklin, taking in his impressive posture. He owns the room, like the pack leader that he is, but there is also a kindness in his eyes. Something that says he strives to be fair and honest. I really am doing my best to not completely fall for him, but it's hard to ignore the butterflies flying through my stomach every time his gaze finds mine. Even harder when they are met by a shit ton of guilt.

"You're his first girlfriend," he adds.

"I'm not his girlfriend."

He chuckles in disbelief, bringing his glass towards his mouth.

"I'm not his girlfriend," I repeat.

"Do you honestly believe that?"

"Yes. No. I don't know."

I would be lying if I said my heart doesn't jump for joy, hearing Reign calling me Franklin's girlfriend. But my mind is screaming 'no', simply because labeling it would make this situation even worse. If we don't label it, I can still pretend it's not real for him either.

That I'm just a girl he's sleeping with.

That I'm just a girl who holds his interest for now.

Fuck, I'm so full of shit.

I've been spending every spare minute with him for the last few weeks. We eat together; we work together; we sleep together; we have amazing sex. I'm pretty sure that doesn't fall under the criteria of 'fuck buddy.' Hell, I think it even surpasses the line above 'friends with benefits.'

Holy hell, I'm his girlfriend.

I stare into his eyes from across the room as everybody around us disappears from my vision. I only see him and his hypnotizing, sea-green eyes. My pulse starts racing at this realization.

I'm his girlfriend.

He trusts me.

Why do I follow the abusive demands of Emerson Jones when I can ask for the protection of Franklin Wolfe?

Why do I continue to comply with what I know when this man has been putting his trust in me for weeks without really knowing me at all?

'Trust is key to me, Kendall.'

I can still hear the words he said when he pushed me against the cold concrete of the stable, and again when I told him about my history with Emerson, echoing through my mind.

Why don't I give him the trust he's given me?

Why don't I tell him the truth?

The corner of my mouth tilts up in a pleased grin as an epiphany hits my brain, a confident voice in my head telling me I can trust him.

That he's not my problem.

He's my *solution.*

That he will protect me if I tell him the truth that has been hanging above my head like a thundercloud, threatening every happy moment I have with him.

My eyes stay locked with his, feeding my confidence. I'm a split second away from strutting across the room and throwing myself into his arms like you see in those cheesy rom-coms, ready to tell him every single thing I've been hiding.

But as always, my luck proves to be pretty much nonexistent yet again. Before I can get my feet to move, I see someone enter the room from the corner of my eye. I feel like my heart stops when I catch a glimpse of his military haircut, followed by at least ten of his men, each of them holding automatic weapons. My eyes widen, then I notice Franklin following my shocked face before the entire room goes quiet and guns are drawn from every corner. I gasp and clutch my chest as Reign moves to stand in front of me.

"Oh, a buffet!" Emerson bellows through the room before his eyes lock with Franklin, whose face remains expressionless. "Do you mind?"

Without waiting for a response, Emerson saunters to the buffet while his men spread throughout the room, clearly unaffected by the two dozen or so guns pointed at them. He takes a shrimp off the table before popping it into his mouth.

"Oh, these are good! Who's your caterer?"

"You've got some nerve, Jones. Walking into our family home like this," Connor growls, his frame seeming to grow bigger, like a real wolf when being threatened.

"I thought I'd already shown you that I've got some nerve?" Emerson wears a derisive smile as he saunters through the room. "I mean, was it not enough? Do I have to be more specific? Do you need more visuals? More blood maybe? I can do that." I wipe away the sweat forming on my forehead at his words while Reign keeps his arm and most of his body in front of me like a human shield. The hairs on the back of my neck stand up with every step Emerson takes closer to us.

First, his eyes find Reign's, then they lock with mine. Fear is stampeding through my veins, the sound of my racing heart pounding in my ears.

I have no clue what he's doing here, had no idea he was going to be here. Is he going to expose me? What if he's here to kill Franklin? The thoughts alone have me wringing my sweaty hands as I take a deep breath, trying to stay calm.

Nice try.

"Reign!" he shouts with a wide, obnoxious grin. "New girlfriend?" Emerson smirks while I blink nervously at his theatrics. Without thinking, I quickly glance at Franklin, instantly regretting it when Emerson follows my gaze.

"Or is she yours, Franky?" he taunts, making Franklin clench his jaw while his hands ball into fists beside his body. Rage fills his eyes, and I can see his chest move while he takes in deep breaths, ready to charge before Killian throws a hand in front of him, holding him back.

"Oh, she *is* yours!" Emerson chuckles, stepping closer towards me. "She's pretty."

I'm feeling extremely relieved that I told Franklin my history with Emerson, but now my fingers and toes are crossed that Emerson doesn't reveal what's transpired between us recently, or rather, what he's been blackmailing me into doing. With a smug look, Emerson chose that moment to narrow in on me, making me think this is it. He's going to out me in front of everyone, sharing with the world how we've known each other since forever. That I've been his little spy.

In my head, I can already see Franklin slipping away from me.

"What do you want, Emerson?" Reign growls at him while Emerson keeps his focus on me, his ominous eyes piercing right through me in a haunting way. Through his menacing glare, he has a silent conversation with me, leaving me praying that the earth will open up beneath my feet. Finally, he breaks our eye contact, turning his focus to Reign.

"Simple. More money. More power," he answers with his arms wide as he continues to saunter through the room.

"Don't we all?" Killian huffs sarcastically while he boldly rolls his eyes.

"Sure." Emerson shrugs before he points his gun at one of the elegantly dressed women. She lets out a screech, her lip trembling before her eyes start to well up, and her body starts to shake. Her husband reaches out his hand to drag her away, but before he can get to her, one of Emerson's guys points his gun at him, making him freeze to the spot. The thick tension in the room is suffocating. Everyone is on edge. I bring my hand up to cover my mouth, feeling like the suspense is going to make me pass out.

With a rapid turn of his head, Emerson's eyes fixate on me, making me gasp for air.

"You, get over here, or I'll shoot her." He's speaking to me. Fuck my life.

"No," Reign roars at the same time I hear Franklin growl from across the room. In response, Emerson cocks his gun, giving me a defiant look, and raises an eyebrow. To everyone who doesn't know of our connection, this looks like nothing more than an obvious threat. But to me, it's a silent command to obey, telling me he will kill her if I don't cooperate.

"It's okay," I whisper to Reign, while I gently push his arm away and step in front of him. My eyes find Franklin, who's scowling at Emerson. When he meets my gaze, he lightly shakes his head as if he's asking me not to get any closer. But I know Emerson better than anyone in this room. He's not joking. He's not playing around. He will kill her if I don't 'play along', as he would call it.

"Tut tut, a little faster, sweetheart." His finger moves closer to the trigger, making me gasp for air while I bring my hand up.

"No, no! L-let her go. I'm coming. I'm here."

Emerson holds out his hand, and I grab it before he twirls me around so that my back is pressed against his chest, his gun against my temple. His hand is cupping the front of my throat, and the back of my head is leaning against his shoulder, making it easy for him to whisper in my ear.

"Leo says hi, sweetheart." I close my eyes in defeat when he murmurs this against my ear. Not loud enough for anyone but me to hear. I'm sure I look horrified as a sense of desperation floods my body upon hearing the name Leo.

Oh God.

"What do you want, Jones?" Killian asks again, his face a steely mask.

"It's time for a new king," Emerson explains while he walks us backward to the open door he originally came in through. "*Bow.* Bow, agree to a tax fee, and this will work just fine." His fingers are pressed painfully into my chin, bruising the bones in my face while he continues. "You may think you're the top dogs, but you won't be for long. Be smart and bow down now before I'll be forced to start a war." He expresses as if he's asking for tickets to the Red Sox.

Finally, Franklin steps forward to take control of the situation, owning the room once more.

"Let go of her. Now." His deep voice sounds completely composed and calm while he shoots me an encouraging look.

"Sure, no worries. You can keep your whore." I can't even describe the relief I feel when Emerson pushes me into Franklin's arms. I quickly wrap my arms around him as he holds me tight against his chest. Then we're moving as Franklin and his men start following Emerson and his crew, who are walking towards the exit. "But I'm serious, Franklin. Tik tok, tik tok. I want an answer within two weeks. If not? I'll take that sweet little cunt of yours and make her my own." He walks out, but not before he halts one more time, right in front of Nigel, who's plastered against the wall in fear. His eyes widen when Emerson looks him straight in the eye.

"Sorry, man. I need to show them I'm serious. Kill him," he says to one of his men holding an automatic weapon. He can't be much older than Nigel and looks nothing more than a troubled teenager with the snapback he's wearing on his head backwards.

Fear filters through Nigel's eyes, and I can literally feel my heart skip a beat when Emerson walks away, and the teen pulls the trigger, several bullets piercing through Nigel before his lifeless body drops to the floor. Screams echo through the room while I look at the dead body in front of me in horror, too shocked to control my breathing. I think I may throw up when I look over at Emerson. He shoots me a wink, then he disappears out of sight. My feet are glued to the floor, unable to move even an inch, while only one thought fills my head.

That could've been my brother.

26

Franklin

I drag her back into the hallway, away from the people who are now circling the dead body in my dining room.

Nigel.

A twenty-one-year-old kid who's been under my wing for the last three years. I promised him I would help him build a future, but instead, he ended up dead under my command.

My heart is drumming in fury, my muscles like tight chords in my body while my fingers enclose around Kendall's hand in a strong grip.

When I look behind me, I find her panting with a horrified look in her eyes. I push her against the wall in the hallway before I take her face in my hands to force her to look at me so I can help her calm down. Goddammit, this will be another thing to haunt her forever. When she told me about her history with Emerson and the way he treated her, I vowed to myself that I would protect her like he never did. But the last five minutes make me realize I'll never be able to do that.

This is my life.

"Look at me, Kenny. Look at me."

Her terror-filled eyes find mine while she swallows hard, clearly doing her best to keep from hyperventilating.

"You're okay. Everything is okay."

"Okay?" she screeches. "He's dead. He killed him."

"I know. Just calm down."

"Calm down?!" Her eyes grow a little wider, her panic only seeming to increase at my words. Most of the people who are part of our organization have seen a dead body in their lifetime, many have seen more than one. They know it's a risk, running with the Wolfes. Even Nigel knew that.

But I hate Emerson for corrupting my girl like that. Scaring the shit out of her, making her feel unsafe when really there shouldn't be a safer place in this city than by my side. She doesn't know that, though. All she knows is that she's spending her time with a criminal who says he will protect her while her ex is a criminal she has learned to fear.

"Come on." I grab her arm and pull her with me, ignoring the staff as I lead her through the large kitchen. Once outside on the terrace, I guide her down a gravel path into the huge garden that is surrounded by roses. The path leads to a small, covered up patio with a bench, sheltered from the rest of the house.

"Sit," I command, pushing her on the bench while she stares at the ground in front of her. Her eyes are frenzied and glassy, making me wonder if she's in shock. I shake my head, unable to process seeing her like this. I crouch down in front of her, holding her knee with one hand while the other cups her cheek, and I look up into her eyes. "Baby, hey. You're safe. Look at me. I will keep you safe. He won't hurt you anymore."

Finally, her eyes lock with mine. I watch as her eyes well up, then a single tear escapes the corner of her eye.

"You can't say that. He will find me."

"Come here, pretty girl." I get back up and take a seat next to her, pulling her into my arms.

"He'll have to go through me first. I promise. I'll keep you safe." She's crying now, so I shush against her hair, keeping her tight against my chest.

Sometimes I forget how fucked up the world is. How my reality is normal to me but completely insane to practically everyone else. I was raised with abuse, murder, dead people, and corruption. Seeing a dead body is a loss, something I mourn, but never for long because I've learned that I have to move on. Stay focused on the next step. When I saw the defiance in her eyes, the first time I saw her in The Library, I assumed she was used to men like me. Used to bending the rules, living on the edge of danger, always looking for more no matter what it takes. I was too caught up in her hypnotizing appearance to see she's truly one of the good girls, the ones who understand the concepts of the criminal world but don't truly realize what it really entitles.

"He's dead, Franklin," she whispers while her hands clasp onto mine as if she's scared I will let her go.

Never.

"I know, baby." I can't even make up some cute story to make her feel better. She just watched him die. He's dead. Emerson Jones killed him to send a message, and he crossed a line that can't ever be uncrossed.

"He will pay for it," I murmur against her head, making her look up at me with big, devastated eyes.

"You're going to kill him?" Her voice is uncertain, as if she doesn't know what she thinks of that idea.

I get it.

It's hard to talk about murder or anything else that's unethical. But in this world, it's really simple: eat or be eaten.

Emerson Jones just tried to eat me. Now I have to show him that I'm the only one eating in this city.

"I may," I reply honestly, not knowing my plan just yet. I may kill him, or I may give him another chance to fall in line. Perhaps he'll do it to save his crew. Although something tells me that Emerson Jones is not going to stop until one of us has a bullet through his head.

I just know it ain't going to be me.

"I … I just," she stutters, tears once again running down her cheeks. It breaks my heart, seeing her shattered like this.

"What is it, baby? Just talk to me." I want to take it all away. Whatever fear or pain she's feeling, I want to take it all away, but I have a feeling I'm one of the things she's afraid of.

Rather, my life.

"I … I can't do this, Franklin."

I cringe at her words, not willing to let her go. My heart feels heavy just thinking about it. I know I once vowed I would never fall in love… In fact; I told my brother I wasn't going to settle down anytime soon just days ago, but I can't look into the future and not see her in it. I can't look ahead and not see her by my side. I never thought I'd share my heart with a woman, but I think she stole it that first night.

"Hey, listen to me." I cup her face forcefully with both hands, making sure she pays attention to every word I'm about to say. "If you are with me, you will never be in danger. I will always keep you safe. My brothers will always keep you safe. I know this isn't what you're used to, and I'm sorry I'm dragging you into this, but I'm not willing to let you go."

She sadly shakes her head, tears streaming down her cheeks.

"That's what I'm scared of. This *is* what I'm used to. Emerson made me watch how he tortured and killed people numerous times. Showing me what would happen to me if I didn't do as he said. When we broke up, I was relieved that my life would finally be less violent. Yet here I am, falling in love with a Wolfe."

Her words cut through me like a knife.

She's right.

I can't promise her a life that is less violent, not now. Not yet.

"Please, Kendall. Don't leave me. I've got plans. I'm not going to be doing this for the rest of my life. Stick by my side. I'll make it worth it." I hate the desperation I can hear in my voice, but I mean every word.

My plan was never to stay on the dark side of the law, to always have to look over my shoulder. The only reason I started the organization I've built was to create something for the future.

A legacy for my brothers.

Making sure they won't have to do the things that I've had to do. Making sure that by the time they have their own families, they can be free, safe, and won't have to worry about anything other than keeping their wives and children happy.

I never wanted to walk this path myself, the one I've created for them, the one that includes a family and children. But if Kendall is another reason for me to get out, I'll take it. I will take it because I want it all with her. I want to wake up next to her, put a ring on her finger, and fuck me one day I want to have kids with her. I feel stupid just thinking about it, and never in a million years would I have admitted this to myself if she wasn't about to slip from my fingers.

"Please," I beg, looking into her troubled sapphire gaze. When she doesn't answer, I suck in a deep breath and wonder if there's more.

"Is there something else you need to tell me?"

She closes her eyes, and for a second I think she may. But then she shakes her head slowly, and even though I don't believe her, I don't push it.

"No."

I squeeze her cold, dainty hands.

"You can trust me, Kendall. Just stay with me."

Finally, she nods, then I press a bruising kiss on her lips while the cogs in my head spin, urging me to break the connection.

"Actually, there is something I need to say to you," she whispers, her red-rimmed, teary eyes breaking my heart.

"Wait." I hold out my palm, suddenly realizing what she'd said. "Did you say you're in love with me?"

She looks up, panic creeping into her eyes while I eagerly wait for her to answer my question.

"I … I…" she stutters, her eyes wide like a deer in headlights.

"Don't be scared, pretty girl." I cup her cheek and offer her what is hopefully a reassuring smile.

"I think I am." The words are rushed as she pushes out the words as if she's afraid she may back out if she waits any longer. A laugh escapes my lips.

"Good. Because this would've been really awkward if you weren't."

"What would be really awkward?" She straightens her body on the bench, a questioning look shadowing her orbs.

"Me telling you I love you," I confess, while she blinks in response.

Finally, a big smile splits her face. Her tears have started to subside, happiness now shining through her instead of fear. I did that. I stopped her panic from escalating and replaced it with joy.

"You do? You love me?"

I growl while I circle my arms around her waist, pressing her to my chest, wishing I could show her with how tightly I hold her, that I never want to let her go.

"Yes, Kenny. I love you." I look down at her, still holding her close while I feel my heart open for the first time in thirty-one years. Loving anyone other than my brothers has always been a liability, a weakness I couldn't afford, so I'd never wanted it. But Kendall Ryan sneaked up on me, it's fucking impossible not to love her.

She's beaming as she looks up at me, her cheek pressed against my chest.

"I love you, too, Franklin Wolfe."

"Good answer." I lean in and press a kiss against her soft, plump lips, vowing not to go another day without them.

27

Kendall

I walk over the Central Wharf, trying to take measured breaths to control my nerves. Last night was intense. Like fucked-up, shitfaced intense.

This morning I woke up, realizing I need to put a stop to things with Emerson, or things will go to shit again real quick. I need to tell him he needs to pipe it down with his unexpected visits before he's going to fuck up his own plan. I'm feeling more confident now that I know I have Franklin in my corner, but I still have to be careful about everything I do and say. If I fuck this up, it will cost me my life. And my brother's.

The salty wind makes my brown hair whisp in front of my face, and I'm reaching up to tuck it out of the way when I reach the bar.

The Alabama Anchor.

I push the door open, and I'm greeted by one of Emerson's guys, who gives me a sinister nod. I raise an eyebrow, daring him to stop me as I keep walking through the room.

Since the first day we arrived in Boston, this was where I

spent most of my time. The inside is dingy and dirty. I cringe, wishing I'd never had to spend more than a minute here rather than the years I wasted between its walls. Now that Franklin has asked me to move in with him, I know that I'll never live like this again. Never have to live in squalor or struggle under Emerson's thumb again.

It's a small bar with room for no more than about twenty people at the same time, but that's not the reason Emerson bought it before he packed us all up and moved us to Boston.

No, it's the door in the back, covered by a black, velvet curtain, that's the real reason he bought this piece of shit bar in the first place. I push the curtain to the side, stepping over the threshold before I descend down the stairs. Before I reach the last step, my nose is greeted by the thick scent of cigars mixed with a hint of coffee. I hear the sound of at least two deep voices.

Well, he's definitely up.

I check my watch while I push the door open farther, two sets of eyes looking at me in surprise. Or annoyance, I'm not sure.

"You're up?" I ask Emerson the obvious. "It's only ten in the morning. I thought you'd definitely sleep in after the busy night you had."

Emerson's tongue presses against his teeth as his lips lift in amusement.

"Morning, sweetheart." He leans back against the corner booth he's sitting in while Cary gives me a suspicious glare. "Take a seat, have a coffee with us. Just like old times."

"Old times would be me bringing you coffee, and those days are over, Em."

"They don't have to be?" He shoots me a wink, causing goosebumps to scatter across my body.

How the hell did I ever fall in love with this douchebag?

"I'm not sure your new girl would appreciate that."

"She'll learn to share," he shrugs. "Just like you did."

I guffaw at the reminder of exactly why he and I will never work. Not deeming his remark worthy of a response, I press my hands on the table and glower at him. His amber eyes brighten in excitement, apparently enjoying my new attitude.

"What the fuck was that stunt last night, Emerson?"

He licks his lips when his eyes move to my boobs, now at the perfect height for him to stare at them.

Right, not the best move, Kendall.

Deciding I have to go with it now anyway, I glance at my boobs before I roll my eyes at him.

"Emerson!" I bark, slamming my fist on the table, trying to get his attention back.

"Hmm?" His eyes find mine again, and I clench my jaw in annoyance.

"What was that stunt?" I ask through gritted teeth.

He brings his coffee cup to his lips and takes a slow sip, probably making me wait just to piss me off.

Son of a bitch.

Finally, he puts his cup back down and lounges back, his arms outstretched over the booth.

"Just a friendly reminder."

"A friendly reminder?" I parrot, harshly, not hiding the fury in my tone.

"The Wolfes need to start understanding that this is inevitable. Me taking over. Regardless of what collateral damage may occur because of it."

"Like Nigel."

"Was that his name?"

"You are fucking unbelievable! You want me to gain his trust, to make sure I will get you your shot, but then you barge in unannounced, killing his men. That's not fucking helping, Emerson."

His face goes rigid, and he leans his forward while narrowing his eyes at me.

Shit.

I know I'm in trouble when his hand quickly reaches for my jacket, forcefully pulling me closer to him.

"Listen up, sweetheart. First, you don't tell me what to do. Second, I've been watching you. They have no clue you're working for me. Unless you told one of those fuckers, but you wouldn't do that, would you?" My stomach recoils in fear as the tip of his finger strokes my cheek.

I shake my head frantically.

"N … No, of course not."

The amount of lies I've been telling for the last few weeks is killing me, but I have no choice, it's for the best.

"Good." I almost fall when he lets me go with a slight push. I quickly straighten, trying to create as much distance between us without running away. I quickly glance at Cary, who dons a smug grin while staring at me with his icy blue eyes.

"Just keep doing what you're doing, and everything will be fine. You got it?" Emerson considers me with that soulless look that still haunts me at night.

I'm eager to get the fuck out of here, so I nod in agreement before I turn around to walk away.

"Kendall?" he calls out when I reach the door to the stairs.

"Y … yeah?" I answer, unable to keep my voice steady while I clutch the doorknob.

"You'd be wise to make sure you're not part of the collateral damage when shit goes down. Or your brother."

I just stare at him, willing the nervous feeling in my stomach to relax.

I hate him. He fucked up my life for a long time, controlling me in every way he could. Trying to literally scare me to death, and even though I still fear him, I refuse to cower like I did before.

My chin raises up before a slight smile forms on my face.

"Of course, Emerson," I reply before I race back up the stairs, getting out of this hellhole as quickly as I can.

28

Franklin

I walk out the front door of the mansion, met by my chauffeur.

"Morning."

"Morning, sir. Where to?" He holds the car door open for me while I lower my head to get in.

"The Peppercorn, please."

"Yes, sir." He closes the door before he sits down behind the wheel and starts the car. We are driving for about a minute when my phone starts to vibrate.

Killian.

"Morning, brother."

"Get to Reign's place. Now," he barks, making me growl in response.

"Excuse me?" I retort through my teeth, not appreciating being talked to like that.

"Whatever, Franky. Just get over here." He hangs up the phone before I can reply, making steam erupt from my ears.

That little shithead.

I sent a quick text to Kenny to tell her I'm running a few minutes late to lunch, as I'm not planning on making this stop last any longer than necessary.

"Change of plans. Take me to Reign's condo," I inform my driver, who nods in response.

I fold my hands in my lap while I peer out the window, fucking pissed off about my brother barking at me like he's the fucking alpha. We all know who's the one in charge here, and I don't let anyone boss me around.

Not even my brothers.

Five minutes later, after having too much time to think, I'm even more furious when the car stops in front of Reign's building and I'm storming out of the car with long strides. When I reach the top floor, I stomp out of the elevator, fuming when I enter the small condo.

My eyes quickly find Reign, who gives me an apologetic look.

Fuck. If Reign has emotions about it, shit must really be hitting the fan.

"What the fuck is going on?" I growl when Killian strides in from the kitchen.

"What the fuck is going on?" Killian repeats, his eyes ripe with fury. "Your girl is a fucking traitor, that's what's going on!" He's yelling, his livid energy making him seem bigger than usual.

My chest lifts with a weighted sigh, walking towards the window to stand next to Reign as I pinch the bridge of my nose.

"Not this again," I grumble while I lean my back against the window frame.

"Yes, this again," Killian shouts, his face turning redder

by the second. "I told you! I told you, and you wouldn't listen. Now Nigel is dead because of that bitch."

My hand reaches up, and I point a threatening finger at him, a fire igniting in me upon hearing my brother call Kendall a bitch.

"I'm giving you one pass for calling her a bitch, but do it again, and I will rip your throat out."

"What?!" A vein twitches in his jaw. His fury is palpable. For a second, I think he may actually have a heart attack. "You're still defending her—"

"Shut up!" I roar. "Shut the FUCK up, Killian!" My eyes are daring him to say another word while I show him my teeth. I hold his angry look for several seconds before I turn my focus to Reign.

"What did you find?" I ask him, knowing that has to be the reason I'm here and why my brother is going fucking nuts over a business school student.

Reign drags his hand over his face, as if whatever he has to say is hard for him to tell me while he slouches in his office chair.

"She's from Clover, Alabama. That in itself isn't the part that's disturbing, since clearly she's not from Boston, but it's the fact that she's from the same town as Emerson Jones."

"Okay," I drawl, waiting for him to continue.

"I did some more digging, and it turns out they went to high school together. Along with at least three of Emerson's guys, and that Josie girl Kendall is living with."

I close my eyes while I let out a troubled breath.

"But that's not all," Reign keeps going. "Turns out they all moved here after high school. And Kendall and Emerson dated until two years ago. They split up because he found some other chick from the good side of town, and he pushed Kendall to the side."

Reign offers me a comforting smile, probably expecting me to lose my shit like Killian just did.

Instead, I smile right back at him before I look at Killian, who is still heaving on the other side of the room.

"I know," I finally admit.

"You know?" Reign's eyes bulge out before he shares a look with Killian.

"Wait, what?" Killian's head moves back and forth between the two of us in confusion.

"I know," I repeat, a little more force behind my words this time.

"What do you mean?" Reign asks.

"She told me after Killian paid us a visit in the office." I shoot him a reprimanding glare. "When we got home, she brought up Killian's suspicions, and I admitted that Killian thought she knew Emerson. She was fucking terrified to tell me, I can tell you that, but she finally admitted Emerson was her ex. The one who used to knock her around."

"He was abusive to her?" Killian slowly moves closer to Reign and takes a seat next to Reign's desk.

Reign nods before looking at his brother.

"Yeah, she told me she was abused by her ex-boyfriend. She didn't tell me to what extent, but it's clear he gave her a rough time. The girl has major trust issues."

"She does," I agree, "but she found the confidence to tell me the truth."

Killian lets out a sarcastic chuckle before giving me another smug grin.

"Okay, if he's just her ex, why did she visit him this morning?"

I slowly turn my head towards him, my eyes narrowing while I feel my heart speed up in my chest.

"Are you still shadowing Kendall?" I ask softly, trying to keep calm so I don't throw my brother through the window.

"You bet your ass I am! She can't be trusted!"

"With whose permission?" I roar, crossing the small space separating us to get to him.

Reign jumps up, quickly pushing me back.

"Franklin! Stop!" he shouts, his honey brown hair flopping in front of his forehead. "He's only looking out for you, for all of us. You'd do the same. It's the same thing you do for us every day."

I take a step back, bringing my hands up in a placating way.

"She was with Emerson this morning, Franklin. I swear. I saw her leave his bar at the wharf, and he was definitely there," Killian explains with a pleading tone.

I shake my head in frustration, annoyed that my brother won't just follow my lead.

"I sent her there."

"You what?" Reign snaps his head back towards mine.

"I told her to go. He owns the house she and Josie live in. I told her to tell him she wants nothing to do with him, and that she will be moving out. She's moving in with me."

"You d—" Killian cuts his words off, jumping from his seat to start pacing the room.

"You sent her to the enemy, even though we don't know if she's part of his crew?" He rakes both of his hands through his hair in frustration. "Why didn't you just ask Emerson over for some supper, you idiot!"

"Shut the fuck up, Killian. And call me an idiot again, and I will throw your head against the wall." I can feel my nostrils flare as I search for some calm through my nose. "She's okay. We can trust her. She told me everything. She's done with him. She is on our team."

"You only say that because you're fucking the girl! You believe her over me?"

"It's not that I don't believe you, Killian." I sigh, feeling like we're going around in circles. "It's just that I know you are wrong."

"I'm never wrong," he huffs, and I can't deny his words.

He never is wrong. He is my most valued business partner because he's never wrong.

About anyone.

"You're wrong about her, though." I fold my arms in front of my chest, giving him a sympathetic yet stern look.

A dry chuckle leaves his lips before he throws a hand up in the air.

"Whatever, I'm out of here. Don't tell me I didn't warn you when she fucks you over."

I ignore him while Reign and I watch him storm out of the condo. I let my head hang when I hear the door slam shut.

"You're in love with her, aren't you?" Reign's words make me look up, and for the first time in years, I see a look of approval in my brother's eyes. I let his words run through my head for a few seconds before I give him a modest smile.

"Shit." I rub my five-o'clock shadow before I roll my lips. "Yeah, I am," I finally admit.

"Good." He nods, a pleased grin on his face. "That's good. I like her. She's a good girl."

"Yeah? You're not on Killian's side with this one?" I ask in surprise.

"I want to be. But I have a good feeling about her, and if you say she came clean to you, there's really no issue."

"She's really moving in with you?" He looks pleased as he leans back in his chair.

"Yeah. At least until this whole Emerson thing is done. I need her close, make sure he can't corner her again."

"She said yes?"

I cock my head and let my smug expression answer for me.

"Well, I'll be damned. Franklin Wolfe got himself a girl," he mumbles with a smile.

"What are we going to do about him?" I nod at the door Killian just stormed through.

"I'll talk to him. But you gotta keep us in the loop, Franklin. If you find out new stuff about her or you're setting up meetings with Emerson and her, we need to know." He gives me a reprimanding look that normally would piss me off. But right now, it actually warms my ruined heart to hear him talk to me like this. Like for once I'm not the enemy, I'm just his brother.

"Alright, Reign. I'll keep you in the loop." I continue staring at him, a small smile tugging at the corner of his mouth.

"Good. You want a drink?"

"Of course," I reply, taking every moment he will give me.

29

Kendall

When Franklin got back to the apartment at the end of the day, I knew something was up. I hadn't heard from him all day since he canceled our lunch plans, and I'd expected him to check in with me after I went to see Emerson. As soon as he explained to me that he was with his brothers and how Killian had been tracking me, I felt like crap. Franklin knew I was going there, but I hate how this is making Killian even more suspicious of me.

'Don't worry about it, baby. It will work out, I promise. Come, get your things. I wanna take you somewhere,' he'd said before he tugged me out the door.

His chauffeur drives us for about fifteen minutes before he stops the car in an industrial area. Franklin gets out of the car before me, then offers me his hand to help me get out.

"Where did you take me?" I ask while I look up at the gray warehouse in front of me.

Louisa's Shots.

"Shots? I'm not doing shots, Franklin. I'm a cheap drunk, and it's not pretty," I admit this while he tangles his fingers with mine and leads me into the building.

"You are? Remind me to get you some wine when we get back then." He chuckles, making me roll my eyes. We walk in, and immediately we're welcomed by the deafening sound of gunshots being fired.

My feet halt as I look around the room for somewhere to hide.

There is a bar to my left, but the windows in front of me have my shoulders loosening, giving me the perfect view of the shooting range. A few tables are scattered throughout the area, but other than an older woman behind the bar, a sullen-looking man seated at the bar, and two people shooting at a target behind the bulletproof glass with headphones protecting their ears, it's completely empty.

"Fraaaaaaanky," I chant his name as a smile appears on his face, "please tell me you're here to show me how good *you* can shoot?" I give him a pleading look, the sexy grin frozen to his handsome face.

"What?" I blurt when he doesn't reply

"Nothing, I just like it when you call me that." He shrugs before he tugs me towards the bar and places me on the barstool next to the old man before he stands behind me.

"Morning, love." The old woman greets me, her smile and heavy Southern accent making me feel right at home.

"Morning, ma'am," I reply, my normally hidden accent now on full display.

She winks at Franklin before turning her focus back to me.

"What can I get the two of you today?"

"A box of 0.22 bullets and two coffees, please. And can I

get the private range?" Franklin moves to my side, throwing a stack of bills on the bar. I rear back and give him a wary look.

"What are you doing? I ain't gonna shoot."

"Yeah, you are." The woman places a box of bullets on the bar before she turns around to pour each of us a cup of coffee. Franklin reaches for the box as I tug at his coat to get his attention back to me.

"I'm not the kind of girl who walks around with a gun," I explain.

"I know that, pretty girl. But you are the kind of girl who walks around with *me.* And I need you to be able to protect yourself if I'm not around. You have to learn how to shoot. Especially now that I know your ex-boyfriend is also my number one enemy."

I grunt in response; he does have a point.

Emerson always told me having a gun wasn't necessary, that he would protect me. But there were times I'd wished I'd at least *known* how to shoot.

"I don't know."

"What's your name, honey?" I turn my head to the woman behind the bar.

"Kendall."

"Nice to meet you, Kendall. My name is Mary-Jane. Where are you from?"

"Clover, Alabama."

"You're from Alabama and your daddy never taught you how to shoot?" One of Mary-Jane's perfectly shaped eyebrows rises up, making me chuckle in response.

"No, ma'am. My uncle was accidentally killed on a hunting trip. No guns were allowed anywhere near us after that. Mama's orders."

She blinks her eyes at me, her lips pursed.

"Well, your uncle was thick as a thumb, if that's how he died. Don't blame the guns, though."

"Oh, that he was."

"Listen, honey." She places her hand over mine, giving me a comforting smile while quickly glancing at Franklin. "You don't look like the type of girl who wants to be a damsel in distress, waiting for her Prince Charming to save her all the time, now do you?"

I shake my head in response.

"That's what I thought. So do yourself a favor, and let this fine specimen teach you how to shoot so you can point his gun at him when he's pissing you off." A playful smile appears on her face as I break out in laughter.

"Don't push it, Mary-Jane," Franklin teases while he places his hand on my neck in an affectionate way.

"Shut it, Wolfe. You may be the alpha in this town, but I'm still your elder. You better treat me as such before I show you *my* gun." She glares at him, her delight evident, as if mocking him is the highlight of her day.

Franklin brings up his hands in surrender before wrapping them around my waist.

"Listen to the old lady, Kenny," he murmurs against my ears, making me bite my lip when the hairs on the back of my neck stand up, thinking about all the different sensations and emotions this man can make me feel.

I look into the sweet, honey-brown eyes of Mary-Jane as she places my coffee in front of me.

"Fine. Let's go before I change my mind." I glide off the barstool, giving Franklin a scowl. I'm still not willing to admit that my nervousness is mixed with excitement.

His verdant eyes stare at me in amusement as if he sees through me. He can't possibly know that I'm just giving him a hard time, and secretly, have always wanted to shoot, but he sure looks like he does.

I roll my eyes, determined to not give him any confirmation, before I open my mouth.

"Where to, Wolfe?"

"Are we back to that?" He pulls a face before he points at a door on the other side of the room. "That way, baby."

I walk towards the oak door, waiting for Franklin to open it before I step over the threshold. The front part of the room is tiny and small, with a coat rack in the corner. Franklin takes the hem of my coat in his hands before he gently pulls it off my body like the gentleman that he is.

"Thank you." I smile.

After he hangs his own coat, I lick my lips, his athletic physique more visible now that it's only covered by his dress shirt. He rolls up his sleeve while I enjoy watching him unveil his sinewy forearms.

"You like what you see, pretty girl?" He smirks.

"Yeah," I admit without hesitation. "Yeah, I do."

"Save it for later." He closes the distance to plant a sweet peck on my lips. Then he places his hand on the small of my back, guiding me towards the door that leads to the private range.

Instead of a row of about ten cubicles, there are only two in here. He pulls a gun out of the holster that's snug to his body before placing it on the shelf in front of him.

"I'll prepare the gun, and you can shoot."

"No," I disagree with a grimace that has his brows raising in question. "If you want me to learn how to handle a gun, I want to learn everything."

He gives me an approving look before he nudges his head to tell me to come closer.

"Okay, so this thing," he points at a small switch, "this is the safety. Make sure it's off when you want to shoot. Flip it when you are ready, but make sure you keep the barrel aimed in front of you once you do. You won't be the first person who shoots herself in the foot."

I hit him with an offended look.

"What?" he chuckles.

"You better watch it, Wolfe, before I shoot you in the foot."

"Feisty. I like it." He presses a kiss to my hair that makes me smile before he continues.

"Hold up your hand, palms up." I do as he says before he places the grip in my palm, then I wrap my fingers around it. It feels lighter than I'd expected as I bring it up towards the target.

"Feels good?" Franklin asks.

I nod in response before he grabs my wrist, tilting my hand.

"Okay, do you see this small button under the trigger? That's your magazine release. Press that, and your magazine will slide right out."

I press the button, my other hand under the magazine, catching it when it drops out.

"Good, now fill it with bullets."

I open the box, putting bullets into the magazine until it's completely filled.

"Now, put it back in?" He confirms with a nod, so I slide the magazine back in until it clicks.

"Alright, put your earmuffs on," he tells me while he puts a set on his head. "Now spread your legs a little, flip the safety, aim the gun with one hand on the grip, the other under the grip, but don't put your finger on the trigger just yet. Just hold it beside it."

I do as he instructs before he moves in behind me, pressing his chest against my back. The warmth of his body makes me want to lean into his body, though I force myself to stay upright and concentrate on what he's saying. He folds his hands over mine before he starts to whisper against my neck.

"Shut one eye, and focus on the red dot. Make sure you can see the dot in the middle of the rear sight. "

A fluttering feeling overcomes me, pulling me from my concentration while the hairs on the back of my neck stand up and I clench my thighs together. I let out a frustrated moan before I move my lips towards his, my hands still holding the gun in front of me.

"I can't concentrate with you whispering in my ear."

His eyes roam my face in confusion until he gives me a seductive grin.

"Am I turning you on, pretty girl?"

"Shut up and step away." I mad dog him, suppressing my smile.

He brings up his hands in a placating gesture as he steps back. Then I bring my focus back to the target in front of me. I assess the gun that's in my hand, marveling at the lightweight, feeling the grips in the palm of my hand. I close my eyes while I suck in a deep breath, completely homed in on the deadly weapon I'm holding.

"Just stay calm. When you're ready, take a deep breath in, then pull the trigger while you breathe out."

I focus my eyes on the target for a while until I finally do as he says, pulling the trigger while I breathe out. A loud bang echoes through the space, and I look forward to seeing where on the target my bullet landed.

"I did it!" I screech, jumping in the air when I see a clear bullet hole in one of the target rings.

The excitement makes me buzz while I give Franklin a big smile, making sure I keep the gun pointed at the target like he warned. When his eyes look at me with pride, I pounce on him, bruising his lips with my kiss. I break the connection and chew on my lip, giving him a lingering look before I turn my head back to the target.

I place my feet firmly on the ground and straighten my stance before I pull the trigger again, when I feel like I'm ready. When this one hits even closer to the bullseye, the determination that was previously tucked deep inside me takes over.

Bullseye.

I'm not leaving until I hit the bullseye.

Franklin chuckles when I empty the barrel, then quickly fill the clip once more, anxious to keep going. My fingers easily place the bullets inside as I smile at my own actions.

I'm not the kind of girl who believes in violence or guns, but I do believe in self-preservation, and I feel like this is another step in being *me.* In learning to trust my gut, in trusting Franklin when everyone keeps saying I shouldn't. I love that he has given me a way to protect myself. I aim the gun again before pulling the trigger, this time hitting the circle next to the bullseye. My eyes start to ache from holding back tears, getting a bit more emotional each time I release a bullet.

My whole life I've been listening to people telling me what I *can't* do, yet here is this silent, brooding alpha who's showing me what I *can* do. What I'm capable of.

Showing me I'm worth showing new things to. That I can

try new things, moving me out of my comfort zone. A comfort zone that wasn't ever really comfortable.

I take another deep breath, smiling, feeling prouder of myself than I have ever felt in my entire life as I exhale and pull the trigger.

Bullseye.

I let out an excited yelp before I quickly enable the safety, laying the gun on the wood in front of me before I turn around and jump into Franklin's arms like a happy kid.

"Did you see that?! I hit it!"

"Of course you did," he cheers, slowly spinning me around, his mouth flush with my ear.

I pull my head back while he lowers me to the floor.

"Thank you."

"For what?"

"Treating me the way you do."

He gives me a troubled look, as if the words hurt him inside.

"You don't deserve any less, Kendall."

I'm overjoyed as I plant another kiss on his lips.

"Now it's your turn!" I clap my hands like a seal, excitement still buzzing through me.

"I don't know. I don't want to steal your thunder," he smirks.

"Oh, whatever. Come on, show me what you've got."

"Alright, you asked for it." He takes the gun, checking the amount of bullets in the barrel before he pushes it back in, flicks off the safety, then brings his hand up to aim at the target.

His head turns towards mine with a smug look on his face.

"Six bullets," he informs me. I feel confused when he

doesn't say more, just keeps his gaze on mine. "Count to six, and keep your eyes on me."

I have no idea where he's going with this, but I start counting.

"One."

Bang.

"Two."

Bang.

"Three."

Bang.

"Four."

Bang.

"Five."

Bang.

"Six."

Bang.

When the last bullet leaves the gun, I turn my head towards the target, and my mouth falls open in awe. The entire bullseye area has disappeared, leaving nothing but a gaping hole, a piece of the rubber wall behind it peeking through.

"What the fuck?"

"Told you, pretty girl." He shrugs while I blink at him.

"Where did you learn to shoot like that?" I gape while he places the gun back in front of him, then leans against the wall, tugging me between his legs. He pulls out his phone, checking the screen for messages before he pushes it back in his pocket.

"My dad," he answers my question.

"Your parents aren't around, are they?" I feel uncertainty trying to creep into my body, but I push it away, remembering how he told me I can ask him anything.

His fingers reach up, stroking my cheek in endearment. "No."

"Want to tell me what happened?" My eyes plead, hoping he will open up to me.

He lets out a deep breath as he rests his hand on my neck; the warmth soothing my skin.

"My father beat my mother to death, and then he took off with his girlfriend." The tone in his voice is calm, without an ounce of anger, which is both surprising and disturbing. My heart falls at his words, and I suck in a shocked breath, covering my mouth with my hand.

"Are you serious?" I ask, my voice muffled by my hand, before I place it over his heart.

"Yeah."

I shake my head in disbelief, wondering how anyone could do that to anyone else. To his children.

"How old were you?"

"Eighteen."

"Holy hell!" I cry out in my Southern drawl. "And then what? You took care of your brothers?"

He drags his hand over his face, clearly having a hard time talking about this, the pain on his face tightening my heart.

"Yeah. I took care of all of us. Then when I got arrested, they were placed in foster care since they were all minors. I got Connor out pretty quick because he was sixteen at the time. But Killian spent two years in foster care, Reign four." He clenches his jaw, almost spitting out the words, clearly affected by the fact that he couldn't keep his brothers together.

"They didn't want to give me custody of the younger boys, saying we'd come from a cycle of violence, my arrest not helping that. It took a whole lot of bribery for me to finally get Reign out when I did, otherwise, he would've stayed in there until he was eighteen."

"Is that why Reign and you don't get along?"

"No," he huffs. "When I finally got him out, I was his hero. The day I was arrested, he hacked into the police system, fucked around with the evidence, and made sure they had to drop all charges against me. But by that time, child protected services already took them, and I had to fight for custody. It wasn't until years later when he found out that I wasn't innocent that he flipped."

I consider his words, a question lingering on my tongue. I'm scared to ask, though, because I'm pretty sure I won't like the answer.

"Why were you arrested?" I bring my hand up to cup his cheek, giving him a comforting gaze. Hopefully, I am silently telling him that he won't scare me away, even though I'm already terrified to hear what he's about to say.

"Second degree murder." He examines my face closely as he says this, waiting for my reaction.

I take a deep breath, letting the words settle in my mind.

My first instinct is to run.

I should run as fast as I can.

I've spent enough time with Emerson to know anyone who can kill is someone you should run away from as quickly as possible. But the feelings I have for Franklin make it impossible for me to leave.

Even though he's a criminal, the biggest, most powerful criminal in the entire city, I can't help but think about how he treats me.

Like a damn queen.

I stayed with Emerson for six years, even though he

treated me like shit. He lied to me; he cheated on me; he abused me; he belittled me.

Yet here is Franklin Wolfe, ruling the city of Boston with his Wolfe pack, admitting every awful thing he's ever done. Never pretending he's any better than he is, but also treating me like I'm the most precious thing in his world.

I don't fear him.

I feel safe with him.

"Did you do it?" I ask, watching his mesmerizing green eyes closely.

"Yes," he says without hesitation, his voice deep and confident.

"Did he deserve it?"

"Yes," he repeats.

I let out a relieved breath, even though I know I would've stayed no matter what answer he gave me. I lean in, tugging his neck closer before I cover his mouth with mine.

I kiss him slowly at first, showing him I'm still here, that I'm not going anywhere. He stays rigid for a few seconds until he parts his lips, sating my craving for him as he moans against my lips.

His grip around my waist tightens as he tugs me closer, his hard cock pressed to my lower belly while I dart out my tongue and lick the seam of his lips.

When his tongue finally finds mine, it searches my mouth in hunger, growing more demanding with every breath.

"There is nothing that will keep me away, Franklin," I whisper against his lips when I press my forehead against his.

A small smile tugs on his lips while I feel one of his hands reach under my shirt.

"Good. Because I told you, there is no stopping me."

As if my words unleashed something inside of him, he

crashes his mouth against mine while his hands move to the front of my jeans to unzip them. He lets out a hungry roar when he pushes his hand down my panties, finding my pussy soaking.

"Fuck, you're drenched," he mutters as he moves his lips to the skin beneath my ear. I'm so turned on, I almost collapse into his arms.

"I know," I mewl, "fuck me, Franklin." My hands reach up to fist his hair, twisting his face towards mine, forcing him to look me in the eye. "Fuck me, Franklin. Fuck me like I'm yours," I plead against his lips.

"You are mine, Kendall Ryan." He rushes to push his dark jeans down, then he does the same with mine while we work to ensure our lips stay connected the entire time. I throw my head back against the wall, anxiously waiting for him to enter me with my jeans pooled around one of my ankles. His lips find my neck again while he lifts up one of my legs, giving him easy access, before he roughly enters me, stretching me wide.

"Holy hell," I screech before covering my mouth, suddenly aware of the fact that we are not home.

"Don't worry about it, baby," he chuckles as he starts to thrust inside me. "These walls are soundproof. Why do you think I took you here?"

"To teach me how to shoot?" I pant, the feel of his shaft rubbing against my walls over and over again, making it hard for me to speak.

"That was just an added benefit. But this," he grunts, pushing me even harder against the wall, "is the real reason I brought you here."

"I'm not complaining."

"Good." He pushes his thumb into my mouth, and

instantly I suck on it, wetting it with my tongue before he brings it down to circle it around my clit.

Long, slow, soft, even strokes that brush my sensitive nub in the most scorching and delicious way over and over again.

"Fuck," I moan while all the tension from the last twenty-four hours releases from me. I'm enjoying the pleasure between my legs, then relishing the sweet agony as his moves become more frantic. I bring my lips towards his, softly biting his lips as he lets out a grunt. "Harder," I beg.

I lower my leg to the ground when his hands move down. He grips my ass as he languidly pulls back several inches, readjusting my body by pushing me against the wall before he starts slamming inside of me again. My head keeps banging against the hard surface, but I don't even care. I'm completely consumed by this man and this moment.

I can feel the muscles in my ass cheeks tighten from the tension, creating a rigid, sore pain. That combined with the sensations he's eliciting by flicking my clit has my looming orgasm more intense by the second.

"Yes! Keep going!" I let out a cry as Franklin continues fucking me at a steady pace, bringing us both closer to the point of release.

Finally, I feel a burst of ecstasy exploding inside me, making my eyes roll back in my head. Franklin drives into me even harder, letting out a feral roar as he slams his eyes closed. I watch him come undone, loving the ecstasy on his panting face, small drops of sweat beading his forehead. When his hips still, I drop a lingering kiss on his lips before I connect my forehead with his. We are both panting, sweaty, wet, and totally satisfied when he snickers.

"Was that a good shot?" he jokes, pulling an unexpected laugh from me.

"A perfect shot!" I feel fatigue settling in my body as I lean against his chest, glad that he can keep me up even while his dick is still inside of me. "Shall we do it again?"

"Next time, baby. Right now, I need to go and see Connor."

30

Franklin

I walk through the front door of the mansion at the same time Connor walks down the stairs.

"What's doin', man?" He grins. "You've got a smile on your face."

"Shut up," I roll my eyes, shutting the door behind me, with said smile still in place.

"I thought you were taking Kendall to the shooting range?" I follow him as he walks towards the kitchen, my leather shoes clicking on the marble floor as we move through the hallway.

"I did."

"Then why are you acting like you just got some?"

The perceptive bastard takes a seat at the breakfast bar while I move to the fridge, pulling out two beers before placing them on the bar. He places the cap between his teeth, opening the bottle before handing it to me while I cock a brow at him.

"You need me to answer that question?"

"You dirty bastard, you fucked her at the shooting range?" A proud look appears on his face while I take a pull from my beer as he puts his between his teeth once again to open it.

"Shut up, Connor."

"What?" he bellows, enjoying this way too much. "You're not the adventurous type, but she pushes you out of your comfort zone, I like it."

I shake my head, leaning my back against the counter while giving him a glare, even though I'm not really irritated. Kendall does push me out of my comfort zone. She makes me want to do better, be better, and fuck me, she makes me want to love and protect her, evoking emotions in me I'd always thought were reserved for my brothers. I didn't take her to the range tonight because I wanted to fuck her, even though the thought had crossed my mind, but because I wanted her to feel as strong as she is. To make her realize she's fully capable of defending herself, even though I will be around to protect her. I want her to stick around for fuck knows how long, and I'm realistic enough to realize that shit can happen. Like it did with Nigel.

For fuck's sake, I sound like a fucking pussy.

"How are you holding up?" I give Connor a sympathetic look as he purses his lips before he takes a pull from his beer. His massive, tattooed arms look even bigger as he raises the bottle, highlighting every muscle in his upper arm.

He's huge.

He's the type who will barely budge when you try to shove him to the side, always trying to maintain the same stoic expression I do, but if he cares for you? He turns into this big teddy bear with the same empathy for all living things like Reign.

"Shit happens," he states, brushing away the grief he's obviously feeling.

"You're allowed to be sad, you know. Just because you're a fucking asshole doesn't mean you're not allowed to have feelings. I know you loved that kid."

"I did," he confesses. "And I will avenge him, but there's nothing I can do to bring him back. So we move on." He shrugs his shoulders, even though I can see the pain in his eyes.

"You called me out here because you found something?"

He nods his head, taking another sip of his beer.

"Yeah, Reign found out where that kid lives."

"What kid?"

"The one who shot Nigel. His name is Damien Johnson."

"Okay," I drawl, not liking where this is going. "What did you do?"

"Busted through his door."

"Then what happened?" I ask carefully, pretty sure I'm not going to like what he's about to say next. He leans forward, resting his elbows on the counter.

"He wasn't there."

I let out a sigh of relief, glad I don't have to go pay off any police officers to cover up my brother's murder.

"So I took his sister," he deadpans.

"Are you shitting me?" I dart forward, scowling as I press my hands on the breakfast bar, ready to pull the rest of the story out of him. "No suh!"

Damn, I hope he's fucking joking.

"Yes suh," he replies matter of fact, taking another pull from his beer.

I rub my hand down my face, trying to keep calm.

"You took *her*? You kidnapped a girl?"

"Yeah, I actually know her," he explains, finally looking somewhat guilty as he drinks his beer.

"You know…? What the…?" I can't believe this motherfucker.

"Yeah, I slept with her a while back," he says this as if he'd lost his favorite toy *a while back* instead of taking a human being against her will.

I rub my hands over my face, staring at my brother, seriously wondering if he has lost his mind.

"You took the girl you once slept with."

"Like years ago, and technically," he starts, the corner of his mouth rising in a sneaky grin, "she offered herself up."

"What the fuck are you talking about? She offered to be taken?"

"Well, no. But she was begging me not to hurt her little shit of a brother. Offered herself instead. I took her up on the offer."

"Connor!" I shout "That's a fucking felony. We don't go around kidnapping women!"

"Well, she didn't want to tell me where her brother was, so I figured we could trade her for her brother. If he loves his sister, he'll take the trade without a second thought. It's a win-win." He says all this with ease, as if he's announcing that he's going to the packie for some bears.

"A win-win?" I echo, seriously concerned about my brother's sanity.

"Okay, maybe not a win-win, but you know what, I don't care. That little shithead killed Nigel. An eye for an eye, Franky. I want him to pay. If I have to do that by taking his sister, so be it." His voice tells me he's growing more aggravated, so I soften my face and loosen my stance. "You would've done the same thing if that had been any of us."

"You are my little brother."

"And he was a little brother to me," he yells, slamming his fist on the surface, pain swimming in his eyes. He's right. During the last few years, Nigel became one of us. A Wolfe without the name, but he definitely was part of us. Even more for Connor, who spent most of his days with him.

"Okay," I concede as I rub the back of my neck. "I get it. But now we'll need to find a way to shut her up once she's free to go."

"I think killing her little brother will shut her up."

"Yeah, that'll probably do the trick," I agree sarcastically. "Where is she now?"

A guilty look appears on his face before he turns away, avoiding my eyes.

"Connor?"

"Your bedroom."

"Goddamm … you're a fucking bigger shit than Reign is right now!" I yell, ready to kill my brother.

"Well, you've been at the apartment with Kendall. Figured, you weren't coming home soon."

"You're an asshole."

"Yeah, well, that makes two of us." He brings his beer bottle up to toast me, a huge grin splitting his face. "Don't worry about it, she's cool."

"She's cool?" I repeat, confused by his choice of words.

"Yeah. Her name is Lilly."

Now I'm not a chatty person in general, but until this moment, I don't think I've ever been speechless in my life. I swear, if I don't die from a bullet through the head, it will be from one of my brothers giving me a heart attack.

"For now, I'm gonna pretend that I don't know about this girl. We already have enough shit on our plates as it is. Don't tell Reign and Kill about her either. We're keeping this between you and me. I don't need any more people knowing you're keeping some girl you fucked hostage upstairs. Don't want to give Killian any more reason to not trust my judgment."

"Cool." He shrugs. "He's still giving you a hard time about Kendall?"

"Yeah, says she's running around with Emerson."

"And is she?" He raises his eyebrows.

"She is," I confess, "but nothing I don't know about."

"You're serious about this girl, aren't you?" Connor takes a pull from his beer with a questioning look on his face. "I mean, you can't deny it because you even quit smoking for her. Something you said you'd never do." He gives me a smug grin, which I return with a glare, resisting the urge to roll my eyes.

"Just admit it, Franky. You're stuck on her."

I exhale deeply, realizing there's no use in denying it. My brothers all have different opinions about Kendall, but they've all noticed that she's not just some girl I'm fucking.

"Are you cool with that?" I ask, knowing he doesn't let anyone into our circle easily.

He stares at me for a while, narrowing his eyes until he brings up the bottle for another drink.

"Yeah, I'm cool with that. She seems like a good girl. But you better be right about Kendall, Franklin." He points his bottle at me with a slight scowl.

"Yeah, I know," I reply, hoping my heart isn't going to cause this to all go to shit.

31

Kendall

I hadn't gone back to my apartment once, not feeling like seeing Josie. She texted me a few times, probably because she heard about the party, but I wasn't ready to talk about it.

Besides, I'm still kinda shaken up about seeing Nigel get shot in front of my eyes. I've been assisting Reign with the funeral arrangements, hoping it would make me feel a bit better, helping someone for a change. Franklin went with his brothers to Nigel's house to pay their condolences to Nigel's mom. Franklin told her he would not only pay for the funeral, but would also provide for her until her last child turned eighteen.

'I can't bring her son back,' he'd said, *'but I can at least give her one less thing to worry about for the next few years.'*

It fucking melted my heart, further proof that my domineering badass has a soul. I think back to how Josie told me to put on the show of my life, and how at the time, I'd agreed with her. But after the last week, after all that we've been through and seeing the true Franklin that no one else sees, it feels impossible to put on any act when I'm around him.

My heart can't put on a show anymore, and my mind is done trying.

However, my conscience is still there, yelling at me every minute of the day, telling me what a cunning bitch I really am. I do my best to ignore it, relishing in my addiction to the way Franklin makes me feel, but I know there is only one possible outcome in this fucked up situation.

No matter what happens, I'm the one at risk, and if this doesn't go as planned, I'm the one who's going to be fucked.

Literally.

It feels like I'm waiting for a tropical hurricane, knowing there is a chance my house will get washed away, but praying it will stay up.

It's Friday afternoon, and I mentally prepare myself as I put the key into the lock, twisting it to open the door.

"Hey," I bellow through the hall once I've opened the door. I throw my keys on the side table in the hallway, heading straight for my bedroom to grab a weekend bag out of the closet.

"Hey," Josie greets me, her look stern and filled with worry when she appears in the door frame.

"Hey." I pop my head out of the closet, then turn back to the weekender in my hand.

"I heard about the party."

"Right."

"You need to stop, Kenny. It's too dangerous."

I hear her, I really do. But let's be honest: I don't have a choice.

"I can't. Not until I know my brother is safe."

"Kenny! You've put yourself in the middle of a gang war. This isn't going to end well."

I stick my head past the closet door so I can face her. Her normally confident face now looks insecure, fear visible in her eyes.

"Emerson put a gun to my head. Did you hear that?"

She gasps for air while she frantically shakes her head.

"Yeah. He put a gun to my head and put me in a headlock before whispering in my ear that Leo said hi. The same Leo my brother ran into last week. I *can't* stop, Josie. I can't just walk away. Emerson won't let me."

"What if Franklin finds out?"

"I told him Emerson and I dated," I confess.

"You did what?" she screeches so loud I cringe. "Why would you do that?"

"To get him to trust me."

She blinks in shock before taking a seat on my bed.

"What did he say?"

"He was pissed I didn't tell him earlier, but he also said I could trust him."

"Right," she says, disdain sewn through her voice, and because I know her so well, I bet she's suppressing the urge to roll her eyes at me. "So do you? Trust him?"

I turn back around to put some tops in the bag before I slam the door shut, scowling at her while I throw the bag on the bed next to her.

"Shouldn't the question be whether Franklin trusts me?"

"He's been with you every single day for over a month, so I think the answer to that question is pretty clear. The better question is, do you? Do you trust him? Do you think he's the lesser evil?" Her deep blue eyes are questioning me in a mocking way, which I seriously don't need or appreciate.

"What do you really wanna ask, *Josie*?" I narrow my eyes at her because I'm fed up with people in my life trying to control me. Telling me what to do like I'm some damn dog.

"Say it," I demand through gritted teeth while I take a step closer, no longer willing to keep my mouth shut.

"What are you doing, *Kendall*?" She emphasizes my name as if she's my mother and I'm the child, defying her. "What team are you on? You better choose wisely."

I just shake my head, annoyed by her question. Annoyed by the lack of support my supposed best friend is giving me.

"My own, Josie. I'm on *my* team." I move towards my bathroom to get the rest of my things. "My goal is to keep my brother safe and to stay alive. That's my fucking team."

"I'm just scared, okay? We know what happens when Emerson gets angry. You need to end this. Let's just pack our bags and go home."

"Since when the fuck do you care if Emerson gets angry?" I sneer at her as I walk back into the room. "You hate Emerson. Besides, you think Emerson wouldn't find me there? That he wouldn't punish me in some kind of twisted way for disappearing on him? You know he won't let me walk like that without some kind of repercussion."

Concern blankets her face, and I examine her. I know she cares; she means well, but I have a weird feeling that sends shivers down my body.

"I just really don't want you to get hurt. Or Jameson." Her eyes look at the bag on the bed while I put in the last of my stuff. "What are you doing, anyway?"

I look up at her, unable to mask my guilt.

"What's going on, Kenny?"

I avert my gaze, knowing she won't approve, especially

after she just spent the last two minutes trying to convince me to break things off.

"Franklin asked me to move in," I explain, pushing out a troubled breath. I grab the handle to the bag, ready to escape, when she gives me a baffled look.

"You're kidding me, right?" she asks before I shake my head in denial. "Kenny, are you crazy? He's a freaking crime lord! The *biggest* one in this city. You can't live with him. What if he hurts you?" she shrieks while she frustratedly runs a hand through her silky, pitch black hair.

"Franklin knows about Emerson paying for our house. He doesn't like the fact that he can barge in here whenever he wants. Besides, he wants me close because of what Emerson pulled last weekend. If I tell him no, he'll be suspicious."

"I thought you weren't going to let any more men control your life? Yet here you are, moving in with the next criminal because he says so."

"Emerson hurt me for six years. I think I will be fine for a few weeks," I deadpan, meaning every word.

Yes, Franklin is a criminal, but definitely not worse than Emerson. At least Franklin treats me good, always making me feel valued, liked. Even loved.

"You can't live with him, Kenny," she hisses, my brows spiking when she steps closer to me. "He's the fucking enemy. Emerson won't trust you anymore."

My lips form a thin line as I become more and more annoyed that I need to defend my choices.

"You know, Josie. You talk a lot about what Emerson wants."

"To keep you safe, yeah," she responds, making me regret my comment.

I'm being a bitch, and I know it. She's only trying to

protect me, just like she has for as long as I've known her. But I can't have anyone talking in my ear right now, not even her. My mind and my heart may be in a constant battle, but I know one thing for sure: I need to do this on my own.

I offer her a sweet smile, hoist my bag over my shoulder as she gives me one last pleading look, showing me the girl I know and love.

"I know, Josie. I'm sorry. I didn't mean it like that. But I'm trying to keep everyone safe here. Franklin trusts me, but he wants me close because of what Emerson pulled last weekend. If I tell him no, he'll be suspicious. Trust me, I'm doing the right thing. Everything will be fine." I place my hand on her shoulder, giving her what I hope is a comforting squeeze.

I know this is what I need to do..

Her expression reverts to the stern one again, clearly frustrated by my answer.

"Don't make me call your parents to tell them their daughter is dead, Kenny," she groans.

"I won't," I promise before I walk out of the door. Damn, I hope that's a promise I can keep.

32

Franklin

The front door closes behind me with a low thud as I walk into the apartment, looking for the head of glossy brown hair that is the reason I'm home early this evening. The corner of my mouth rises when I find her beaming at me from where she's curled up on the couch. She's wearing black leggings with a black sweater, looking tiny as fuck, almost disappearing into the large piece of furniture.

"Hey, pretty girl."

"Hey, you." I throw my jacket over the back of the couch before I lean in for a kiss, the smell of her honey tasting skin making me growl in longing.

I've never imagined myself coming home to a woman waiting for me on the couch. But now that she is, I wouldn't want it any other way.

"Did you get your things?" I mumble against her lips between kisses before I place my arm under her butt, lifting her off the couch. I turn around to seat myself against the soft cushions while she straddles me, making her screech in excitement.

"I did," she replies, her smile waning as she wraps her arms around my shoulders.

"Did Josie say anything?" I watch her face continue to fall, then her eyes, as the words leave my mouth. I reach up a hand to tuck some hair behind her ear, then clasp her chin, tilting her head up so she's looking at me. "Did she?"

She nods her head while her ocean blues drown in her tears, making me clench my jaw.

"She told me I couldn't trust you. That you were the biggest criminal in the city, and she didn't want me to get hurt." The volume of her voice lowers with every word, and I hate that her so-called best friend can fuck with her head like that.

"Are you scared I'll hurt you, baby?" I scrutinize her face, not wanting to miss the slightest change in expression. "Do you feel like you made the wrong choice?"

She immediately shakes her head, her eyes welling up.

"No." The tone in her voice is firm. My heart relaxes as I let out a relieved breath. "You won't hurt me. I know that. I'm just sad that Josie and I aren't on the same page anymore, and I don't want to lose my friend."

"I will never hurt you." I cup her neck, tugging her face closer until her forehead is pressed against mine. I carefully swipe away the tears sliding down her porcelain cheeks.

"Sometimes we have to let go of our old lives, to fully commit to the new ones. But in most cases, it's worth it. I'll make it worth it, pretty girl. I promise." I kiss her tears, her eyes, and then her lips, hoping to demonstrate the affection I have for her. When she moves back to look at me, she brings one leg up to get off my lap before she snuggles against my side, her small hand draped over my stomach.

"When I first came here with Emerson, I was so happy that my best friend decided to come with us. I was in love with Emerson, but having Josie here made me feel less lonely in this new city. We used to do everything together, especially because Emerson was busy, starting up a new business. She was my anchor, but at the same time, she tied me down. I couldn't talk to her about Emerson because she's always hated him. She always pushed me to leave him, and she was right. She's always been right, and I should've listened to her. Anyway, I always expected that she would welcome someone new. That she would support me when I fell in love again. When I found someone who treated me right. I guess she doesn't want that either." She stares across the room while I run my fingers up and down her arm.

"Sounds like she's a snake," I reply, which makes her chuckle. Apparently, she doesn't realize that I completely mean it.

"I know girls like Josie. They want all the attention. They want to be the center of attention all the time. She probably can't stand the fact that she's no longer your center of attention."

"Yeah, I guess so." She tugs me even closer, like she's scared I'll leave. I withhold a snarl as I think about her words.

I don't like Josie.

We've never officially met, but I've heard a lot about her. She sounds like one of those girls who wants to be involved in every single faction of the underground, fluttering her eyelashes to get doors to open up for her.

A cunning little cunt is what Killian would call her.

The type of girl who would sell her grandma if it would benefit her. I don't want to trash her friend in front of her, so I'm glad Kendall's staying with me from now on. Or at least until this whole Emerson threat is handled. Or until I'm certain she's safe.

33

Kendall

My phone vibrates in my hand as I traipse through Franklin's office to leave some documents on his desk. I glance down at my phone, a smile forming on my face when I see the name on the screen.

Franklin.

"Good Afternoon, Mr. Wolfe. What can I help you with?"

He stays quiet for a long moment, then I hear him clear his throat, followed by his deep voice.

"Okay. From now on, you are not allowed to say Mr. Wolfe unless we are in the same room and you're naked."

"Franklin!" I reprimand while an excited chuckle leaves my lips.

"Don't say shit that turns me on through the phone, pretty girl. Especially when I won't see you for another three hours."

"Fine." I roll my eyes while I hear him mumble to someone next to him.

I'm standing behind his desk, looking at the only picture in his office. It's a picture of the boys with their mother when they were younger. Or I assume it's their mother, since she has the same hypnotizing green eyes as all the boys. Her honey blonde hair is long, almost touching her waist, and she has a beaming smile that reminds me of Reign. Franklin is standing next to her like the strong rock that he is, a serious expression on his face like it usually is. He can't be a year older than fourteen, yet you can already see the pain in his eyes. My heart aches for him.

"Why are you calling?" I finally ask when the mumbling stops.

"I need you to take the papers home with you."

"You mean the ones we talked about this morning?"

"Yeah, they're in my drawer, stashed away in the double bottom." I take a seat in his chair and open the drawer to my right. I reach in to pull out the folders inside, then do my best to open the fake bottom while my phone is tucked between my head and my shoulder.

"How do I open this?" I grumble when the lid won't budge.

"There's a button on the side of the drawer," he explains before I lower my head to look closer. I spot the silver button that could easily be mistaken for a screw but seems bigger than the rest. When I push the button, the double bottom pops open.

"I feel like a damn spy," I joke when I pull the documents out of the small space.

"Well, next time, make sure the owner of the documents doesn't know you're taking them." I pout when he chuckles.

"Don't mock me, Franky. I would make a great spy."

"Oh, would you now?" I can hear the playfulness in his

tone, and I put on a seductive look even though he can't see me.

"I seduced you, didn't I?" I purr.

He lets out a full belly burst of laughter that is infectious as fuck.

"What?" I screech, trying to suppress the laugh sitting on my chest.

"You didn't do shit, pretty girl. We both knew you were mine the second I walked through the door of The Library."

"Shut up, asshole." I smile, looking through the documents I pulled out of the hidden compartment. "What do you need me to take?"

"There's a folder with a black logo on it saying Lupus Equus, LLC. Take that, and put the rest back in the drawer, please."

"Alright, I'll see you tonight," I reply, hearing the sounds of him getting into the car on the other end of the phone.

"See you tonight, baby."

I hang up the phone as I go through the documents until I find the folder he wants. I put it to the side before I put back the rest of the documents. I'm about to push the hidden compartment closed before my hand lingers, wondering what else is in there.

My gaze automatically moves towards the door, contemplating my chances.

I'm alone at the office, and I just heard Franklin get into his car, so I have time. Not wasting any time, I push the button again, and the lid pops open. I take out the documents once more, my heart galloping as I quickly glance through the documents, wondering if there is anything in her I can give to Emerson, something that will appease him or at least keep him quiet for a while. I slowly scan the surface of each piece of paper when I finally find something I can use. I let out a triumphant squeal as I fold it up, shoving it in the back pocket of my jeans, when I hear the door open.

Fuck.

I quickly grab the documents and put them back in the drawer, then I close the lid and put the original folders back on top, shutting the drawer just as Killian walks in.

His eyes find mine before they look in the direction of the drawer, quickly looking back at me with a vicious glare.

"What were you doing?"

"N … nothing."

He lowers his chin, hands on his hips. He looks both handsome and terrifying in his black leather jacket, his green eyes seeming even brighter against his five o'clock shadow.

"Then why the stutter, Ms. Ryan?"

I take a deep breath, then lift my chin up in faux confidence, knowing I can't slack off now.

"You just make me nervous."

He slowly walks closer, every step heavy and calculated like he's the Wolfe and I'm the prey.

Fuck me.

"Why do I make you nervous, Kendall?"

"Because you clearly don't like me." I scowl, silently reminding myself I have Franklin on my side.

"You're right. I don't. I know you're up to something."

"I'm not *'up to something'*," I repeat, folding my arms in front of me while I lean back in the chair. He presses his hands against the wooden desk, hovering above me like he may start spitting poison any second now. "Your brother asked me to take this folder out of his drawer to take home." I hold the folder up in the air with a daring look. "You can call him if you don't believe me."

He eyes the folder, his stern expression fixed in place.

"You can't fool me, *Kenny*," he snarls. "I see right through your little act. Don't think you can fuck my brother over, or I'll be there to shoot a bullet through your pretty little head."

I keep my eyes locked with his, doing my best to stay calm while he keeps staring at me as if he's about to jump over the desk and choke me any second now.

"I know, *Killian*."

"Good." He slams his palm on the desk, causing me to flinch and suck in a shocked breath that makes him chuckle. The bastard's enjoying my discomfort. "Get back to work, Ms. Ryan."

I watch him turn around, grab one of the folders out of the archive drawer next to the door, then give me a vicious look and exit the office. I stay frozen in place, scared to move even an inch, until I hear the door close behind him.

Holy hell.

34

Kendall

There's a nervous flutter traveling through my stomach the next morning when I walk into the *Alabama Anchor*.

It's hard to believe I spent so many of my days in this cellar bar, either serving drinks or just hanging around with Josie. At one time, this bar felt more like my home than the apartment Emerson and I lived in. In the apartment, I was always on edge, not knowing what kind of mood he would come home in. But at the bar, I was constantly surrounded by other people, giving me the sense that I was protected. Emerson was always less intense with other people around because he didn't want spectators present while we fought, or because having other people around made him less tense.

Pushing the door open, I quickly notice him sitting at the bar, a whiskey in his hand, while he looks at something on his phone. The blonde behind the bar gives me a glare, as if I'm interrupting her private time with the boss, and I give her a scowl in return.

"Sweetheart, so nice to see you," Emerson quips, a big smile appearing on his face.

"Hey, Em." He raises up one arm, silently asking for a cuddle, so I move in to give him a side hug. His smoky cologne enters my nose, making me swallow in discomfort while he daringly strokes the small of my back. His sweet smile kinda throws me off, reminding me of the guy I once fell in love with. I haven't seen this side of him in a long time, since Boston made him the criminal that he is. The longer we lived on the East coast, the less of this Southern boy I saw. God, the number of times I prayed he would come back to me.

He never did.

Or maybe he was never really there.

Maybe this was always the real version of Emerson.

Cold. Cunning. Crushing.

"How are you?" he asks, nudging me towards the barstool next to him before he turns his body my way, our knees touching while he twirls a strand of my hair around his finger. I narrow my eyes at him in suspicion, wondering what he's up to.

"I'd be better if you would stop hurting innocent animals," I purse my lips.

"What do you mean?"

"Don't play stupid. I'm talking about those two dead horses. I get you want to stick it to Franklin, but can't you do that without murdering perfectly healthy animals?"

"I haven't touched his horses."

I huff in response, not believing a word he's saying.

"I mean it, sweetheart. I haven't. I don't have to fuck with his horses to piss him off."

"Oh, no. I forgot. You just need to put a gun to my head if you want to piss him off."

"I'm sorry about that. You know I would never hurt you. But I didn't fuck with his horses."

There is a sincerity in his eyes that I haven't seen in a very long time but still recognize.

"You didn't?" I ask, confused.

"Sweetheart, Franklin Wolfe has a lot of enemies." He drags my stool closer to his, so I'm seated between his legs. Then he lays his hands on my quads, massaging them.

"What are you doing, Emerson?"

"What?" he questions, the grin on his face reminding me of how handsome he can be. "I've missed you."

My heart stops for a second, knowing where this is going.

I've seen it so many times. Every single time I had the balls to leave him, he would call me saying he got me something, that he wanted to talk, or that I needed to pick something up from the bar.

Yet every single time, his true intention was to woo me back into his arms, which I did like the love-struck fool that I was. Because it's true, I was and probably still am a love-struck fool.

The only thing he doesn't know is that my heart no longer beats for him.

Even though it's a fucked-up situation, my heart is now held by a Wolfe.

"Emerson." I shake my head and remove his hands from my legs before I glance at the woman behind the bar.

He follows my gaze, and he turns towards her as well.

"Eve, can you give her a vodka lime, then give us a minute?"

I observe her, watching as a fake smile appears on her face and she flutters her lashes at him.

"Of course," she coos, her grin in place until his focus goes back to me, then she gives me a dagger shooting look.

I huff in amusement, assuming she's his latest fuck buddy as I turn back towards him.

"I mean it, Kenny. I've missed you."

"That's not what you said when you kicked me out for … Laura? Was that her name? Or Laurie? Maybe it was Lauren." I'm teasing him with a hand on my chin while Eve puts my drink in front of me. I mumble a thank you before she leaves the bar, heading upstairs.

"Come on," he whines, a pleading look on his face as he squeezes my knee, "don't be like that. You know you'll always be my girl. You're my weakness. And I am yours."

"Yeah, you sure as fuck are." I grab my glass, downing it all at once before I close my eyes to let the alcohol settle in my body. It's only two in the afternoon, but considering the situation I'm currently in, I feel like I deserve a free pass.

"I know you still feel our connection," he replies, completely misinterpreting my response.

Yes, he is still my weakness.

But not because I love him.

Not because I want him back.

Because I obviously have a hard time breaking loose.

Because I have a hard time holding my own against him.

As if lady fortune is finally turning my luck around, my phone starts to buzz in my back pocket. I pluck it out, holding it beside my body to make sure Emerson doesn't get the chance to see the screen.

FRANKLIN: You've got this pretty girl.

I hold back my smile, grateful that he somehow knows what to say and when. My confidence rises again, making it easier to focus on the reason I'm here, reminding myself why I should stick to the plan.

"I've got what you want," I finally say.

"Meaning you?" His tongue darts out to lick his lips in what I'm sure he intends to be a seductive way. I'd love to rip that tongue right out of his mouth.

"No." I scowl, wanting to give him a bit of a hard time. "I've got papers that will help you overthrow the Wolfes."

"Like what?"

"I've got a list of all his horses, their steroid suppliers, and the politicians who are his regular gamblers. I even have photos of corrupting evidence, putting some influential people in very sensitive positions."

His eyes widen in surprise before the corner of his mouth curls up.

"How the fuck did you get your hands on those?"

"He actually thinks I'm only giving you this." I pull a list from my back pocket and place it on the bar. "This is a list of all his businesses, shell companies, and investments."

His brows hug together in suspicion.

"Why would he give you that?"

"He found out we have a history. I had to make it seem like I'm setting *you* up instead of him."

"I'm impressed, sweetheart."

"Franklin trusts me." I raise a shoulder. "He showed me his secret spots. All I had to do was take it out. Which was a pain because one of his brothers doesn't trust me. You were right, he's been tailing me."

"Glad I taught you how to shake off people back in the day."

"Yet I can't seem to shake you." I offer him a sardonic smile, even though I mean every word of it.

Surprising the hell out of me, he leans in to press his lips on mine. Automatically, my hand reaches up to stop him while my head jerks back.

"What are you doing, Em?" I press my fingers to his lips, keeping my head pulled back like a turtle so he won't kiss me again.

"I want you, sweetheart," he murmurs against my fingers before I let them fall and shake my head. I have no clue how this Emerson Franklin thing will end. All I know is that I'm hoping to still be alive in the end, and that Franklin Wolfe makes me feel more confident than I ever have. He's shown me I'm worth something when Emerson always made me feel worthless. I'll probably end up with a broken heart after this, but I'll be walking away with a lot more self-worth. Saying no to Emerson Jones is part of that.

"You've belittled me, you've hit me, you've threatened to kill me, and you don't listen to me. You basically treat me like trash until you find some other girl. Then when you're done with her, you come back to me, temporarily treat me like a princess until the entire cycle starts again. I don't want that anymore, Emerson."

"I know, baby. I fucked up. I know. Let me make it up to you." He leans in, pressing a soft kiss under my ear that makes me close my eyes in disgust and huff out an annoyed breath.

"Em," I scold, trying to ignore his lips on my most sensitive spot.

He brings his head close to mine, pushing his nose against

my cheek.

"Don't tell me you think Franklin Wolfe is any better," he whispers, his hand digging into my thigh in a threatening way. Quickly, I slap his hand away before gripping his chin with force.

"Don't be ridiculous." I hold his face in a dominating way, feeling damn proud of myself. "But you've treated me like shit for too long. Don't think some sweet words are going to lure me in again."

Hunger appears in his eyes as he grabs my wrist, tugging it down so his chin is free again.

"I don't know where this side of you is coming from, but it's damn sexy, sweetheart. But okay. I hear you. I promise I'll do better."

He presses a peck on my cheek, his hand resting against my neck.

"Don't get ahead of yourself. Let's just get this over with, and we will see how it goes after that, okay?" I glare, our lips mere inches apart.

His tongue darts out, sliding along my lower lip daringly, while I keep my mouth shut in defiance.

"Alright, sweetheart."

He leans back, so he's fully in his seat, resting his head on his hand while his elbow leans on the bar.

"You got those docs?"

I reach into my bag to grab the folder before throwing it on the bar.

"So now what?" I ask a minute later while he quietly peruses the papers with an impressed look on his face.

"These are pretty good, sweetheart. I can make him go out of business with this information. But," he starts with an ominous tone, making me sigh in annoyance.

Of course, that couldn't be the end of this.

"I still want him dead." His playful expression is instantaneously replaced by a threatening one. I sigh in disappointment. I'd really hoped that these documents would avoid any more bloodshed, other than maybe mine, but I should've known better.

"Why, Em? Can't you just destroy his rising empire? Take over his businesses? Run him out of town like a dog with his tail between his legs?"

"You wouldn't understand, sweetheart. You're just a little girl in a—"

"A big man's world, yeah, yeah, I know. You've told me many times," I interrupt while I roll my eyes. "I'm guessing you need more from me?"

He takes a card out of the back pocket of his jeans before he places it in front of me on the bar.

"Ask him to take you out to this new restaurant on Friday. I'll take it from there."

I take the card from the bar while I look at him warily.

The Fort Maple Kitchen.

"This is that new place. It's yours?"

"No need to worry about that, sweetheart." He gives me a sweet smile, one that's supposed to be loving and caring, but it takes everything I have to not puke.

I nod and grab my bag before heading towards the stairs, knowing there's no use in trying to convince him otherwise.

"I'll win you back, sweetheart," he shouts to my back.

I turn around, giving him a demure smile.

"Does he have to die, Emerson?" I ask once more, hoping maybe I can avoid more bloodshed.

"Yes, sweetheart. He has to die." His answer is stated firmly. And it's my cue to get the hell out of dodge.

35

FRANKLIN

Listening to the dial tone, I get out of the car and head into the office. When she doesn't answer, I curse into the empty space, a wave of concern showering my body.

When I told her to go to meet Emerson this morning and give him the entire list of all my businesses to make him believe he has the upper hand, I knew I was taking a risk. It's the reason I didn't tell Killian and Reign. Especially Killian, who would go nuts. He doesn't trust her, and now that she hasn't been answering her phone for the last two hours, I'm starting to wonder if he was right. She came clean, telling me about Emerson, but I can't help hearing this tiny voice asking me if I was foolish for believing her.

I flop into my desk chair with a growl before I dial her phone again.

It rings five times before finally I hear something on the other side of the line.

"Hey." Her voice seems small and emotional, creating a tight grip on my heart.

"You okay?"

"Yeah, I'm good." I can hear her cover up a sniffle.

"Why are you crying, Kendall?"

"I'm not. I'm good. Really."

I exhale loudly while I pinch the bridge of my nose before I reach into the drawer next to me to pull out a pack of cigarettes. Even though I've mostly quit, I need something to take my mind off the nerves I feel right now.

"How did it go?" I ask as I take one out and light it, taking a long toke, the smoke filling up my lungs. Unfortunately, the toxins don't help me relax.

"Good. Just as we planned. I gave him the list."

"Good," I retort, blowing out the smoke. "Where are you? I've been trying to reach you for a few hours."

"I'm at the condo. I just needed to pick up some things I forgot." She sounds sincere, but still I have the feeling she's not telling me everything. I wish I could look her in the eyes right now. A stone is forming in my stomach, and I try to push the feeling away by taking another drag off my cigarette.

"You need to let me know where you are, pretty girl. It's not safe now that half the city knows you have links to the Wolfes. I'm sending a car to pick you up."

"I'm fine, Franklin."

"Kendall?" I imagine her being frozen to the spot right now after I say her name in a deep, commanding tone.

"Yeah?"

"Trust is key." I'm aware of the accusation that is hiding behind my words, but I don't care. I've surrendered to her actions, and I hate not being in control.

She stays quiet for a while until I hear Josie's voice in the background.

"You can trust me, Franklin. I have to go. Josie's here."

Before I can respond, she hangs up on me. I slam the phone on the wooden surface of my desk before I scrub my hands over my face.

This better be the right decision.

36

I end the call when I hear Josie's footsteps coming down the hall. I hold the pen in a firm grip while I sign my name at the bottom of the letter before putting it in the envelope. I lick the glue line and am sealing the envelope when she appears in my doorway.

"You're here," she states, surprise in her eyes.

I offer her a genuine smile before I straighten to stand and hand her the letter.

"If anything happens to me, I need you to give this to my parents."

For a moment, her eyes widen in shock, but then the judgmental look I'm sadly getting used to seeing alters her face.

"Stop it, Kendall. You're scaring me. Whatever you are doing, break it off. Let's pack our bags and fucking go. I'll go with you." She folds her hands in front of her like she's praying, refusing to take the letter.

"We can't, Josie. I need to do this. This has to end, and if I run, I'll be risking more than just my life." I push the letter against her chest, grabbing her shoulder with my other hand as I lock my eyes with hers.

"Don't worry. Everything will be okay. I promise."

"You can't promise me that!" she shouts. "You need to stop! It's too dangerous. You can't go and fuck around with two of the biggest criminals in this city! Let them kill each other! But you have to get the hell out of the city to make sure you don't become collateral damage."

"It's too late for that, Josie. I already am collateral damage. All I can do now is play along and hope my family doesn't get hurt. Or *you.*"

"What do you mean?"

"You're the closest thing to me in this city. If anyone wants to hurt me, you're the easiest option right now. I can't risk that."

"We don't have to risk shit if we just leave!" She shrugs my hand off her shoulder while she raises her hands in the air in frustration. "Let's go home, Kenny."

I shake my head, determination written on my face.

"No. I know you want to protect me, and I love you for it. You're the best friend I've ever had, and I'm grateful for all the moments you protected me like family. But I have to do this. Please give this to my kin if something happens to me."

Tears are forming in her deep blue eyes, and my throat works hard to suppress my own.

"Please don't do this, Kenny."

I reach out to grab her shoulders before I pull her against my chest, wrapping her in a tight hug. She responds by doing the same, squeezing me hard.

"I'll be fine, Josie. I love you."

When we finally let go, I quickly grab my bag from the bed and walk out of the bedroom without looking back, knowing I'll break down if I do. I pause when my hand circles the handle of the front door, taking a deep breath before I exhale slowly and walk out.

"FRANKY, ARE YOU IN HERE?" I open the door to his office, finding the answer to my question when I'm met by his mesmerizing green eyes. I felt his irritation through the phone after I didn't answer the first few times, and the stern look on his handsome face has me grimacing while I hold still in the doorway. I knew disappearing on him wasn't the smartest thing to do, and it definitely doesn't help with any trust issues he may have, but I needed to write that letter in peace. After seeing Emerson this morning, I knew that I had to finish this, no matter the consequences. But I'm not a Jones nor a Wolfe, so I need to make sure my family will get closure if things go south.

If the plan turns to shit and I'm left with nothing more than a body riddled with bullet holes.

"Come here, pretty girl." The muscles in his face relax as he gives me a smile.

A warm feeling envelops me as I round his desk. He turns his desk chair to face me, and I bring my hip up to perch on the edge of his desk. Before I'm fully seated, he grabs my waist, spins me around, and tugs me onto his lap, the heat of his chest warming my back.

"You scared me," he growls against my neck in a reprimanding way, making the nerves between my legs wake up.

"I'm sorry." I turn my head so that our lips are almost touching, looking into his eyes.

"Don't do it again," he grunts before practically bruising

my lips with a powerful kiss. "Did you do what you needed to do?"

I nod my head and turn my body towards him so I can run a hand through his hair.

"I'm sorry I scared you."

"It's okay. You wanna go out for supper tonight?"

I shake my head.

"Let's order in tonight," I say, while I leave a trail of kisses down his neck. "That way we won't have to wait for dessert."

"Hmm, sounds like a plan."

"Speaking of dessert, there's this new place in the Central Village that just opened a few weeks ago. The *Fort Maple Kitchen*. Have you heard of it?" I lean back to look at him, appreciating the smile tugging at the corners of his mouth.

"Yeah, I've heard of it."

"Have you been?"

He shakes his head, the smile now gone and his usual stoicism back in place.

"Will you take me?"

"Sure."

"This Friday? Like a date?" I beam at him with an excited smile.

"I thought we skipped the whole dating phase?" he teases, to which I slap his chest in response.

"Fine," he agrees with a soft chuckle. "I'll take you on a date, pretty girl."

37

Franklin

I look up when she enters the room wearing a black dress that brings out her curves in all the right ways. The sleeves are long, wrapping around her toned arms, and the waistband accentuates her slender figure before the fabric flares out over her hips.

Her make-up is slightly darker than normal, showing off her blue eyes. I drag my teeth over my lower lip, ignoring my dick's reaction as I whistle through my teeth.

"Damn."

"Is that good or bad?" she asks, strutting towards me in her black heels.

She wraps her arms around my neck while I wrap mine around her waist, her floral perfume invading my senses.

"Definitely good. You look gorgeous, baby. Are you ready?"

She lets out a troubled sigh, making me frown before the corners of her mouth turn up in a big smile.

"Yes, I'm ready."

A few minutes later, we're seated in the backseat while my chauffeur drives us to the restaurant. I grab her hand, giving it a tight squeeze before I bring it up to press a kiss on top of it.

"I like this," I confess.

"Like what?"

"Dating you. You getting dressed up for me. Being able to show you off."

The little minx sticks her tongue out at me.

"You talk like I'm one of your horses."

"You're definitely prettier than my horses," I respond dryly before she pulls back, slowly looking me up and down.

"I like *you* like this."

"Like what?"

"Relaxed. Fun. Joking with me. Playing with me. I like seeing the Franklin that no one else gets. Like this version is reserved just for me." The look in her eyes changes as if she says the words with a heavy heart, so I reach over, stroking her cheek with the back of my hand.

"I *am* reserved just for you, Kenny," I assure her as the car stops in front of *The Fort Maple Kitchen*.

"We're here, sir," my chauffeur says from the front seat.

"Thank you. Just park around the back. I'll text you when we're ready to leave." I let go of Kendall's hand to get out of the car before I offer her my arm to help her out. She locks her arm with mine, and I take the moment to press a kiss against her temple. "I can't wait to peel this dress off your body when we get home."

She releases a chuckle as we walk into the restaurant where we're greeted by the host.

"Good evening, sir. Do you have a reservation?"

"Wolfe."

Recognition flashes in his eyes before he gives me a tight smile.

"Right. Of course. Follow me, sir." I glance around the restaurant while he leads us through it. It seems quiet for a Friday night, with only three groups of people sitting at the shining black tables.

A few faces look at us as we walk through the restaurant, some nodding at me in recognition, though I don't acknowledge them.

The host leads us to a section in the back of the restaurant that's vacant and separated by a translucent room divider, giving us the privacy I prefer, yet the vision I need to stay in control of my surroundings.

"Here you go, sir." He guides us to a small table in the middle of the area. "I'll make sure you won't be disturbed. Can I get you a bottle of wine to start with?" He pulls out Kendall's chair, and she gives him a friendly smile as she takes the seat while I sit down across from her.

"A whiskey for me. And a vodka lime for my girl."

"Yes, sir." He nods before he takes off, then I stand up, lifting my chair and moving it so I'm next to her seat instead of across.

"This is really nice." She places her hand over mine. Her cheeks are a little flushed, a wary look detectable in her eyes.

"It is. Who told you about this place?"

"Oh, Josie told me about it, a few weeks back."

We make small talk until the server comes back with our drinks. I eagerly grab my glass, holding it up in the air to make a toast. She mimics my move, grabbing her glass and lifting it up while she breathes out through her nose and forces a tight smile.

"To you, Kenny. I'm a lucky bastard to have found you."

"It's only been five weeks. May not want to jump to conclusions." She makes the joke, but she looks like something is nagging at her. "With me around, your luck can turn any second."

I lean in, bringing my lips close to hers.

"Stop trying to push me away. I told you, there is no stopping me. You're mine. Get used to it."

She opens her mouth to say something when I hear a commotion coming from the main dining area of the restaurant. When I turn my head towards the sound, I hear Kendall gasp for air. I watch as Emerson walks through the door, followed by eight of his men, guns drawn.

"Everybody out," he hollers, his command reverberating through the restaurant.

They all get up, scurrying out of the restaurant while I mentally prepare myself for what may happen as I quickly glance around, looking for options.

"Oh God," Kendall cries in a whisper next to me.

My attention snaps to hers, looking into her eyes with an intense focus. I need her to stay calm and follow my lead, or this whole thing will go to shit.

"Relax. Breathe."

She nods wildly before she grabs her glass, taking a big gulp of the clear liquor just as Emerson reaches our table, giving us both a stomach-churning smile.

"Sweetheart! I hope I haven't kept you waiting. How are you holding up?" His focus being on Kendall has me clenching my jaw in anger while my mind races to process his words. His boys strategically line themselves up, making it impossible for us to leave the restaurant, not that I was planning on going anywhere, anyway. I'll avoid any massacre at any time, but I sure as fuck won't run with my tail between my legs either. The move makes me chuckle, thinking about how predictable Emerson is, yet also realizing we're in a pretty fucked up situation.

Kendall closes her eyes as if she can't bear to watch the scene that's about to unfold. Her throat bobs as she opens her eyes again, giving me an apologetic look that has the grip she's had on my heart tighten by the second. I grab her wrist, trying to reassure her, but she shakes her head, ripping her arm out of my grasp, the tears welling up in her eyes.

Suddenly, it's like my body is grounded in place as a heaviness seeps into my muscles. I blink, yet whether my eyes are closed or not, I keep seeing the same image.

Killian's face appears behind my retinas, telling me I can't trust her. Killian's advice has always guided me, but I let my heart take over this time. Even though I knew it was stupid as fuck. My nails leave indentations in my palms as I fist my hands tight.

I gave her my heart, believing she'd take care of it, and now all I can do is watch as she holds it in her hands, having no clue what she's going to do with it. I internally shake my head, realizing the mistake I've made by putting my life in the hands of a woman I've known for only five weeks. Ever since I was little, I worked my ass off to give my brothers what they deserve, to make sure their kids would have a better start at life than we had, and now, when I'm almost there, I'm letting it all get fucked up by a woman. I reach into the side pocket of my slacks, hoping they won't notice as I press the button on the side of my cell, making sure it will dial the latest caller.

This better fucking work.

Emerson holds out his hand, and she grabs it, averting her gaze before he tugs her under his arm. I keep a straight face, taking deep breaths, trying to stay calm while surrounded by his army of douchebags. Calmly, I hold my drink in my hand, swirling the liquid around while I wait for him to talk, avoiding looking at Kendall.

"Have you been good to my girl?" he jibes, making me squeeze my glass so tight, I'm surprised it doesn't shatter.

"Better than you have."

"I doubt that. Otherwise she wouldn't be coming back to me, right?"

I don't answer, pressing my lips into a flat line, glancing at Kendall. She looked gorgeous when we walked out the door. The strong, beautiful young woman I fell in love with the first time I walked into The Library. She piqued my interest instantly, even though she was hiding her fierce personality under a thick shield of insecurity, making me desperate to break down her walls. I hate how she turns into a shy little kitten when Emerson Jones comes around the corner, since she's a fucking panther when she's at her full capacity.

I wait patiently until she glances back at me, our eyes locking in a silent conversation.

"Is she? Going back to you?" I question him, arrogantly cocking my head.

He narrows his eyes on me before shooting me a bored look, unaware of Kendall's hand moving towards her thigh while I maintain my tight scowl.

"What does it look like?" He presses his lips on her hair, his eyes still locked with mine. I break out in a chuckle when I realize what is going to happen. He just looks at me in confusion.

In a split second, Kendall pushes away from him, grabbing the gun out of her thigh holster and aiming it at him. His eyes widen in shock, yet before he can react, she shoots him in the knee, making him crumple to the floor, then points it back at his head. I take this moment to grab my gun and point it in front of me. His men now on edge with their guns cocked, taking a step closer, ready to fire.

Before anyone else can, I pull the trigger, firing a bullet above Emerson's head as a warning.

"Don't move," I roar to the men who are now frozen, looking at their leader with severe displeasure on their faces. The shot literally brought Emerson to his knees, yelping in pain while cursing out all kinds of shit in anguish.

"You stupid bitch," he spits in anger while Kendall keeps her gun pointed at his head.

She looks fierce as fuck, and my heart fills with pride, knowing she's all mine.

For a moment there, I doubted her, thinking she was going to fuck me over in the end. Fuck, the amount of stress I endured in those ten seconds probably took off at least five years of my life. But as soon as I saw her reaching for the gun I'd given her, that all disappeared, replaced by a feeling of triumph, knowing it took a lot for her to find the courage to defy Emerson like she's doing.

Now all I have to do is get us out of here alive.

I lean back in my seat, taking a sip of my drink while I glare at Emerson, who's still giving me an evil look while he holds his leg in pain.

"It looks like you put your eggs in the wrong basket, Emerson."

His eyes rise up to Kendall, any affection he had for her thirty seconds ago now completely gone.

"I should've known you were going to fuck me over."

"Oh, shut up, Em. I've done everything you ever wanted. For years, you tormented me and terrorized me, only to butter me up when you felt like it. You treated me like shit while I kissed the ground you walked on. But no more. I'm done." I'm so proud of the ferocity emanating from her as she spits all of this at him.

I quickly glance towards the entrance of the restaurant when I hear the sound of footsteps, finding a black-haired girl running in with a panicked look on her face.

"Stop!"

Josie.

Kendall and I share a confused look, keeping our guns in the air while she pushes through the human wall to get to Kendall and Emerson.

"This has to end! Kendall, don't do it. You'll regret it for the rest of your life." She moves next to Kendall, looking down at Emerson with a pleading look on her face while I narrow my eyes at her, not sure what to make out of the situation. "Just put the gun down, and let these bastards fight it out. You've got him now, Emerson. Let Kendall walk. We'll go back to Alabama."

Emerson grunts in response while I monitor the situation in front of me. I subtly shake my head at Kendall when she glances at me in question, not sure what's going on either.

Kendall turns her attention back to Josie.

"I'm sorry, Josie," she says, the emotion in her voice clear. "You're right. This has to stop. But Emerson will never let me go. He will always try to control me."

"Please!" Josie tries again.

"No." The finality in her voice fills me with pride. When the pleading look on Josie's face is quickly replaced by a cunning glare, I suck in a surprised breath.

That little bitch.

She pulls a gun from her back pocket, placing it against Kendall's forehead.

"Josie, what the fuck are you doing?"

"You wouldn't listen." Josie shrugs a shoulder. "Lower your gun."

The tone of her voice is calm, completely clear of worry. Kendall's concerned face moves back and forth between Josie and Emerson, who is now grinning at me with an evil smirk.

"Josie, you know how badly Emerson treated me. He hit me. He terrorized me. You're the one who told me to leave him so many times." It's clear that Kendall is totally perplexed as she looks at her best friend. I can see how she's struggling to keep it together, wanting to stay strong but not knowing what to do.

"You fucking deserved it. You're a little girl, always needing someone else to tell you what to do. He quickly got sick of you, but you were like a little puppy, following him around even when he kicked you to the curb. *Multiple times*."

38

Kendall

I blink in shock as I take in Josie's words.

"You fucking deserved it. You're a little girl, always needing someone else to tell you what to do. He quickly got sick of you, but you were like a little puppy, following him around even when he kicked you to the curb. *Multiple times.*"

I shake my head, my breath hitching as I do my best to ignore the dizzy feeling in my head. I squeeze the grip of the gun, feeling the cold sweat forming on my palms as I turn my head to fully face Josie. Her dark blue eyes are glaring at me, while the corner of her mouth is curled in a snarling grin, similar to the one Emerson used to give me on a daily basis. My skin feels tight on my body, slowly suffocating me while the last few years of my life with Josie flash through my mind.

Brief moments when she would fight with Emerson… Can I trust my memories? I have no clue what's wrong and what's right, what's real and what's fake until her words fully sink in.

'He quickly got sick of you.'

"Oh my God, you're sleeping with him." My eyes widen in shock.

"Ding. Ding. Ding. Sweet Jesus, it took you long enough."

"What the hell? How long?" I demand through my teeth. I barely get the words over my lips, my voice crackly as fuck from the dryness forming in my mouth.

She rolls her eyes at me with a smug grin, as if she's enjoying my naivety.

"What? You really thought *you* were the reason I moved out to Boston with y'all?" Josie says with spite. I turn my head towards Emerson, who is now looking up at me with a guilty expression, pursing his lips in aggravation when he looks at Josie. "I told you she would screw you over, Em baby."

"Shut up, Josie," he growls.

Her eyes darken at his words, and she cocks the gun, making me flare my nostrils.

All these years, I didn't just get played by the man I loved, but also by my best friend. Fucking my boyfriend behind my back like a fucking skank.

I take a deep breath, resisting the urge to slam the grip of my gun against her face when I hear a soft growl behind me, reminding me that Franklin's still sitting at the table, literally having my back.

Thank fuck I listened to my heart instead of my head.

I saw the uncertainty in his eyes when Emerson walked in, but nothing made me more confident about finally closing this chapter of my life than the love of Franklin Wolfe. He didn't just build me up; he showed me what kind of foundation was hidden behind the thick walls I had surrounded myself with. He showed me I was worth loving when I've been surrounding myself with people who don't know the meaning of the word. I was scared as fuck when I told him how Emerson had me in his grip after he shot Nigel. But even though my mind told me to run, to hide, and never come back, the thought of a life without Franklin by my side was more terrifying than the wrath the Wolfes may have descended on me after confessing my true agenda.

He saw me from the very first moment he walked into The Library, truly saw me, and he never took his eyes off me. It has been only five weeks since he took a seat at my bar, but if I have any say in it, we'll be together for the rest of our lives.

There's a seed of a smile on my face as I cock my head and move my gaze back and forth between Emerson and Josie.

"I guess he's not that interested in you anymore, *Josie,*" I mock, causing the muscles in her face to tense up. My head hurts, the thoughts pounding away at me. I'm gonna need a minute to get over this, to grieve our friendship. I don't know how I'll do it, but I sure as fuck know I'm not going to let anyone bounce me around like a basketball anymore.

"He's been interested for the last seven years, *Kenny.* I'm pretty sure he'll be fucking me tonight, not you," she snarls.

"Shut your mouth, Josie," Emerson mutters.

"You mean the seven years when he was my *boyfriend*, and you were nothing more than a dirty little secret? Nothing more than the cheap fuck he kept on the side? Did it hurt? Did it piss you off when he would beg me to come back to him while you gave your best effort to make me pack my bags and go back home? You're his side chick, Josie. And that's all you ever will be." A chuckle escapes my lips, and I hear Franklin snicker behind me.

I pull back my shoulders, feeling more confident by the second.

"Or is she the one, Em? She's the one you're going to marry? Knock her up? Buy a mansion out in the country?" He brings his head up, glaring but keeping his mouth shut. "That's what I thought. It's not too late to leave, girl," I say, pointing my gun towards the door before bringing it back towards Emerson's head. "You're clearly not needed here, so how about you walk out the door with the little dignity you still have left?"

"Shut up, you Wolfe whore," she screeches.

"I told you she was a cunning little bitch." Killian's voice resonates through the room while Franklin's men appear, blocking every entrance, making it impossible for anyone to leave.

"Never said I didn't agree with you," Franklin booms from behind me, still sitting in the same spot, sipping his whiskey as Emerson's guys turn around, now pointing their guns at the three Wolfe brothers and the small army behind them. Panic washes over their faces when they realize they're outnumbered.

"You okay, darling?" Reign gives me a nod, a worried look on his face.

"I'm not sure," I reply honestly. He responds by giving me a wink, trying to comfort me.

"Put the gun down, girl." Killian's legs are wide, hands on his hips. His eyes are dark as he glares at Josie, looking at her like she's his prey, and he's anxiously waiting until he can rip her apart.

"You put your guns down, or I'll shoot her through the head." I look at Josie when I hear the worry lacing her voice, wondering if she would be capable of pulling the trigger.

Even though she's trying to display the same lack of emotion I've seen when she kicked her latest booty call to the curb, there's also a hint of anxiety peeking through that is clearly fucking with her confidence. It's like my super confident best friend is shrinking by the second, and for once, I actually feel stronger than her.

"No, you won't," Killian counters, an arrogant look on his face. It's the same look he gave me many times before, a slight scowl that will make you do whatever he wants. I don't know how he does it, but with his handsome face and smooth appearance, he's fucking intimidating. When my eyes lock with Josie's again, there's no denying her panic, making me break out in laughter.

Mistake on my part.

My grip loosens a little, keeping my focus on Josie, and it's clearly noticed by Emerson. Unexpectedly, he jumps up with his good leg, slamming my arm to the side, and knocking it against Josie's face before both of us fall to the floor. The rest of the room breaks out in chaos while Franklin jumps on Emerson. When gunfire rings in my ear, I quickly crawl to the nearest table, tipping it to the side to take cover behind it. Everyone scatters through the restaurant, most scurrying to take cover, others trying to take out anyone in their path. I suck in a desperate breath when I look to my right, seeing Franklin and Emerson wrestling. I glance around me to make sure nobody's coming for me when I notice a gun laying on the floor, not close enough for me to grab it without being an easy target. I cautiously peek above the table, taking in the war zone in front of me while I try to think despite the deafening sound of people fighting, guns firing, and the sound of my racing heart in my ears.

I'm looking at Josie, her unconscious, limp body sprawled over the marble floor, when Killian shoots two of Emerson's guys as they try to run away. Two more dead bodies are on the floor next to Josie, and Killian is now punching another guy. Reign jumps over the bar, disappearing behind it before he pops back up, grabbing one guy by the neck before slamming his head down on the bar, knocking him out. My heart has never worked this hard, and I do my best to ward off the panic seeping in as I scan the situation. I decide my only option is to duck back behind the table, so I do, pressing my back against it while I close my eyes and take deep breaths to prevent having a panic attack.

You can do this, Kendall.

I let out a grunt before I get up and look over again, my gaze landing on Connor, who is punching one of the guys repeatedly, even though the guy is in no state to defend himself anymore. Connor is unaware of Cary, Emerson's right-hand man, who is about to jump him from behind. I quickly leave my shelter and throw myself to the floor, grabbing the gun before I point it at Cary, his arctic eyes locking with mine. My finger pulls the trigger, and he jumps to the floor. I guess I missed because he gets back up, running towards the entrance as fast as he can. I follow him with the gun, firing shot after shot before he bursts through the door, disappearing out onto the street.

"Shit," I mutter as my eyes find Connor, who gives me an approving look before his face falls at something behind me, making me turn around.

Emerson stands behind me, the barrel of his Glock aimed at my head with an evil smirk on his face. From the corner of my eye, I see Franklin doing his best to get up off the floor.

My eyes go dry from how wide they are, and it feels like my heart stops when I look into the barrel, my throat filled with needles as I realize this is it.

"Goodbye, sweetheart." Emerson beams at me before he pulls the trigger, and everything goes black.

39

Franklin

I sit beside the bed like I have for the last twenty-four hours, holding her hand and occasionally pressing kisses against her forehead, anxiously waiting for her to wake up. I paid a fuck ton of money to get her home with top-notch carers around the clock. The doctor said she will be fine, and I know she will.

She's a tough one.

She proved that when she faced all her demons in one go and defended my brothers, even though she is anything but comfortable with guns. During the last weeks, she's shown me what she's capable of and the woman she becomes when given some attention and acknowledgment. Like personal humans, she just needed a little nurturing. And I plan to give it to her for the rest of her life.

"She still hasn't woken up? Pshh. I have to say Franky, are you sure she's the one? She seems a bit lazy," Killian jokes as he walks into my bedroom, followed by Reign and Connor.

Connor quickly slams his palm against the back of Kill's head.

"Ouch, I was joking!"

"No mocking the new Wolfe," Connor barks at him with a glare before he takes a seat on the edge of the bed while Reign and Killian lean their backs against the wall.

"New Wolfe? Isn't that a bit hasty?" Killian looks at me with a questioning look. I lift up a shoulder before I give him a small smile.

"I'm not letting her out of my sight ever again, so we may as well make her a Wolfe." He huffs in response while Reign and Connor break out in laughter.

"You've spent your whole life saying you'd never settle down with anyone, then this sassy bartender walks in, and he starts to plan their wedding before she's even agreed to marry the bastard." Connor snickers.

"I like her. I don't mind sharing my name with her. She'll be a great addition to the family, plus she pisses Killian off, so that's always fun." Reign casually folds his arms in front of his body, giving me a tight but approving look. I can't help but let my face split in a beaming smile, surprised by his nice words.

The last few weeks, Reign has seemed less agitated with me, and I can slowly see him opening up to me. I'm pretty sure Kendall is responsible for that, and it has nothing to do with Reign actually starting to like me again, but I'll take it, anyway.

I give him an appreciative look, making Killian roll his eyes.

"If you two are going to start hugging shit out, I'm going to start thinking I'm in some alternate universe, so don't push it now," he says while running a hand through his brown hair.

My lips part, wanting to tell him to shut up before Kendall's stirring beside me makes me snap my focus towards her. Slowly, her eyes start to flutter open as she swallows hard, licking her lips, trying to take in her surroundings. Connor reaches over to the nightstand to grab the glass of water the nurse put there before holding the straw to her lips to help her take a sip.

It's an endearing sight, seeing my bulky, tattoo-covered bear of a brother care for her, already treating her as one of our own. She eagerly closes her lips around the straw, then she takes a small sip. When I stroke the soft skin of her cheek, she turns her head to face me.

"Hey." She smiles.

"Hey, pretty girl."

"I can't be in heaven. I'm pretty sure Killian was planning on sending me to hell."

We all chuckle while she eyes him with derision. I can finally take a deep breath, my heart full at seeing her spunk back.

"Sorry about that." Guilt forms in his eyes as he steps away from the wall, hands clasped behind his back.

"Don't be. You weren't wrong," she says. Her voice is still hoarse, and the fatigue on her face is clear, yet she's still the most stunning woman I've ever seen. "You were an asshole. But you weren't wrong," she continues, still speaking to Killian. "Are we good now?"

"Yeah, we're good."

"Good to have you back, Kenny," Connor pipes in, squeezing her hand. "Reign, Kill, let's give these two a moment." He gets up, eyeing his younger brothers, who silently follow his lead as he walks out the door.

Killian follows Connor out of the room, while Reign

pushes himself off the wall, slowly sauntering towards the bed.

"You had us scared there for a while, darling." He gives her a mischievous grin, making me roll my eyes. "Don't do it again."

"I'll see what I can do," she replies.

"Good, because I like my brother better when you're around. So I kinda need you to stay." He drops a kiss on her forehead before he strokes her hair in a loving way. "Get some rest."

She gives him a small wave as we watch him walk out of the room, then I turn my head to my girl. I lean forward, softly pressing a kiss to her lips.

"What happened?" she asks, looking fragile and lost. "The last thing I remember is Emerson's glaring eyes staring into mine with a gun pointed at my head."

I let out a troubled breath. I don't really want to relive the memory because it's something I'd rather forget. The moment Emerson had a gun that close to her head, ready to pull the trigger, still flashes through my mind whenever I close my eyes. Not to mention when she knocked her head on the table. For a minute, I'd thought she broke her neck, and in a panic, I couldn't find her pulse. I'd literally roared in agony. It's a moment I want to forget, but I know I never will.

"When Emerson pointed that gun at your head, I jumped in front of you, pushing you to the side. You hit your head on one of the tables before you hit the floor, knocking you out."

"But I heard the shot. Oh, my God, are you okay? Are you hurt? Did he shoot you?" she rambles, worry swimming in her eyes.

I place my hand over hers.

"Calm down. I'm fine. He didn't hit me."

She nods, letting the words settle in before her eyes widen. "You almost took a bullet for me."

"I didn't, but I'll take every bullet for you if I have to, Kenny." Her eyes well up, and before I can tell her to not cry, a tear escapes the corner of her eye. I swipe it away with my thumb before I cup her cheek, and she leans into my touch, placing her hand over mine. She enjoys our connection for a few beats before she gives me a wary look.

"She betrayed me." Tears leak from her eyes while she looks up at the ceiling, not needing to tell me who she's talking about.

"She did."

"That little bitch. Where is she?" That fierce look of hers that I love appears on her face, the same one she had when she found out her best friend was just as bad as her ex-boyfriend. I give her cheek a gentle squeeze, happy to see she hasn't lost her spirit. I let go of her face before dragging my hand over my own face, knowing she'll probably need a minute to process this.

"She's gone, baby."

"Gone? Gone where?"

I roll my lips before I lock my eyes with hers.

"She was standing behind you when Emerson fired that gun. He shot her right in her chest. She's dead."

Her hand moves up to her mouth after she sucks in a shocking breath. She shakes her head in confusion while she blinks a few times.

"I don't know how to feel," she confesses.

"You can feel however you like."

"What about Emerson?"

"Connor took care of him."

"Is he gone?" she asks me, a wary look on her face.

"He's gone."

She stays quiet for a while, and I just sit next to her, keeping an eye on her to make sure she's all right, watching how her brain tries to process everything she's learned in the last few seconds.

"Is it weird that I'm sad?"

"Of course not. She was your friend." I squeeze her hand reassuringly while she stares at the wall in front of her as she silently nods her head.

"What happens next?" she finally asks.

I move my face close to hers, our lips almost touching.

"Whatever you want, pretty girl."

40

Kendall

The sweet smell of the red maple trees stimulates my senses while I close my eyes for a second, trying to enjoy the moment. The sun is warming my face as I climb onto the stage, ready to finalize what I've been working so hard for. I thought there would've been shame when I had imagined climbing this stage as a twenty-five-year-old graduate, but I feel nothing more than utter pride.

"Congratulations, Ms. Ryan." The college president shakes my right hand while handing me my diploma cover with the other.

"Thank you," I smile in return.

My eyes are roaming the audience, looking for those mesmerizing green eyes that make my heart stop every time they lock with mine.

I turn the tassel of my cap to the left when Reign's cheering voice catches my attention.

"YAAAAAS, KENNY!" he shouts through the crowd, the

way he's clapping his hands like an excited toddler making me chuckle. Killian and Franklin are standing next to him. Franklin's lips curl into a panty melting smile, and he gives me a wink before I turn to walk off the stage to return to my seat.

I stay in my seat, clapping for the other students for the next fifteen minutes before the college president finally gets to the last and best part. We all get up after he has his final say and prepare for the part we've all been anticipating.

"I hereby present to you the class of 2020." Before he can finish his sentence, the crowd breaks out in cheer, and we toss our caps in the air. I jump in laughter, falling in the arms of my fellow students even though I have no clue who they are since I didn't really connect with anyone. My eyes are welling up, and by the time I'm pushing through the crowd to launch myself at Franklin, tears are streaming down my face. His arms wrap around me while he spins me through the air, my face buried in his shoulder.

"You did it, Kenny." His deep voice warms my ears and instantly comforts me inside like only he can.

"I did it."

I lean back before smashing my lips against his while he puts me back on the ground, still keeping his arms around my waist. When I look into his eyes, they're filled with lust, making my cheeks heat.

"What?" I ask him after he continues staring without saying anything.

"Can you wear that tonight?"

I look down at my light blue gown before grabbing it between my fingers.

"You want me to wear this?" I ask, confused.

"Yeah," he replies, making me quirk up an eyebrow. "With nothing underneath."

I look up at the sky and laugh before jokingly slapping his chest. He pulls me flush against his body, bringing his lips to the skin below my ear.

"I'm not joking, pretty girl," he croons, leaving a lingering kiss between every word that has me closing my eyes, savoring the moment.

"Jesus fuck, get a fucking room." My eyes snap open to see Killian roll his eyes.

"Yeah, for fuck's sake, Franky. Give us a minute to congratulate the girl," Reign says as he pushes Franklin off me in mock anger.

Franklin's jaw tics and he scowls while his brother wraps his arms around me in a tight hug.

"Congratulations, Kenny."

"Thanks, Reign."

"You nailed it," he says while he lets go of me, making room for Killian to do the same.

"Congrats, girl," he whispers in my ear before he gives me a genuine smile.

Killian and I had needed some time to adjust to the new situation, to one another, and even though he's been nice since the day he learned I was never betraying Franklin, it still took some time for him to loosen up with me. I guess it took him a while to fully realize that I was not part of some scheme to bring down the Wolfes. That I really am in love with his brother. He put in a lot of effort to get to know me, and over the last few weeks, I feel that he's really starting to accept me now.

"Thank you, Killian."

"You do realize you're fucked now, right?" Reign grins.

"Why is that?" I hold my diploma case in front of my body while Franklin takes the moment to pull me back against his chest, resting his chin on my shoulder.

"You'll be working for us now until the day you die."

"That is true," Franklin chimes in, giving me a kiss on my cheek.

"What?" I screech. "What about free will and all that shit?"

"You lost that the second he laid his eyes on you, girl." Killian pulls a face as if I'm asking the stupidest question in the world.

"That's also true," Franklin agrees.

"Yeah, you're a Wolfe now. You'll be doing the books, making us money. Doing our laundry." Reign sums up the tasks on his fingers, that innocent grin of his radiating.

"You better not be talking about your dirty underwear, Reign, because I sure as fuck ain't touching those."

"Wait? Not even mine?" Franklin grouses, making me turn my face towards his.

"Maybe. If you play nice." I brush my lips against his, bringing a smile to his face.

"I never play nice, pretty girl. But I know for a fact that's how you like it." He softly bites my lower lip.

"Hmm, maybe," I muse.

"What, you're gonna do his laundry but not ours?" Reign pouts, acting offended as he dramatically places his hand on his heart.

"He'll be giving me orgasms in return, so yeah."

"We can give you orgasms? Killian is great with his mouth, and I have magic fingers." He holds his hand up in the air.

"I am good with my mouth." Killian nods his head in agreement.

"Don't fucking make me disown the two of you," Franklin growls, pointing his finger at his brothers while I let out an amused chuckle, loving the banter between all of them.

"I'm kidding." Reign brings up his hands in a placating gesture while Killian mumbles an "Okay."

"I'll pass. One Wolfe is all I can handle." I lean into Franklin's chest while he nuzzles his nose against my neck.

"Good answer. Come on, let's go. We're taking you out to supper." He links his hand with mine, tugging me with him as we walk down the road to where his chauffeur is waiting for us.

We've almost reached the car when Connor comes peeling around the corner, the tires screeching as he comes to a stop in front of us in his all black truck. He jumps out of the truck, and we freeze on the sidewalk, wondering what the fuck is going on when we see that his face is red, and he looks flustered with what appears to be panic in his eyes.

"Why don't you assholes answer your phones!" he roars, slamming his palm on the hood of his truck, fuming in fury.

"We shut them off for the ceremony," Franklin deadpans.

"Don't *fucking* do that!"

"What's going on, Connor?" Franklin's voice is steady and calm, as if he's completely unaware that his brother is about to lose his shit any second now.

He clenches his jaw, averting his head as his Adam's apple moves along his throat. When he looks up, he gives us a look I will never forget. What I'd thought was fury has been replaced with a level of desperation that breaks my heart.

After what feels like minutes but is probably only seconds, he finally locks eyes with Franklin.

"They took the kid."

THE END.

ACKNOWLEDGMENTS

First, I wanna thank you, my reader. I hope you sure as fuck enjoyed this one because this one was hard! It didn't fly from my fingers; I wasn't unstoppable writing this, and I definitely didn't feel confident about it for a long time. In fact, I had week-long breaks in between, but I did it anyway. This one was hard work, and I'm grateful you picked it up.

Second goes to my husband, simply because he's my person, for life. But also because I run around with my phone all day, squeezing in words wherever I can, plotting any new books, checking my sales or whatever I'm doing that is book related, and he's okay with that because he believes in me. I hope you're right about Franklin, baby. #fingerscrossed.

Third goes to Madelon Cornelisz, my alpha. She didn't do shit for this one, in fact she hasn't even read it because she was too busy feeding her baby (I guess I can let that one slide), but I know eventually she will read everything I write and I appreciate the hell out of her.

Next up is Katie Salt. I'm so grateful to have you in every single way. You help me grow my business bigger, write my books faster, and keep my head sane when I get confused as fuck about every new thing we learn. Thank you for being an amazing friend, colleague, person, and know that you're my people. Meaning you're stuck with me for life. <3

My fourway, I love you. Don't worry, this is not some kind of polygamy thing, although I'm sure y'all reverse harem lovers would totally dig that. They are there when it matters, and I'm happy we've got a circle where we can rant, bullshit, joke and celebrate.

Jordan, Rion, and Lea. I love you. You guys go in one breath for me because you've been there since the beginning, and I don't think I want to write another book without you. You're not only my beta's, but in the last year you guys became so much more. Thank you for all the time you invest in my books and me. I can't wait till I can buy the three of you a drink. Or two. Maybe six. Hell, screw that, let's do ten.

Sheryn, I have to tell you I hate the time difference but luckily we always find a way to catch up, and make it work. Your words always motivate me, and I'm glad I found a great friend in you. If you could just move to Europe in the near future, that would be great <3.

Rachel, I didn't expect you to binge this one, because well … you're busy as f*ck. But you did, and you gave me the confidence to send it to the others! Thank you for giving me your time and let's have drinks… SOON!

Brianna, girl, you deserve a medal! Thank you for putting the time in my book even though you were sick as hell. You didn't have to, but you did anyway, and that means the world to me!

Mallory, you were a breath of fresh air that I needed for

this one. Your feedback really polished my book, and I'm happy I reached out to you!

And last, but definitely *not* least, Kim. Thank you once again for polishing my book, supporting me in every way, and giving me everything you know to help me grow. I truly appreciate everything, and I'm really grateful that I'm part of your clientele. I'm dreading the day you'll ever stop, so … please don't. LOL.

ABOUT THE AUTHOR

Billie Lustig is a dutch girl who has always had a thing with words: either she couldn't shut up or she was writing an adventure stuck in her head. She's pretty straight forward, can be a pain in the ass & is allergic to bullshit, but most of all, she's a sucker for love.

She is happily married to her own alpha male that taught her the truest thing about love:
when it's real, you can't walk away.

Check out www.billielustig.com for more info

ALSO BY BILLIE LUSTIG

The Fire Duet:

Chasing Fire

Catching Fire

The Boston Wolfes:

Franklin

Connor

Reign

Killian

Contemporary Standalone by B. Lustig:

8

CPSIA information can be obtained
at www.ICGtesting.com
Printed in the USA
LVHW110946300722
724783LV00020B/538